LET SLEEPING MURDER LIE

CARMEN RADTKE

Let Sleeping Murder Lie

By Carmen Radtke

ISBN 978-1-9162410-5-3

In fond memory of all the places I've ever called home.

NOVELS BY CARMEN RADTKE

CHAPTER 1

Five Years ago

*D*onna Dryden watched her husband's precious golf trophy arc through the air and shatter against the fireplace.

Glass shards rained onto the stacked bricks Ben used for repairing the wall of the stupid old hearth. If he'd paid half as much attention to her as he did to the crumbling house and the management of the farm land, she might feel bad about leaving him. Instead she felt wildly jubilant. A few days, and she'd be rid of this crumbling manor house with its constant draught and smell of antiquity. She'd be rid of her father-in-law with his silent criticism and his lumbering presence. No more Ben and his indifference to her wishes.

As for the money he'd have to pay her for the divorce

settlement ... She'd earned every penny of it, by staying buried in the back of beyond after being promised they'd return to London as soon as Ben's father had recovered from a mild stroke. That was two years ago.

At least she'd found happiness, more than she could ever say about her marriage.

A fierce draught made her shiver. Typical Ben, she thought, leaving a window open to make this icy place even more unbearable. That was her last conscious thought as a brick came down on her skull.

Present Day

Eve Holdsworth lined up the books in the in-built shelf. To an uninitiated observer the order must appear senseless. Genres were jumbled together, colours didn't match, and an alphabetical search would drive an orderly mind demented. Eve sorted her books by a different system, like she approached most of her life. The yardstick was affection. If she loved a book, or a writer, or a place, it automatically went to the top.

Unfortunately, that also meant she let herself be influenced by people she'd never met. She'd first come to her mother's birthplace England attracted by fantasies of charming, if slightly eccentric village life, where Miss Marple observed from her rockery or through lead-pane windows, Miss Read dispensed sensible advice, and men played darts in the back rooms of thatched country pubs.

After ten years she should know better, but in a stubborn display of optimism or, as she admitted in those rare moments of clear-eyed honesty, of disinclination to cut her losses and start all over in another country, she'd rented yet another quaint cottage in yet another quaint village.

Eve stepped back and admired the room. Her armchair, her mahogany writing desk she'd purchased at an auction a week after her immigration, and her books made this an instant home. She'd developed the knack of travelling light. Apart from her bed and her computer, everything else could be sourced from charity shops and returned there when she moved on.

The ivy-covered white-washed cottage was peaceful too, bordering on the too quiet and as close to a cliché as Eve could find. What was the point of living in a village straight out of a romance novel if her house didn't at least look the part?

Which was why her new bedroom faced a stand of trees that meandered towards miles of woods, and fields lined the roads leading to the nearest market town.

Her stomach rumbled. She'd promised herself a lunch at one of the three pubs, and then she'd stroll around the village. The real estate agent had shown her around on her first visit, but Eve preferred to explore on her own. Just like she preferred solitude to the company of the wrong people. Luckily her job as a freelance Spanish translator offered her the freedom to indulge herself.

Eve marched past the welcome-sign that boasted a population of 1870. She wondered if it would be amended thanks to her arrival, or if this figure bore as much connection to facts as the image of good ol' England bore to present day UK. Although, warts and all, she still liked it. And Puddleby, as she'd dubbed her new home in a nostalgic nod to Doctor Doolittle, gleamed in the sunshine. Lead-paned windows shone, the pastel coloured cottages and terraced houses begged to be put on a picture postcard, and a small brook babbled under a low bridge.

If the village offered more jobs than at the local dairy cum post office, the rent would have been outrageous. Eve crossed her fingers, hoping this place would stay a quiet backwater ten miles from the nearest main road.

It was all as quaint and wholesome as a Constable painting, if Eve ignored the two grizzled men with faded tattoos all over their bare calves. One of them even sported one on his scalp. Through the sparse hair Eve spotted a Union flag and the words "Made in Britain". She shuddered and headed in the opposite direction.

Several gazes followed her as she entered the faux-Tudor "Green Dragon". The old-fashioned theme was kept up inside, with burgundy velvet upholstery, oak and gleaming brass. The bartender should have worn a figure-hugging wench's costume instead of a blue boiler-suit.

At a corner table dozed an old woman, and two elderly men leant on the counter, leisurely nursing their pints, as Eve joint them.

"Could I have a menu?" she asked.

The bartender whom Eve guessed to be in her early to mid-thirties, same as herself, handed her a laminated list. Sandwiches, grilled sandwiches, paninis – there didn't seem to be much demand for lunches. On a blackboard, the specials of the day were listed. Home-made soup with crusty bread and steak-and-ale pie.

Eve ordered the soup, aware of unspoken questions. But since she'd rented the cottage for six months and intended to be on friendly, if remote terms with the local population, she decided the make the first step. Also, the menu, while sparse, was without typos or punctuation atrocities, and the soup hit the mark as well.

"This is excellent." She flashed her teeth in a well-practiced ingratiating smile; enough to feel warm and genuine, not so much people would think she was desperate to become one of them. "I'm Eve Holdsworth, by the way. I've moved into Ivy Cottage."

The bartender returned her smile with the same level of detached friendliness. Eve warmed towards her.

"Nice to meet you. I'm Hayley, and over there in the corner is my nan, Letty Trowbridge. She owns the 'Green Dragon'. Fifth generation."

"That's impressive."

"You American?" one of the two old men asked. Eve's accent must have given her away, since she took great care when it came to her vocabulary.

"On my father's side. My mother's a Londoner."

"One of those," his friend said. Eve wasn't sure which of her parents he disapproved of, but experience told her the American part of her genes was the likely culprit.

Hayley gave her a small, apologetic shrug. Eve waved it off and sat down in a cosy corner by an unlit fireplace.

"Sorry about them," Hayley said when she cleared Eve's table. "They're not used to strangers."

"Surely people do move in? It's a picture-perfect place, at least from the outside."

"Yes, but they're usually old age pensioners, dreaming of growing their own veg or winning prizes for a cottage garden. Not that that'd ever happen around here." Hayley swiped a few crumbs off the table. "Or it's folks like me, coming home after a stint away." She motioned towards her still dozing grandmother. "Granny couldn't handle the pub any longer."

"Must be tough," Eve said.

"It has its compensations. Anyway, if you need anything or have any questions, feel free to ask."

"Thanks. I will."

"And if you want to meet more of the locals, we do bingo afternoons on Thursdays and pub quizzes on a Monday evening. Some customers are even under forty."

"I'll bear that in mind," Eve said.

Hayley noticed with amusement the sly glances that followed Eve out of the door. A young, attractive woman could count on receiving attention, welcome or not.

Eve followed the brook into the woods. The soft soil under her feet muffled any sound. Birds flew up and settled back down as she strolled past. She'd expected the path to be well-trodden, but the overgrown bits indicated otherwise. Conceivably the country-dwellers had enough of nature in their back yards or toiling in the fields.

Eve knew her perspective of country-life was simplistic. It suited her that way. She had enough subjects to dive deeply into to do with her work, and keeping everything else refreshingly easy, unencumbered by too much thought, was her idea of relaxation. When she spotted flowers she liked, she could enjoy them as much as any expert without knowing name, preferences and taxonomy.

Fish darted through the shallow water. Eve suspected that although she could see the occasional pebble, at this stage it could be called a creek, or a stream. It was definitely a lot wider than in the village, where the bridge seemed excessive to cover something about two feet wide. But with an elderly population, health and safety would be a concern too.

She marched on. The late March sun slanted through the canopy and warmed her enough to tie her jacket around her waist, and she'd picked up a branch to use as a walking-stick. She'd spent the week indoors, cleaning, packing and unpacking. This walk would make up for her recent lack of fresh air.

The cabin came as a surprise. Eve had ventured from the path because she thought she'd heard a cry coming from somewhere on her left. After a few hundred yards ducking under trees and getting snagged by thorny twigs, she stood in a small clearing. A fence ran along on the outside. The cabin had an unused air, with its grimy windows, but looked to be in good repair.

A little owl perched on the roof top and cried. Its yellow eyes met Eve's astonished gaze before it buried its head under a wing. Eve tiptoed away, careful not to disturb the bird.

She promised herself to buy a pair of binoculars when she went to town. Bird-watching in groups had never appealed to her, despite her British side, but on her own it might be different. And the owl had looked at her, as if sizing her up.

Eve returned to the proper path, to find that she'd been out for over an hour. Ahead of her, a small figure cast a fishing rod into the water. She hesitated for a few seconds before she turned around to head for home. For one day she'd had enough human interaction, and most anglers disliked interruption anyway.

CHAPTER 2

The next day after lunch and a spontaneous shopping expedition, Eve set out in her newly bought walking shoes and with a backpack containing a thermos of hot tea and a pair of lightweight binoculars recommended for bird-watching. She'd noticed lately a largely sedentary lifestyle made her back ache sooner. Since the nearest gym was ten miles away and the evening classes in yoga and seated exercise sounded as enticing as watching paint dry, an outdoor hobby with a specific goal – to watch the owl – seemed the best solution.

She crossed her fingers for luck. She'd heard often enough it took a measly twenty-one days to form a habit, but in her case the theory proved wrong. What she could confirm after vigorous self-experimentation was that it took barely twenty-four hours to backslide. Repeatedly.

Perhaps this would be different. "Please," she said under her breath. "And please let me stop talking to myself. It's embarrassing."

She should have marked the spot where she'd left the path, Eve thought as she ambled along the creek. The trees all looked the same. There should be two with low-hanging branches where she bumped her shoulder, but that was her only clear recollection. A smarter woman would have tied a piece of fabric to a tree or snapped a photo.

Her luck was in. The angler was back as well, reeling in the line.

Eve cleared her throat as she approached, in an effort to politely announce her presence. It failed, although she was barely a metre away.

"Excuse me?" she said.

The angler spun around at a speed that took her by surprise, because he didn't look the nervous type. He watched her with wary eyes, another thing that surprised her. She might have disturbed his solitude, but for no more than a minute or two. Nevertheless, Eve felt at a disadvantage.

"I'm looking for a cabin?" Since when did her pitch change when addressing a stranger, and since when did she end a sentence with a dangling question mark?

The man righted himself. Eve sensed a subtle change in the atmosphere, from disinterest to annoyance.

"Why?" he asked. His voice and his appearance were a lot more attractive than his demeanour. She'd not be intimidated by his brusqueness.

Instead she opted for the same brand of friendliness she'd used with Hayley. She fished the binoculars out of her backpack. "I came across it yesterday, and I saw an owl sitting on the roof."

A semblance of relief came into his eyes. He was probably an animal-lover, intent on keeping away anyone who'd disturb the bird, Eve hazarded a guess.

"I got these field glasses to watch it from afar. I wouldn't go near it, I promise," she said.

He touched the price tag stuck to the body. "Your first field trip?"

"We all start somewhere." Eve hung the binoculars around her neck and held out her hand. "Eve Holdsworth. Before you ask, I only just moved to the area, so if I put a foot wrong, blame my ignorance of local affairs."

"Ben Dryden." He leant the rod against a tree. A faint smile crinkled the corners of his dark blue eyes which were set off by a light tan and dark blonde hair. His handshake was firm and lasted long enough to make up for his less than friendly welcome.

"If you could point me in the right direction, I'll be out of your hair." She gave him what she thought came off as a non-committal smile, one that said she could take or leave his acquaintance and was not in the least interested in a flirt. Two years of uninterrupted singledom could do that to a woman.

"That cabin is private property." Ben took the hook off the rod, a wriggling worm still attached to it. A bucket at the side contained water and three fish trying to swim in the confined space.

"The fish are not dead." Eve instantly chided herself for her trite remark.

"I'm not killing them. They'll go into another pond."

"Couldn't you use a net, so they don't get hurt? Anyway, the cabin. I'm not going to trespass, I promise."

"Because you want to see the owl."

She nodded.

"The place has a bad reputation," Ben said.

"Why?"

"The owner's notorious. If you stay in the area, you'll find out soon enough."

Eve felt the blood drain from her face. "Is it drugs?" The last thing she wanted was to stumble unwittingly upon a crime lord and his henchmen. She'd taken a few self-defence classes ages ago, and she tended to have a key clenched between her fingers when she walked home alone at night, but she'd be no match for well-trained career gangsters.

"Heavens, no," he said, regarding her with faint amusement. "You must have lived in pretty rough places."

"Life on the mean streets." She imitated a heavy drawl, to lighten the situation. To be fair, she had witnessed a mugging during her childhood in Portland, Oregon, and another one in Bristol.

"You might find life in these parts pretty boring," he said.

"I like the lack of distraction. Essential for a free-lancer." Lower rent counted as an added attraction, allowing her to travel to places like Paris and Rome, where she could imagine herself in an old Audrey Hepburn movie, although she wouldn't confess that to anyone.

Ben picked up rod and bucket. "If you follow me, I'll show you the way."

The path allowed her to walk next to him. He was about five inches taller, but she easily fell into the same rhythm with him. Much better than rushing to keep up with him, Eve thought. She suspected he slowed down for her, another point in his favour. She glanced at the bucket, relieved she didn't have to see the gutted fish she'd expected.

They arrived at the tree her sore shoulder remembered only too well. "Wait," she said.

Ben stopped at her request. She pulled a red cotton string out of her pocket and tied it in eye-height around the two trees flanking the opening.

Rotting pine needles and small twigs rustled under their feet. One hundred yards from the fence, Ben said, "I've got to head back now, but you'll find the cabin straight ahead."

Eve felt a pang of disappointment but hid it behind a smile. "Thanks for guiding me."

"No problem. Maybe I'll run into you again."

She perked up. "Do you come to the village pubs? The 'Green Dragon' seems pleasant."

"I'm not much of a pub-goer these days." His smile took some of the sting out of the rebuff, but not enough. She'd pretty much asked him for a date. Eve mentally slapped herself. She really must feel lonely. Or spring affected her in undesired ways.

She gave him a casual wave and marched on towards the cabin. The owl perched on the roof as Eve had hoped, and the binoculars allowed her a close look at the creature with its stern impression on the white and brown face. "Now what?" she asked herself. Did merely looking at the owl count as bird-watching, or did the pastime require serious study of the avian world?

Eve peered through the lenses. She'd count to see how long it took the bird to blink. That would make her feel more engaged instead of searching for something to do with herself.

The owl blinked, and Eve left.

Hayley polished glasses as Eve pulled up a bar stool. Half a dozen men and three women stood around an ancient dart board hung at a wall. A chalk-board helped them keep track. Half empty pints stood on a table. They seemed to ponder something momentous, because Eve's entrance made no impression at all.

She ordered tea with milk. Hayley offered her a caddy with a rich selection. "I keep this for bingo nights," she said before Eve could ask. "Much safer than to risk another drunken brawl."

The word another hung in the air, like Ben's bait. Eve decided not to ask as she selected a fragrant Earl Grey. Let Hayley offer information at her own volition, and she'd be much more forthcoming. In Eve's experience, no bartender liked to be pumped for titbits.

"Had a good day?" Hayley set down pot and cup, and a china cow with milk.

Eve showed her the binoculars. "I've taken up bird-watching."

"There's a group you could join if that floats your boat." Hayley shuddered. "They're constantly searching for new blood, and believe me, that's not simply a turn of phrase. Marching for miles at the crack of dawn, through mud and thistles, and when you can't tell one bloody warbler from another, they'll tear you apart." She gave the gleaming counter a quick wipe. "Still, it's a nice hobby I suppose."

"I'm not much of a joiner." Eve stirred her tea. "I just prefer to have a purpose when I go for a longer walk. Otherwise I'll slack off after a week or so."

The discussion at the back ended with one of the women, a septuagenarian with a mass of flame-coloured hair pouring out from under a woollen hat, taking up the darts. Her lack of aim was only equalled by the force of her throws. The dart-tips penetrated the wall left of the board. Pockmarks in the plaster led Eve to think it was a regular occurrence. The discussion started anew.

"That's a pity," Hayley said. "They always look for reinforcements at our local am-dram. Our donkey's ass moved away, and that could be the end of the group."

Eve's blank stare elicited a chortle from Hayley.

"We do nothing but the panto each year. It's good fun."

Eve lied, "I'll think about it."

The dart game got heated. Hayley ignored it.

"Do you know anything about a cabin in the woods? I was told it's got a bad reputation," Eve said.

Hayley dropped her polishing cloth. "What cabin?"

"A little place, about two or three miles further down the stream?"

"How did you hear that?"

Eve added an unnecessary splash of milk to her tea and stirred it again. "A guy I met mentioned it. Tanned, blonde, thirty-something. His name was …"

"Ben Dryden."

"Yes." Eve didn't know why she was surprised. Bartenders knew everything, and everyone.

Hayley picked up her cloth. "The place has a bad reputation alright, as does the rest of the property. And the owner."

"But why?" Eve asked.

"A woman was murdered there five years ago. No conviction, but ask most people here, and they will swear to one thing. It was Ben who killed his wife."

CHAPTER 3

*E*ve spilt her tea down her shirt. "He's a killer?"

"According to popular opinion." Hayley held out a box with tissues. "Mind you, he had an alibi of sorts, but there was no other suspect."

One of the dart players shuffled over, an elderly man with bow-legged knees and white stubble on his chin. Hayley put a finger on her lips, as if to warn Eve away from the subject.

"Hiya, Bob," she said instead. "Another round of pints?"

He gave her an affirmative nod and shuffled back.

When she had delivered the beer to the players, Hayley gave Eve an apologetic look. "Sorry if I scared you."

"That's fine. I just didn't expect that." Something in

Hayley's voice made Eve ask another question. "Do you believe it? That Ben did it?"

"Not really, but then the Ben I knew ages ago would've raised hell until the police caught the culprit, not roll over and keep shtum while folks here treat him like a leper."

Eve shuddered. "But in that case, why didn't he simply move away?"

"Because he can't. He's looking after his father. The old man's in a wheelchair, and it would kill Adam Dryden to leave the place. Generation after generation of Drydens. Ben sunk all his money in it a while back, just to keep the house and some of the farm land." Hayley leant closer to Eve. "People reckon that's why Ben did her in, for his father's sake. Because Donna wanted a divorce and the settlement would have meant selling up."

That was all Eve found out in the pub. But she needed to know more. Luckily, the ubiquity of the internet made it easier to satisfy that urge. Less than two minutes search, and she scrolled through archived newspaper articles. They were sparse enough with the information, though.

Five years ago, on a wet Thursday night, Ben Dryden had returned from a business meeting in Manchester to find his father drugged with sleeping pills and his wife Donna lying in the living room, her head bashed in with a brick from a pile used for repairing the fireplace. Ben called the police and was instantly suspect number one, and, as it turned out, the single suspect in the case.

His meeting had ended early enough to be home in time for the murder, but a dinner bill from a restaurant and a receipt plus footage from a petrol station gave him an alibi. The CCTV showed a silver Volvo like Ben's and a man in a grey suit resembling his get out of the car.

A heavy downpour had set in a few minutes earlier, so the footage was fuzzy enough to allow for ambiguity. The post mortem had substantiated that Donna Dryden died while her husband was still close to two hours away, but then again time of death was hard to pinpoint to the exact minute.

Eve rubbed her eyes. No wonder Ben was set free, but from the newspaper reports she'd found she could understand as well why the locals thought of him as a murderer at large.

Judged by the photos, Donna had been pretty, glamourous even, with a perfectly styled golden bob and enough make-up to make Eve feel dowdy with her tousled copper-brown curls and freckles. She needed to pay more attention to her looks. She also needed to stop envying a woman who'd been bludgeoned to death aged thirty-one.

Eve pushed away her laptop. Hayley was right. Her new acquaintance didn't appear like a cold-blooded criminal, but also there was no evidence of an impassioned outcry for justice or resounding declarations of his eternal love for his slayed wife.

And to stay here, where he'd forever be a pariah, smacked of self-flagellation, she decided. Ben could install a nurse to look after his father, who according to the reports had suffered a mild stroke prior to the murder and received treatment at home. Donna's death triggered a second, much more serious stroke.

Eve glanced at her backpack. She had two choices. The first was to give up her new hobby and stay away from the woods so she wouldn't run into Ben again. The second option was to seek him out. He probably could do with a friend.

Except, what if his alibi was phony, and she sought the company of a killer, in the middle of nowhere? She'd strolled into the woods twice, and apart from Ben hadn't seen a single soul.

Staying away was the only sensible option.

A can of self-defence spray rested in Eve's right coat pocket, her hand sweaty around it. "This is stupid," she told herself. Traipsing straight into the lion's den, although she'd left a note in the cottage, explaining where she was headed. It would help with inquiries should her lifeless body be found in the undergrowth.

Her foot caught on a tree root. For a second, she lost her balance. Eve swore softly under her breath. It served her right for not paying attention to her surroundings and getting silly ideas. There would be no inquiries because nothing bad would happen to her. All she did was take a healthy stroll to check on a bird of prey. There might be a nest somewhere, with eggs, and perhaps a mate for the little owl.

Even if Ben were guilty, he'd gone for five years without another murderous incident, and he surely must have been tempted, if the locals were anything like the people she'd grown up with in half a dozen states all over America.

Eve pulled her hand out of the pocket and wiped her brow. The sunshine packed considerable heat in sheltered places. Nerves had nothing to do with her sweating.

Ben stood in his usual spot, rod in his hand and bucket at his feet.

Eve sauntered ahead. The corners of her mouth ached from the strain of being upturned in case he spotted her. He didn't. *Just as well,* she thought. *You're here, bird-watching, not Ben-spotting.*

The red string she'd marked the trees with sat

untouched. She moved onto the clearing and scrambled in her backpack for the binoculars. She trained them on the cabin. A perfunctory glance showed her an empty roof. The owl could be anywhere. Maybe flirting with a mate. It was only considerate in this case to sneak away, in case she disturbed something avian.

Ben packed up as she made her way back to the main path. She waved; a restrained gesture that indicated friendliness without being overly enthusiastic.

Ben must have caught the movement out of the corner of his eye because he turned into her direction and gave her a quick salute.

Eve grinned despite her earlier doubts as she strolled closer. Another two reddish fish with white bellies swam in the bucket.

"Are you restocking something?" she asked, trying to remember what he'd said during their first meeting.

"A pond."

"Wouldn't it be easier to buy them in an aquatic store?"

"My dad's fond of the Golden Orfe that swim in this brook. He's in a wheelchair, so spotting them is a bit of a treat for him."

Eve feigned ignorance. "That must be tough for him. Does he live close by?"

"We still share a house, a couple of miles away."

"That's amazing," she said. "I can't imagine living with my dad. My mom, at a pinch, if she was alive, but he and wife number three would drive me crazy." She stopped herself. The point was to get Ben to talk, not to reveal her own private thoughts. A change of subject was asked for.

She peered into the bucket. "They're really not hurt?"

"Supposedly they don't feel pain the way other animals or humans do. I certainly hope so. A hook's better than having them get entangled in a net and drown."

She shivered. There must be a subject without morbid undertones. "Are the woods always this deserted? It's spooky."

Ben appeared surprised. "The forest? In this direction, mostly yes. If you walk the other way from the village, you'll come across occasional benches, a picnic table and a few things for kids to climb on, if I remember correctly."

"Then I'll stick to this side."

That garnered her another smile. Her hand no longer felt sweaty, and she'd almost forgotten about the self-defence spray.

"If you want to, I can give you a tour one of these days. Unless ..." Ben let the sentence peter out, but he'd said enough for her needs.

"I'd love that. If I'm not taking up too much of your time," Eve said. Self-preservation prompted her to add, "I'll let Hayley know I've had a better offer from you. She's busy enough, running the pub."

"I wouldn't say better, but you're right about Hayley. Is she still single-handedly running everything?"

"That's the impression I got." Eve waited for a reply, but none came. She fished a dog-eared business card out of her backpack. "Here's my number. I'm flexible."

A better offer? She cringed as she replayed the conversation in her mind. There must have been a better way of informing him people would have a clue about her whereabouts. Instead she'd sounded as if she was trying to flirt with him. Maybe she should have told him the truth: she felt comfortable in his presence, a sentiment that hadn't changed, but she also was aware of the suspicions resting on him, and only a stupid or infatuated woman would blindly follow him.

That's what she should've said. She also should have gone shopping if she wanted to dine on something other than tinned soup or a frozen pizza. Another trip to the "Green Dragon" seemed in order.

The pub pulled in a good-sized crowd in the evening. All

but two tables were taken, although most customers stuck to liquids.

Hayley had a helper behind the bar, a dark-haired young man who was strapping enough to be accepted by the blokes and handsome enough to be liked by the half dozen women. Even the two who seemed to be part of a couple glanced at him more or less covertly when he stepped out from behind the bar to deliver trays full of pints. For the single women, the young bartender appeared to be the major attraction together with razzing the single men.

Eve felt tongue-tied, although no-one talked to her to test her theory. She stood squeezed into the spot between bar and juke-box, waiting patiently for her turn to order.

"Sorry it took so long," Hayley said five minutes later.

Eve dismissed it. "No worries. Are you always this busy in the evening?" She studied the menu. "I'll have fish and chips, please."

Hayley wrote Eve's order down. "I wish. The local rugby team scored a big win. The lads are celebrating a possible promotion to the next league." She motioned towards the young man. "Dom should be celebrating too. He's their flanker, but I had no-one else to fill in."

"That explains the stares."

"That's small-town fame for you. Your usual table alright?"

Eve relaxed. If a few visits entitled her to a usual table, she'd made a good choice for her new local.

The crispy hand-cut fries and sole wrapped in golden batter seconded that. The bar area was still busy when she finished her meal, but the drinking had slowed down enough to leave Hayley breathing space. The customers all wanted to chat with the man of the hour anyway.

Hayley carried a water bottle and two glasses over to Eve's table. "Do you mind if I sit here for a few minutes?" she asked.

Eve made space for her. "Are you this nice to all newcomers?"

"If they pass my nan's test."

Eve looked around but couldn't see the old lady. "Where is she?"

"Running the kitchen." Hayley pointed at Eve's clean plate. "As you've noticed yourself, she's still the best chef for miles."

"Tell her these were the tastiest fish and chips I've had in ages." Eve smiled, making her next remark sound like an afterthought. "I ran into Ben again. Do you think I should change my birdwatching sites?"

28

"Depends, doesn't it." Hayley gave her an inscrutable glance. Eve prayed her face didn't change colour.

"On what?" she asked, satisfied with her casual tone.

"Were you scared?"

Eve thought back. She'd felt a frisson of nerves, but the idea that Ben could harm anyone seemed as likely as if the drinking crowd would turn on rugby hero Dom. She also had her self-defence spray, although Britain's alternative to pepper spray, which in most countries except here was perfectly legal, was a joke in comparison.

"See?" Hayley said. "You've got your answer."

"But what do you think?" Eve asked.

Dom hollered for assistance.

Hayley rose. "I think I'd better get back to work."

Hayley chuckled as she closed the door behind her last customer and rinsed the tap-heads in preparation for tomorrow. Eve's feigned disinterest couldn't fool her. It seemed Ben had lost nothing of his appeal for intelligent women since their college days. The sports stars had always had their fair share of impressive female fans, but Ben didn't do badly for a young man who preferred Shakespeare to soccer and conversation to cricket. Not that he'd ever taken advantage of it, to Hayley's knowledge.

That was another thing about him. Ben had morals, and standards, which made him the perfect target for a wife who turned out to lose interest in a man dedicated to his father. It also made it easy to believe that he'd been a hypocrite all along, instead of a gentleman with a heart of gold.

Hayley sighed. Of course, there was that other side to Ben too, the obstinate side and the pride with which he'd kept everyone away in those last five years. And the fact he didn't care what people thought of him, which in turn convinced them further of his guilt. He kept out of their way, and they kept out of his.

Except Eve seemed to get through to him. Hayley yawned. Past midnight, and she needed to be up at seven. She really should hire more help.

Eve gazed through a chink in her curtains at the moon. It had reached the stage in between where she always failed to know if it was waxing or waning. A moon stuck in between, where it could go either way. Like Ben Dryden. Either she forgot about him or she found out more. If he was guilty, which seemed highly unlikely, considering the public information, she'd get the hell out of Dodge. If he was innocent, it would be pleasant to get to know him better. All she knew was that he had a soothing voice and a smile that lit up his face, if she could coax one out of him.

Eve pulled the duvet over her head; much easier than getting up and closing the curtains properly. She needed utter darkness to think through her plans. For a brief instant she remembered a documentary she'd watched, about women from all over the world falling in love with men on Death Row after exchanging letters. Nonsense, she told herself. She'd never be that gullible, apart from the fact that she wasn't falling for Ben Dryden, and that odds were good he'd never killed a single human being.

CHAPTER 4

*B*en stooped over his father's wheelchair and wrapped the woollen throw around John's spindly legs. Despite their best efforts the draught in the lounge persisted. Donna used to complain about it.

Ben's stomach lurched. He had successfully stopped thinking about his wife for a long time, but since he met Eve, Donna popped up in his mind unbidden, and unwanted.

He must have winced. John looked at his son. His body had shrunken after the second stroke left him permanently crippled, but his mind stayed sharp as a tack, and his vision was clear enough to read his son's face.

"Problems?" he asked as he moved his heavily veined hand towards Ben's shoulder. John's right side had suffered the brunt of the damage. He could still feed himself with his left hand and button up his shirt, he could even lift himself out of the wheelchair to use the bathroom, but in a not too far future he'd need help for that too.

"Bit of a headache," Ben said. They never spoke about Donna. There was no need to.

Ben checked his watch. Chris Ripley, John's massage therapist, should arrive any minute. He'd been with John since that first small stroke seven years ago, when weekly massage and physical exercises kept the old man upright solely with the aid of a cane. Since Chris' partner during that period was on an active army tour, he also was available at short notice. Since Donna's death, Chris came three times a week.

They'd turned Ben's old nursery into a treatment room, with a hospital bed, bars along one wall and a powerful space heater which was switched on for ten minutes before the massage. When his father had to give up working the land and found himself without savings, Ben had sunk most of his money into doing the necessary repairs. Replacing the old wiring throughout had not featured on the list. They only used the space heater under supervision. The wiring in the main part of the building was new and should last while John was still alive. Ben didn't intend to plan any further ahead.

The doorbell rang. Chris had his own key, but he always waited to see if Ben was home before letting himself in.

John's eyes lit up as he saw his massage therapist. At thirty-five, Chris combined an easy-going personality with just enough sympathy for his patients to develop a bond without becoming too attached to them. He reserved a mildly flirtatious manner for the mature ladies in his care and a man-to-man attitude for his male patients.

Ben appreciated the arrangement. Chris did more than help John physically, he supplied entertainment and outside interest for a man no longer able to go out and about himself.

It also meant that Ben could enjoy a few precious hours of freedom without feeling obliged to stay close by. On days without Chris he rarely went further than the stream, in case his father needed him. They'd rigged up a system where John could call Ben on a mobile phone attached to the back of his wheelchair. The phone was voice-controlled. For emergencies John also had an alarm button on a string around his neck which would connect him with the local emergency services.

Ben knocked on wood. So far, they'd never needed it, but it helped him feel on top of things. Life would be easier if his father would be able to let go of this place, but his attachment to the house and the land was built into the very fabric of his existence. That's why Ben had no choice but to come back and save it, no matter the personal price. Donna had never been able to understand the necessity. But for John, this wasn't an outdated money-pit, it was the centre of his life.

Ben snatched his waxed jacket from a hook in the hallway. They'd cleared the pathways as much as possible for John's wheelchair, which meant removing most furniture. The Georgian coat-stand dating from his great-grandfather's days had brought in a three-figure sum at auction.

Ben wondered if he should change his long-held plans to go to the movies and take a stroll in the woods instead. It had been nice to talk to someone who knew nothing about him, or about Donna, for a change. But Eve Holdsworth would still be around tomorrow or the day after and seeking her out felt like an admission of his loneliness.

Eve kept an eye on the old-fashioned wall clock. Keeping busy usually helped, but despite her best efforts the hands of the clock moved at a pace that allowed her to watch her fingernails grow.

She climbed onto a rickety chair and buffed the exposed wall beams with beeswax although they already gleamed. She reached a stage where she'd do anything to distract herself.

When the phone rang, she lost her balance. The chair fell, and she saved herself with a jump that ended with her scratching her hand on an empty picture holder.

Eve sucked on the bleeding graze as she picked up the phone. No wonder her heart beat so fast after this brush with catastrophe, she told herself as she said, "Hello?"

"Eve, darling."

Eve's hope deflated. She knew that voice. It belonged to a woman who only called when she had an urgent assignment to fulfil and needed Eve to cram in a week's worth of work into half the number of hours. An email from her was always welcome, because it would contain a reasonable deadline. A phone call instead was a reason to break out into cold sweat, although at least the payment was prompt and almost generous.

Eve listened to a long string of instructions, to which she agreed without complaint. Then she put down the phone and swore. By now she had developed an impressive list of invectives. They served as an antidote to the pain of agreeing to the job.

Five days for a list of translations that would comfortably take twice as long. While being a freelancer afforded Eve the luxury of working from home, she still could but dream of reaching the coveted state of being able to pick and choose, at least if she wanted to eat regularly.

This meant she had to forego her walk, and her owl-watching, and her brief chat with Ben Dryden unless she'd be willing to work until midnight.

She glanced at her backpack, and her computer, and again the backpack. One last sigh and she brewed a pot of strong coffee to boost her concentration while she tackled the job from hell.

Ben waved Chris off and locked the door. He bolted it as well and shuttered the windows. Although there were no valuables left in the house apart from his computer equipment and a few cumbersome antique furniture pieces, he did this diligently. There'd been one attempt to break in, shortly after Donna's funeral, and while the door held fast, two lead-pane windows shattered under an onslaught of rocks. Wrapped around them was paper bearing the single word Murderer.

John dozed in front of the fire. After the massage he needed extra warmth.

"Dad?" Ben put a hand on John's shoulder, knowing his father enjoyed the physical contact, although he'd openly snort at the sentiment.

The old man grunted and opened his eyes. "I wasn't napping, if that's what you think. Just resting my eyes."

Ben stifled a grin. He only needed to worry when his father admitted being tired, or lonely.

"Sandwiches and soup okay?" he asked.

Ben cut the sandwiches into small cubes. In the beginning he'd tried to find a daily help to clean and cook for them, but no-one local wanted to set foot into the house of horrors, as they no doubt dubbed it.

Ben and John had fallen into a routine that was uneasy at first, with the many unspoken things between them that would never be discussed now, with his father so helpless. Over time the tension eased, or at least it did for Ben. His father needed him. That was all there was to it. In a way it helped, to be forced to focus on the present, with no dwelling on the past and no useless dreams about the future.

In rare moments of self-indulgence, Ben allowed himself fantasies of freedom. No-one to judge or fear him, no-one to protect, no-one to care for.

"Like Robinson Crusoe," he said to himself as he tested the soup to make sure it wasn't too hot. But Robinson would have gone out of his mind if it hadn't been for his faithful companion, Friday. Ben still had a few friends left, but they were few and far between, and mostly down in London. As for his old mates, no-one but

Hayley had believed in him. If anybody else had given Ben the benefit of the doubt, they'd hidden it well.

Tomorrow afternoon he'd go down to the stream. Maybe Eve would come again. A few words with another person, that wasn't much to ask for. It wouldn't last long, he knew that. One day people would tell her about him and on her face would be that sickening look of hurt and fear.

Soup dripped from the ladle over his shirt. He wiped it away and went to fetch his father. After dinner John would watch television for a few hours while Ben sat in his study and worked on his software coding, or they would watch something together. Their lives were as small and clearly defined as the cells of a beehive.

Maybe he didn't deserve more, not after Donna.

There she was again, buzzing around in his head unbidden and unwanted.

They'd been married for six years, first putting off having children to enjoy their independence and then no longer interested in any offspring, at least not together.

She'd been pretty, even underneath all that carefully applied make-up and the Marilyn-Monroe-hair that turned more and more into a work of art the further they grew apart.

Had they ever been happy after that first rush of

hormones, or did they marry because everybody else around them seemed to get hitched? How many of the memories resembled the original moments at all and how much were reshaped by time, retelling or suppressing them?

What he did remember in every excruciating detail was their last long conversation. It should have been a fight, but by then he hadn't cared about the why or who. He only cared about the effects on his father. With good reason, as the second stroke proved.

"When you go out today, don't forget to take the card for your business account," Donna said. She didn't bother to make eye contact. Instead she studied her fingernails. They were painted blood-red, a detail that stuck in his mind. He rarely noticed anymore, and since she moved out of their bedroom there were few occasions anyway to really see her. Or reasons why he should want to.

"I won't," he said.

"You're not asking why?" She looked up, a mixture of defiance and bravado in her voice, tinged with anger.

"Sure. Why?"

"Because I've cleared out our joint account. Two more days, and I'm out of here, out of your life, Ben Dryden, out of this miserable god-forsaken rural hell."

He remembered a pause before he said, "Is there anything I can help you with?"

"Anything you can help me with?" Underneath her make-up her face went pale. "That's all you have to say after all these years?"

"I assumed your mind is made up." Her sudden anger bewildered him. It was at odds with the happiness he'd felt in her since she decided their marriage was over."

"It is," she said. "Absolutely. I wish I'd done it ages ago. And the money I've taken is only a down payment on what you owe me. I want every single last bloody penny that's my due. I don't care if you have to sell your precious paddocks to do it."

"Does my father know?"

"He will. Believe me, he will."

"I see." He'd picked up his briefcase, a monogrammed leather affair she'd given him for his first birthday as a married couple and left. What disturbed him most about he scene, was his utter detachment.

Donna was dead before the end of the day.

His father's cough jolted Ben back into the present. "Ready to eat?" he asked as he wheeled John's chair into position.

"I hope the soup isn't too hot again."

~

Eve made a pact with herself. She'd work non-stop for two hours, take a ten-minute break to stretch or have a snack, and then work for another two hours. The mulling over the subject of Ben Dryden would be strictly limited to her thirty-minute lunch break and after she'd finished her word count for the day.

Usually she spent her jealously guarded idle periods during urgent assignments browsing properties in places she might one day want to live in, but she could do that any day. Allowing herself to think about Ben on the other hand would prevent it from turning into an obsession. As it was, part of the fascination stemmed from the cloud of suspicion shrouding him. Probably, at least. It appealed to the carefully hidden romantic in her, and to the lover of mysteries.

Her alarm shrilled. The deal was on, and the first two-hour period began in earnest.

When she'd reached her word count shortly before midnight, her eyes smarted and her brain felt too fuzzy for any coherent thought. But it didn't matter much. There was always tomorrow.

CHAPTER 5

*B*en perched on a three-legged foldable stool by the stream. Fish shot past his line, oblivious of the hook, especially because he'd not baited it. He had enough fish for the small pond outside the house, and the rod served more as an excuse, although he wasn't sure if for himself or someone else.

He glanced towards the path. She wasn't coming. Of course she wasn't. By now Eve Holdsworth would have heard every single theory about him and his murderous ways. He wondered if the rumours stuck with Donna or if he'd reached the status of a Bluebeard, with any number of unsuspecting females barely making their escape alive.

It would be too late now anyway, even if she appeared against all odds. He needed to get back to John. His father had coughed all through the morning, and a regular chest-rub with peppermint and eucalyptus oils might help.

Ben pulled in the rod, once more ready to return to his duties.

Ben only half concentrated on the film they watched. Instead, he concentrated on his father's physical state and fretted over it in silence. John seemed to cough less, and his breath was less ragged, but he picked up colds and little ailments with an alarming frequency. It was the dampness in the stone, and the climate with its lack of sunshine and the constantly changing temperatures. Ben had tried to take his father away on a holiday in the sun for years now, but the old man resisted stubbornly.

"I was born here, and I'll die here," was John's constant refrain. "I didn't prance off to Italy or Spain when I was in my prime, and I'll be damned if I make a spectacle of myself now in this blasted wheelchair." He'd discounted the doctor's opinion too, and so he and Ben had stayed home, season after miserable season.

What John needed, what they both needed was a change of scenery, and if Ben was honest, a separation at least during the days. He longed to be somewhere he could explore, carefree and without worrying about a bone-headed old man, just for a few weeks.

As things were, his father's physical condition had imprisoned him almost as much as if he'd been convicted for Donna's death. Except in his case there was no early release for good behaviour. The only thing that would set him free was to see his father gone or confined to a nursing-home, which was sure to finish him off in a matter of weeks.

"You're awfully quiet." John's speech was still slow, but on good days the slight slur hardly mattered. Today was such a day, despite the cough. Ben had trained himself to notice any changes to such an extent he'd do it automatically. "Business problems?"

Ben forced himself to a chuckle. "No, simply trying to remember a few things. Anything that's not in my electronic diary gets forgotten." The last thing he wanted John to do was worry about money. Never, ever again. He'd take care of that.

John lifted his good hand to tap at his temple. "Still the best diary I've ever had. Keep it all up here. Nothing's ever forgotten. My body may not be what it used to be, but there's still light on in the attic."

He wiped his mouth. His right hand rested in his lap, the muscles all but wasted away. His zest for life had its up and downs, but so did Ben's. It had taken him a while to accept his status as a pariah, and to learn to hide his true feelings from everyone, most of all John. Sometimes he suspected them both of playing some kind of masochistic game, where they both set themselves up for more pain. At least John never had to experience what it had been like to walk through the streets and have people either flee or spit out after him. Parents pulled their children aside when they saw him. He'd deliberately slow his walk to a crawl, so they got a good look at the wife killer in their midst.

Like with most taunts, people grew tired of it. There might even be a new generation of children who'd never heard of bogeyman Ben, but he couldn't be sure. He'd grown weary of the self-flagellation his trips to town amounted to, and John preferred to be taken to a proper city for doctor's visits and the rare shopping trips.

Ben suspected that the old man relished his isolation. Ben, and then Chris, were all the company he wanted since his wife died shortly before Ben's fifteenth birthday. Maybe that's why John had kept Donna at arm's length, because she took a place off-limits to anyone. Or because he'd sensed how much she'd disliked the sacrifices needed to keep the Dryden's place in the family.

The credits rolled. Ben switched off the television. There she was again, popping up in his thoughts. The ghost of lovers' past. Except that she'd long since stopped loving him and he'd grown indifferent too. A psychologist would have a field day with him.

Eve gasped for air as she came out of her total work immersion. Her brain fizzed and her eyes needed to refocus, but it was done, with a comfortable hour to spare until the agreed deadline.

She splashed cold water over her face. She could barely remember when she'd last brushed her teeth or changed out of her pyjamas. She took a sniff at her armpits and recoiled. What she needed now was a long shower, a decent meal and a walk to clear her head.

The "Green Dragon" had a sleepy air. Hayley's grandmother dozed in her usual spot, Hayley slouched next to her with a book, and the bar stools sat surprisingly empty.

"Hello, stranger," Hayley said as Eve tiptoed closer, trying hard not to disturb the old lady. She'd forgotten the name.

"It's only been - ", Eve counted the days on her fingers. The exclusion of everything apart from work impacted her normal functions. "Five days."

"You could have been lying dead in your cottage. Or in the woods." Hayley's grin indicated a joke.

"Thanks for your concern," Eve said.

"I would have been worried if the postman hadn't mentioned some female swearing like a trooper. At first, he thought you were yelling at a man, but the words 'weaselly turd-blossom of an expression' confused him."

"I was working. And now I'm starving."

"The kitchen opens in fifteen minutes." Hayley took a cloth and gave the gleaming table next to her a perfunctory wipe. "You haven't been out much, then?"

"Not at all."

"And your bird-watching?" Hayley's innocent look could have fooled anyone.

Eve shook her head.

"If you're going after your lunch, you might want to check your buttons. In case you run into people."

Eve glanced down her shirt. How did she not notice that she'd buttoned it wrong? She groaned and moved towards the restroom. Some things needed to be done in private. "I'll be back in a moment."

Hayley whipped out a notepad and pencil, the soul of efficiency. "Can I take your order in the meantime?"

Eve strolled under sun-dappled trees with a sense of accomplishment. The money would be in her account within a week, early bluebells and scillas, if she identified them correctly, scented the air and she had no more obligations for a week.

Since she'd managed to suppress any thought of Ben Dryden during her work bout, she might not even walk any further then the owl's nest.

It had rained two nights ago, and a few muddy spots squelched under her boots. She peered closely at the trees to find her markers, so closely that she gave a start when a voice behind her said, "We meet again."

Eve had practised what to say to Ben, so the last thing she'd intended was to blurt out, "Did you have anything to do with the death of your wife?"

CHAPTER 6

The words had barely left Eve's mouth when she saw his expression turn to frozen. She took a step back. "I'm sorry." It should have come out loud and clear, but instead sounded like a rasped whisper.

"That's okay," he said. "If you hadn't brought it up, I might have."

Cold sweat formed in her armpits, a sign of stress. She should have felt fear too, but she didn't.

Birdsong interrupted the silence. A blackbird swooped onto the path and fell greedily upon an earthworm.

"I thought it's the early birds that catch the worms," Eve said in another bout of inanity.

"The answer is, I don't know."

"What?" Her mouth fell open. She shut it with a snap.

"I didn't do it, if that's what you mean." He ruffled his hair, the single sign of agitation in his otherwise calm demeanour. "But I wasn't there to stop it, and I don't know the why, so how can I be sure there wasn't a way for me to prevent her death?"

"It must be hell, to have all these questions and no answers." Eve's chest felt hollow. She would have liked to touch Ben, to show sympathy, but didn't dare.

"I manage quite well not to dwell too much on it." He leant against a tree, his eyes half-shut against the sun.

"Have you never tried to find out?"

"Who do you think would talk to me? In the public opinion I was judged and found guilty as soon as the news hit the stands. And I have faith in the police."

"But – ", she started.

He interrupted her. "It almost killed my father. I'm not letting him be upset over a wild-goose chase."

"Hayley said he's in a wheelchair."

"He'd had his first stroke before we moved in, but the murder and me as the main suspect triggered a second, big one."

"He was home that day?" she asked. The news reports

had stated that fact, but with little additional information. And they'd called John disabled.

"In a drugged state. Someone put sleeping pills in his tea." Ben abruptly shoved his hands in his pockets and turned away from her.

"I'm sorry," Eve said again. "We don't have to talk about this."

"No. I understand. It's just not my favourite topic."

"How about work? Or hobbies? Favourite places?" She smiled, hoping he'd lighten up.

They fell into an easy step as they discussed the merits of Oscar Wilde, whose plays they both loved, and the overrated-ness of "The Da Vinci Code". Eve marvelled at the breadth of his bookish knowledge and then chided herself for being a snob. It said more about her doubtful taste in men when it came as a surprise to find an attractive specimen who could easily compete with her in terms of knowledge about literature and film.

Ben stopped himself halfway into a discourse about the merits of Terry Pratchett's reimaginations of Shakespeare when his phone buzzed. "I need to get back, but maybe we can continue our conversation another day?" he asked.

Eve nodded her head graciously. "*When shall we two meet*

again? I hope not in thunder, lightning or in rain." It was the best she could come up with.

He flashed her a small smile. "The weather forecast for tomorrow is good."

Eve held out her hand. He shook it with the same warm, reliable grip she remembered. Definitely not the hands of a murderer. How his wife could have intended to leave him was a mystery. She might conceivably have another chat with Hayley. But not too soon. That would be prying.

A hush fell over the "Green Dragon" when Ben strolled in. Shocked glances burned into him before the regulars shifted away. He could hear sucked-in breaths and muttered insults, but Hayley's presence prevented any loud outbursts. She did not take kindly to raucous behaviour in her pub, not matter who or why.

Eve sat at a corner table. Her face lit up when she spotted Ben, but he gave her a quick sign to ignore him. There was no need for her to get involved.

"Red wine, please," he said.

Hayley's grin warmed his heart as she held out two bottles for his inspection. He selected the right one, an Australian shiraz.

"Tosser," a wizened man with half his teeth missing mumbled and pretend-accidentally elbowed Ben.

Hayley glared at the old man. He shrank into himself. The rest of the customers at the bar backed away from Ben as if he had the plague. He inwardly shrugged it off. He'd expected a lot worse when he decided to enter the lion's den.

"How are things?" Hayley leant on the bar and rested her chin on her hands after pouring his drink.

"Can't complain." He sipped his wine, with all the outward signs of a man enjoying an after-work drink with mates.

Three men, among them the old guy who'd found his spine, gathered in a huddle.

Hayley whistled. They looked up.

"Any strange incidents and you're banned," she said, baring her teeth at them in a strangely threatening beam.

"Aww, Hayley," the old man whined. "You know us."

"I do. And we're clear." She focussed her attention on Ben again. "What do you think of my remodelling?"

He turned around, in the leisurely fashion of a man at ease, and scrutinised the framed photographs of famous pubs all over the world. These weren't prints, but clearly private pictures. When he looked closely, Hayley appeared in all of them. But the gleaming wood and brass were all how he remembered the "Green Dragon".

"I'm glad you haven't changed it too much," he said. "Never change a winning team."

Ben left, after savouring his wine. He sensed the change in the atmosphere, from anger to bewilderment, the longer he stayed. If it weren't for Hayley, somebody would have knocked into him by now, hell-bent on starting a fight that would send him to hospital. But Hayley wouldn't stand for any trouble. Although there were two more pubs in town, none of them could compete with the "Green Dragon". Being banned by the Trowbridges was the worst form of punishment.

Ben's stomach muscles relaxed as he opened his car. He'd wanted Eve to see what being associated with him really meant, but he appreciated being spared a physical fight.

Eve didn't realise she'd held her breath until Ben was safely out of the door. The insults were kept low enough to hopefully escape Hayley's hearing, but their nastiness angered Eve. If people behaved like this, five years after the murder, Ben's life must have been insufferable in the beginning. There was but one way forward. Somebody needed to solve the case of the late Donna Dryden.

Eve glanced around. She could easily imagine the men and a few of the women mixed in the crowd to get riled up and go after Ben with pitchforks, or whatever rural implements they had handy. She understood why Ben kept a low profile, and she could understand his worry about his father. The one thing that perplexed her was the fact that while the case remained unsolved, a murderer remained at large. A murderer who might easily strike again. And ben should have cared about that.

She walked home, lost in thought. If Ben for some strange reason declined to take action, she would do it herself. If she hadn't misread this evening, she would also be able to count on Hayley for her mission. While she at first thought the exchange at the bar might have revealed stronger feelings on Hayley's side than old friendship, in hindsight Eve changed her opinion. Hayley had behaved in exactly the right way to show support without drawing too much attention to it or demonstrating softer emotions. If Eve was right, Ben had two defenders willing to ride to his rescue.

That would be tricky though. The biggest snag Eve could see for her sleuthing was how to elicit information from Ben without his noticing.

She struggled to keep her eyes open. She'd leave that

problem to another day. After five years under a cloud, time was no longer of the essence for Ben. She'd have to tread carefully anyway, if she wanted to gain anybody's trust. While people loved to gossip, men just as much as women, her experience in British small towns had proven most people to be disappointingly discreet the second they found her out as both a foreigner and an urbanite at heart.

Maybe she should don a hand-knitted cardigan and talk gardening, or did that only work on television? Hayley would know, Eve thought as she drifted off. Best of all, Hayley might have an idea or two about the real culprit. Once she had a trail, the rest surely would fall into place.

After breakfast, Eve decided to start with the victim. What in Donna Dryden's life made her worthy of murdering? She tapped her teeth with a pencil as she scribbled down this question in a pocket notebook. Although it could be phrased better. What made her the target? Who stood to gain?

She enlarged the question marks. Her handwriting all but guaranteed the illegibility of her notes to the uninitiated and making letters or punctuation bigger were her variation of doodling. Eve, to her deep regret, couldn't draw her way out of a paper bag.

The newspapers she found online had used a headshot and an old photograph from a party, which probably were provided by friends for a few quid. Both showed a young woman with an almost doll-like pretty face and slightly crooked teeth. Those teeth were the sole irregularity. Apart from that, the photos gave no clue of her personality apart from a penchant for eyeliner.

It was hard to imagine the woman in these photos with Ben, but he would have changed. Especially after finding his wife dead and himself as the prime suspect. For a fleeting moment she wondered if he could have changed enough to have been capable of violence once. She pushed the thought resolutely aside. He had an alibi, and besides, Hayley believed in his innocence. Few jobs demanded more insights in the human nature than running a pub, and Hayley and Ben been acquainted since their teenage years at least.

Eve tapped the pencil again, only to miss her teeth and hit her lip with a sharp metal end. The skin promptly broke and she tasted blood.

Eve licked it off.

Blood; there must have been blood on the scene. It would have spattered, even if it was in barely visible droplets. Police used flashlights and chemical sprays to detect them, if she remembered correctly. Eve wrote, police report? Coroner?

It would be a lot easier if she could simply ask Ben. Instead she had to rely on her own ingenuity.

She returned to the first article, which said that at the time of her death Donna Dryden worked part-time in a clothes shop in the market town. That would explain at least part of her frustration. The article said she'd been an assistant boutique manager in London before that. She must have found her new life quiet and boring.

Hayley would be able to tell her more, if Eve could catch her alone. Or find out when Hayley was off-duty for a change. Until then, it couldn't be that hard to find the shop where Donna had sold pants with elasticated waistbands and sequinned tops that fell apart after the second wash. Harder would be finding someone who knew her then and still worked there. In Eve's experience, the people you wanted to stay, invariably moved on. Like she did herself.

Eve silently apologised for her snobbery. "Paula's Parlour" was neither cheap nor tasteless. It might not cater to the rich and beautiful that sauntered through Chelsea and Kensington on killer heels, swinging it-bags and wearing statement coats, but she'd gladly browse here for a new outfit. Or at least pretend to.

Eve rifled through the tops on a rack. She'd seen two

shop assistants at work, one behind the till, the other one folding tee-shirts with the precision of an automaton and the speed of a snail.

She counted under her breath to see how long it would take for one of them to approach a customer.

"Are you looking for anything in particular?" Exactly three minutes later the folder gave Eve an encouraging smile while keeping clear of Eve's personal space. Eve smiled back at the thin dark-haired woman. She took her to be in her forties, old enough to have befriended Donna, if she had known her.

"I don't know." Eve sighed, careful to exaggerate her slight American accent. "It's so hard to say what really suits you. On my last visit, I had such great advice from a lovely lady, but that was, gee, years ago." Eve held a shimmering satin wrap blouse up and tut-tutted. "That Donna knew exactly my style. Much better than me. She doesn't work here anymore, does she?"

The sales assistant took the hanger with the blouse out of Eve's hands and exchanged a worried look with her colleague behind the till.

"Donna, you say? Oh dear." She led Eve to a velvet pouffe and made her sit before she pulled up a second pouffe.

Her colleague joined them, clucking her tongue. She was at least sixty but valiantly fought the losing battle against her age. "You must be very brave, love," she said to Eve.

"This will come as a shock, but our dear Donna is no longer of this world."

Eve clutched her chest. "Oh no. But she was so young." She lowered her voice, half hating herself, half enjoying her newly discovered acting talents. "Was it the big C?" She was met with two blank stares. "Cancer? It's taking so many."

The younger sales assistant shook her head. "Much, much worse. She was murdered, in her own home, I'm sorry to say."

Eve gasped. "Murdered? A burglary?"

"That's not what the police think. There was nothing missing."

"It was the husband who did it." The older woman relished her big moment. "Everybody knows, although the police couldn't prove it."

"Because he wasn't there when it happened," the younger woman said. This conversation seemed to have played out with a certain regularity, Eve thought, because there were no pauses.

The older shop assistant snorted. "Then why did Donna run around with a hang dog look for months, and suddenly she was floating on air? If you ask me, that's when she made up her mind to leave him, but he wouldn't let her."

"It could have been someone else." The younger woman glared at her colleague. Eve kept quiet, hoping to be forgotten in this flow of narrative.

"Like who?" The older woman tapped her foot.

"I'm not naming names, but Donna did have an awful lot of lunch dates, and she did get picked up by this handsome fellow sometimes. And I don't believe in a week of Sundays that was her husband."

"Why shouldn't Donna be friends with a man? Anyway, I didn't see him for weeks before it happened." The older woman crossed her arms over her chest.

A man. That sounded promising. "What did he look like?" Eve asked.

"Tall and broad-shouldered and ever so charming." The older woman snapped her mouth shut, as if registering Eve's presence anew, after forgetting all about her.

Eve wished she'd had another choice instead of asking, but it couldn't be helped.

"I think I'll try on that blouse," she said, hoping the women would pick up their discussion while she was out of sight.

She was lucky. As she twirled in front of the mirror in the dressing room, she caught the words "friend in the corner charity shop". To make her day complete, the blouse flattered her looks. It would be mean not to buy it, after profiting from her skilful interrogation.

As Eve paid for the blouse, she asked, "Is there any kind of vintage shop close by? I've promised a friend in the States a few photos for her blog."

"We only know Kim Potter's place. You can't miss it if you turn left at the traffic light. It's called 'Helping Hand'," the younger woman said. "That's where we take damaged clothes."

"Only good things, mind," her colleague said. "Clothes we couldn't sell with a good conscience, but which need a bit of mending or a good clean. In 'Paula's Parlour' we only stock quality garments."

"I can see that, and you've been wonderful," Eve said, lifting her glossy bag with her purchase. "I can't thank you ladies enough." Her American accent almost slipped. She brought it back in full force. "Y'all have a great day, you hear."

Eve's luck ran out when she located the charity shop. It supported half a dozen local causes, from a hospice to an animal shelter, and the spotless window displayed a better class of goods than the usual knick-knacks and musty clothes Eve had grown accustomed to.

Unfortunately, the shop also sported a Closed sign, with a handwritten notice taped underneath. "Closed until further notice for illness." Eve noticed two dog bowls for food and water in a corner of the room as she peered inside.

An elderly woman joined her. In her hands she held a bulging shopper with albums.

"What a shame," she said. "I hope it's not the doggy again. Poor Kim. It almost killed her when she had to give him up for a bit a few years back."

Eve made a non-committal noise in her throat.

"Inseparable, the two of them." The woman shook her head. "Could be Kim as well, I suppose. This dreadful tummy bug that's going around! My grandchildren have been laid up for days."

"Awful." Eve made a suitably sad, concerned face. Inwardly, she cheered. With any luck, Kim would remember Donna, and hopefully even the mystery man, unless he turned out to be Ben after all, who'd met his wife for lunch. The shop assistants didn't seem to know him, but maybe Donna didn't want to introduce him as her husband. Having an admirer gave her more of a mysterious air than a simple date with her spouse.

The traffic conspired against Eve too. She arrived back to find the pub crowded, with Hayley rushing to serve what appeared to be a meeting of the ladies' bowls and lawn croquet club, judging by the embroidery on their pink shirts. She'd come back later, she decided as she went to pick up her backpack.

Her afternoon stroll led her along a path devoid of people. Only the owl perched in its customary spot. It turned its head away as soon as it spotted her. She could swear she saw a smirk hovering over its beak.

The pub was still crowded on her return, so Eve headed home again for a ready meal. She decided to drop Hayley a note, which also meant hunting for an envelope in her odd drawer where she stuffed everything she intended to put in its right place one day. Only work correspondence and receipts got filed straight away.

Most people probably had such a drawer, she thought. Although personal messages happened mostly online these days, five years ago people still wrote letters, or diaries, or printed out photographs. If she could lay her hands on Donna's things, she might find a clue. Except she couldn't very well ask Ben to have a good old snoop in his deceased wife's things, if he had kept anything at all. Drat.

She sealed the note to Hayley. Until she heard back, there was nothing else she could do.

Eve dropped the envelope behind the bar. Hayley still rushed around. The bowls and lawn croquet club had gone from afternoon tea to pre-dinner drinks to happy hour, judging by the stack of dirty cups and glasses.

Hayley's grandmother gave her a quick wave, but she too pitched in behind the bar.

Eve lit a fire in the woodburner. The crackling logs and the flickering flames helped her relax. Keeping an eye on the fire also gave her something to do. She cherished a leisurely pace after a bout of frantic work, if she had no fixed plans. This though was the opposite. She badly wanted things to happen, and inactivity was hell.

She could get in touch with her father, something she only did once in a blue moon. They hadn't been close since her mother died. His second wife had declined to publicly acknowledge Eve's existence because it made him appear old, as she'd explained on their wedding day less than a year after he'd been widowed. The marriage didn't last, but the damage did. He was now on to wife number three. Their rare conversations were as meaningful as those she had with her mother who'd need a séance to communicate from beyond the grave.

Still, he was her family. A vague sense of duty, and the need for a distraction, made her type away at an email which would have to pass a few tests before she hit send. There would be no mentions of birthdays, or politics, or money, or health issues, in case they made her father uncomfortable. These limitations made the emails between Eve and her father read like a cross between weather reports, a realtor's magazine due to her frequent moves, and with the new addition of the owl to her repertoire, soon also a birdwatcher's diary.

That was the only good thing about climate change, she thought. Although the term as such fell under a strict no-no and it doomed life as they knew it, it kept the communication lively. Her father's emails spoke either of too much snow, too little snow, too much rain, a drought, or storms that should never have happened.

Had he always been this boring and colourless? As a child she'd adored him and his big chuckle which had died along with her mother. His subsequent choice of spouses had been less than satisfactory, at least from Eve's point of view. He stopped coming to visit her soon after she'd moved to England, during the reign of the second wife. She'd stopped visiting him shortly after. They saw each other at weddings and funerals, if at all.

Eve hesitated as she read through her insipid text. Should she add one x or two? Three were over the top and might raise her stepmother's hackles, in case it led to Eve asking for a favour.

One x looked a bit too detached. She groaned as she added a second x and pressed send when the door-bell rang.

Hayley handed Eve a bottle of wine and her jacket to hang up. "A housewarming gift," she said.

"Thank you for coming."

"I hauled in Dom. He's having a ball with all this harmless adoration, and they'll all be gone within the hour. Like Cinderella, only their night out ends way before midnight."

Hayley pulled a chair close to the fire and sat down.

"Won't the men come in for a nightcap?" Eve asked.

"Not when the Pink Panthers are on the loose."

Eve must have looked perplexed, because Hayley said, "The unofficial club name. They toyed with changing it to Pink Cougars, to scare the old blokes, but it didn't catch on." She glanced around openly. "Not a bad place. Bit mumsy for you, I'd have thought."

Eve shrugged. "I don't tend to notice after a while. It's stupid because I'm a sucker for the outwards appearance. In any case I've only rented the cottage for a year."

"That's a hell of a long stretch to live with mustard and aubergine walls."

Eve held up the bottle. Hayley waved it away. "Tea would be nice. And then we can chat about whatever you want to know so badly. Unless you invited me over for my pretty eyes and witty conversation."

"More like your animal magnetism." Eve added a handful of slightly crumbling biscuits to the tea tray.

Hayley suppressed a yawn. "Don't let me nod off. It's the fire, and the fact that I get up earlier than any self-respecting rooster."

"I was kind of hoping you could tell me about Donna Dryden."

Hayley's biscuit dropped into her tea. "Why?"

Eve paused. "Erm ..."

"I mean it," Hayley said. "I need to know before I spill any beans. Is it because of morbid curiosity, the lure of the potential bad boy or do you have an honest to God crush on him?"

CHAPTER 7

*E*ve stared at her guest. "I don't have a crush on Ben Dryden, or anyone else."

"Okay."

"Also, I'm not a thrill seeker or publicity hound."

"But?" Hayley asked, clearly expecting more.

"The way people treated him the other night. Is it always like this?"

"No. Normally, they'd have spat behind his back or with a bit of Dutch courage, called him out for a fight." Hayley might as well have spoken about her grocery list for all the emotion she showed.

"That's horrible."

"What do you expect? Especially if you're not one of the

boys, which Ben isn't. He never got drunk with the locals, he had a posh job, a family tree longer than my arm, and a wife who thought she was slumming it."

"Donna wasn't popular?" She shouldn't enjoy hearing that, Eve silently admonished herself, but she did. Which would have been pathetic and despicable, if it hadn't held the promise of yielding a new crop of murder suspects.

Hailey shrugged. "I think Donna was simply lonely here and out of her depth. She'd married a charming guy with a charming life and a charming place in London, and as soon as his old man is in trouble, that's over."

"Ben and his father must be close."

"Looks like it. But why do you want to know if you aren't interested in him?"

Eve felt her cheeks grow warm. She moved away from the fire. "I like him as a person, and I want him to have a normal life again. I'd want that for anybody."

"Nice sentiment, but that's not going to happen as long as he stays, and he'll stay until his old man pops his clogs."

"Or the case is solved."

Hayley snorted in disbelief. "After five years of a big fat nothing?"

"Is it so unlikely?" Eve asked. "If Ben is innocent, someone else got away with murder."

"He didn't ask you for your help, did he?" Hayley gave her a shrewd look.

"No," Eve said. "He'd much rather be treated like dirt than let anything upset his father. It's crazy."

"But you don't intend to honour his wishes."

"Would you? I thought you're his friend?"

"I am. If you really want to dig up the past, I'll see what I can do to help you. It'll take me a while to remember most things though."

"That's fine. I'll make a list. Just tell me, did you like Donna? And did Ben love her?" Eve half dreaded the answers.

"Hard to tell," Hayley said after an interminable pause. "She might have been perfectly nice, for all I know. It's always hard to be the new one in a small town, and the odd one out. I wasn't here for most of that period myself, but when I was, I never got the impression she felt like she fitted in when I met her, and she took it out on Ben."

"In what way?" Eve hoped she sounded noncommittal. She couldn't imagine Ben playing doormat to a harpy, but some men did that. Like her father, with wife number two.

"Icy glares, snide remarks when she thought nobody would hear her. Silly stuff, really, but hard to shake off," Hayley said.

"And Ben?"

"He's not that easy to read. He took it all on the chin, but I have not the foggiest if that was because he loved her and felt guilty about dragging her here or because he didn't love her and felt guilty about dragging her here." Hayley's eyelids drooped. "Sorry. If you don't want me to fall asleep on the spot, I've got to go."

Eve's conscience pricked. "I shouldn't have asked you to see me after a long day. Shall we talk another time?"

"You better believe that. If you're doing a Sherlock, you need a Watson. Just smarter and better looking."

An ally and new friend, Eve thought as she snuggled under her duvet a little later. This mission couldn't fail.

The next day dawned grey, with the clouds hanging low enough to dampen anyone's spirits. Except for Eve, who took the threat of rain as a good sign, especially if it held off until she needed it to pour down. Maybe a drizzle would be enough for her purposes, but she preferred a good drenching.

She set out under a gunmetal grey sky, wellies on her

feet and a flimsy umbrella in her backpack. Nobody could think of her as unprepared as she strolled along the stream.

Ben stood in the place she now considered to be his spot. His face lit up as he saw her. "I didn't expect to see you today."

"Neither rain nor sleet nor gloom of night," Eve quoted. She had no idea why the unofficial US postal service's motto had popped into her head, but it seemed to fit.

She took out her umbrella. Up close it looked pathetic. "Maybe not sleet."

"Listen," he said.

A sudden breeze ruffled the leaves but that was all. She gave him a puzzled frown.

"There's no bird song," Ben said.

"That means what?"

A fat drop hit her in the eye, followed by a bucket load of rain. Eve had her answer. She flinched. She wrestled with her useless umbrella; after all she'd bought it for this very reason, but a little bit of protection would have been welcome after all. She wanted to look wet and in need of shelter, but not like a drowned rat.

Ben pulled up the hood of his waterproof jacket. He took her arm and said, "We'd better make a run for it."

"Where are we going?"

"My home is closest. Unless you mind going there."

Eve could have punched the air in triumph. Instead, she settled for saying, "That sounds like a good idea."

Ben's home lay fifteen minutes at a brisk pace behind the wooden cabin. Eve glimpsed a tree hollow with something feathery inside, maybe her avian alibi. Her wellies squelched in the few muddy spots, but most of the path stayed solid. That was interesting. Not that she'd expect footprints after five years, should the killer have used this escape route, but Donna had died on a rainy evening. Maybe her assailant had left muddy foot prints. She'd need to ask Hayley or find a way to see the police report.

Eve shivered as they reached the house, a forbidding two-storeyed manor with a half-timbered front. The two wings were lower and made completely of grey stone.

Her wet jeans clung to her legs. Rain ran down her collar and onto her back. She hoped this visit was worth risking a cold.

Ben led her through a side door into a small boot room. The smooth flagstones ran unevenly towards the wall, and the door. He took her jacket and handed her a towel from a cabinet.

She dabbed her face dry and ran the towel through her hair.

"That's better," she said.

"Would you like to dry off in front of the fire before I run you home?"

"Yes please."

She placed her wellies next to Ben's boots on a wooden rack and followed him into a large room with shabby furniture, a few what must be ancestral portraits, and a large fireplace. Only the antlers and stags' heads were missing to make it a country house cliché. For a second, she could understand why Donna hadn't felt at home, although with a white-washed ceiling to bring out the dark beams and the brown wainscoting that ran halfway up the walls replaced with something lighter, this room could be comfortable.

Eve reined in her thoughts. She wasn't here to critique the interior design.

From another room she heard a mechanical squeal. The wheelchair, she assumed.

"Where's the bathroom?" she asked.

Ben pointed towards the hallway. "Upstairs, second door on the left. It's better equipped than the one down here."

Eve clasped her backpack and slipped out of the room. While the ground floor had come straight out of a period picture, the second floor returned her to the present with its ankle-deep silver carpet and pale blue walls.

The bathroom boasted two large oval sinks, and the amount of chrome, glass and marble tiles with a subtle pink and gold thread running through them convinced Eve that this had been Donna's design. Not such bad taste after all.

Eve quickly opened the cabinet to see if the dead woman had left anything else behind. No. All the contents of the rooms confirmed were that Ben took his dental hygiene seriously, he used quality care products, and he had two aftershaves. Also, since one lonely toothbrush stood in the holder, he definitely had no regular overnight visitor.

She battled the urge to snoop in the master bedroom. If she got caught, she had no excuse. She could have told Ben the truth, that she would have loved to see anything left behind by his wife, but he probably would tell Eve to go to hell.

The fire crackled as she came down with her face washed and her hair brushed. A slick of lip balm gave her the satisfaction of looking fresh without obvious make-up.

An elderly man who must have been easily Ben's size before ill health shrunk his body, gave her an unreadable look. The right side of his face was slack from the bushy eyebrow downwards. A shock of brown hair sparsely threaded with silver looked too youthful for the rest. He held little resemblance with his son, but that could be due to his physical changes.

Eve held out her hand and gave him her friendliest smile. "Thank you for letting me seek refuge in your home, Mr Dryden."

Ben raised his eyebrows at his father. The old man lifted his left hand and touched hers briefly. "You're welcome, Miss –"

"Eve Holdsworth. Please call me Eve."

"We don't have many visitors." A few consonants came out slurred. Ben wheeled him closer to the fire. This must be where the body was found, Eve thought. How could they not mind, or at least change the floor where Donna's blood must have pooled around her head? Or they were used to generations being born and dying in the same house, a thought she found horrific.

She warmed herself in front of the fire, trying hard not to scan the floor for dried blood spatters. If the old man hadn't been around, she'd have asked Ben for a bathrobe and taken off her wet jeans.

"Is Chris not here?" Ben asked.

"He had to leave early. Another patient, thinking she'd sprained something or other. Damn fool woman." John's gaze flickered towards Eve. *This is a test,* she thought. She kept her silence.

"Did he give you your massage?"

"He'd never leave without doing his job." A hint of affection broke through the crusty façade. "Aren't you offering your new friend a seat?"

The words new friend held a hint of derision. Was the old man jealous? He was used to having Ben to himself, Eve thought. Or possibly he wanted to protect his son from making another mistake, although there was no reason to misinterpret the situation.

"Coffee?" Ben asked.

"That would be great." Eve's nerves were on edge as she watched Ben leave the room.

John struggled with the controls of his wheelchair. No wonder he preferred Ben to push him.

"Can I help you?" Eve asked.

He struggled harder to get moving. Finally, he grunted in defeat. "Get me to the table. Please."

She wheeled John in place. He reached for a notepad, probably another left-over from Donna, Eve thought. A white cloud covered most of the paper, with a light-blue background giving it a whimsical look at odds with the Dryden men.

John's hand searched in a side pocket of his wheelchair. He produced a pen.

"I could write a note for you," Eve said. A small pause developed. To her, it felt like a battle.

He pushed the notepad towards her. "Write, ginger nuts. Cram of tomato soup. And health bars. Chris likes them."

Eve noted the three items. "Is that all?"

"You're not afraid to be here, are you?"

That coffee took awfully long. "No."

"There is no money."

Eve looked at him, incredulously. "You seem to have the wrong idea."

"I'm simply telling you. That's all. You wouldn't be the first to think she's struck – there you are, son."

He gave Ben a lopsided grin as his son approached, a tray in his hands.

Interesting. John had seen his daughter-in-law as a gold-digger. What a pity Ben interrupted them. She could hardly pick up the thread again.

They drank their coffee wordlessly, the only sounds the

crackling of the logs and John's slurping. He had a special cup, hand-crafted by the looks of it. It made it easier for him not to spill his drink.

Eve got up and gazed out of the window at a dripping clump of trees. The rain had stopped, and the sky was cloudless and blue. The flagstones glistened.

"I'd better get going," she said. "Thank you for your hospitality."

"Not at all," Ben said, more to his father than to her. "We could do with a bit more company."

John fixed his gaze on her face. His right eyelid blinked slower than the left. She forced herself to return the gaze without moving a muscle. Everything with John seemed to be a test. She intended to pass.

Eve rubbed her thighs on the drive home. The still damp jeans felt uncomfortable, but it had been worth it. She'd breached the threshold.

"There's a blue throw on the back seat," Ben said and switched the heater on high.

She half-turned and grabbed it. Together with the blast of warm air it helped with the chill.

"I hope my father didn't say anything to offend you. In which case I'd apologise."

"It's fine," Eve said.

"He used to be full of life. It's hard to be reduced to this."

"He's got you."

"Yeah, well. Not much, is it?"

"It seemed enough for him. Although I didn't get the impression he likes women much."

"He didn't like Donna, in the end."

"Why? Because she wanted to leave you?" Eve kept her tone light, to make it sound like a normal conversation and not an interview.

"I didn't ask him. They rubbed along well enough before it became obvious we'd be here for the long-haul. Or at least that I was going to stay."

Almost home. Eve concentrated on the road.

"Where was she going to live? London?"

"No idea."

"But you had to cancel her movers, didn't you? Or a rental contract?"

"No." A nerve in the left corner of his mouth twitched.

"Sorry," she said. "What shall we talk about? Do you bowl? Or play laser tag? Anything at all."

"I own a pool table. And I used to play golf in my youth."

"Pool's nice. Maybe we could play one day."

"Maybe," he said.

Ben stopped his car in a deserted lane, two hundred metres from Eve's cottage. "I would drive you to the door, but it might be easier for you not to be seen with me."

"I'm not a coward."

"Being smart doesn't equal afraid."

"Can I offer you a drink?"

"I need to get back to my father. But I appreciate your gesture."

Eve entered her home wrapped in the throw. Now she needed to clean and return it. Her cottage seemed suddenly empty and soulless despite its character charm. She thought back to Ben's living room, and the bath room. Like Donna, she never left much of a mark wherever she went.

She peeled off the jeans. Where did Donna intend to live, if she hadn't rented a place? There could be but one answer: Donna had planned to move in with the mystery man her former colleague mentioned.

CHAPTER 8

The fire burnt low as Ben faced his father's inquisition. He'd sat in the car for a good twenty minutes, unwilling to go inside. He wondered how much Eve knew about Donna's murder. There'd been lurid stories in the cheap rags, milking every gory bit and making up things to fill the gap.

He deliberately stepped onto the spot where he'd found his wife. It had taken him two years before he could bring himself to do it, and even today he tended to avoid it. It felt like walking on her grave.

"Pretty woman," John said, not looking at his son.

Ben made a disinterested sound.

"Known her long?"

"Why? Anything wrong with her?"

John pushed himself off the table, using his left hand, and turned the wheelchair forty-five degrees.

"Let me do it," Ben said automatically. 'Where do you want to go?"

"I want to look you in the eyes." John's speech slurred much more; the effort had exhausted him.

Ben planted his feet in front of the wheelchair and shoved his hands in his pockets. "Alright."

"Promise me you won't make another horrible mistake."

"Dad. This is my life."

John closed his eyes and wheezed.

Ben softened. "I've barely met her. It's nice to have someone else to talk to once in a while, that's all."

"You don't need another Donna," John said.

Ben clenched his hands inside his pockets. "She's dead and buried, Dad. Leave it alone."

"I want us to be happy. As far as that's possible."

John's eyes opened. They had a moist film clouding them. This, for him, was as close to expressing sentiment as he allowed himself.

"Don't worry, Dad," Ben said. "We're a team." They were, they always had been since his mother died, although sometimes it hard been hard to accept the fierce protectiveness John hid from the rest of the world. That was a lesson Ben wished he'd never had to learn. Love always came at a price.

"You look tired," he said. "Why don't you take a nap and I'll wake you for dinner?"

At least his work could be relied upon to distract him, and his computers never asked awkward questions. He pushed John's wheelchair to his father's room and returned to a world without unplanned complications.

Hayley pulled up the duvet until it came up to her nan's chin. Letty had what she euphemistically called a hibernation day on her sofa. It meant that her arthritis had kept her awake all night and the medication wasn't enough to dull the pain.

Hayley stroked her grandmother's cheek. The skin was soft under her touch, despite the wrinkles. Letty clasped Hayley's hand and pressed it against her face. "You're my good girl," she said, her voice thin and shaky. "I don't know what I'd do without you. I'm sorry to be such a nuisance."

Hayley gave Letty a kiss on the forehead. "You're never a nuisance," she said as she listened for noise from the pub downstairs. Dom had instructions to ring a bell if he needed her, but he tended to be overly optimistic about how much he could take on. But everything seemed quiet, which suited her. She rarely could sit down for a good chat with her nan. Talking shop wasn't the same.

As much as she valued Letty's support, it was hard to keep her nan from overdoing things. The doctor said cooking and helping and being a vital part of the business she had built helped keep Letty going. The problem was to prevent her from doing too much. As convenient as it was to live over the pub, it also meant she could nip down whenever she thought she was needed.

"Your new friend seems nice," Letty said.

"New friend? Oh, you mean Eve. I'm glad you think so." Hayley put a small container with two painkillers next to the water jug. "Ben seems to like her too."

Letty's eyes fluttered open. "Ben Dryden?"

"That's why he came to the 'Green Dragon' the other night."

Her nan lay still.

"You don't think he had anything to do with what happened to his wife?" Hayley asked.

"No, although – ", Letty struggled to prop herself up. Hayley pushed a pillow under Letty's head. "I've always wondered if he doesn't know more than he lets on." Letty sank back against the pillow. Her eyes closed.

"I'll let you sleep," Hayley said. "We can talk later."

She gently closed the door behind her. There wasn't much that escaped her nan. Why would Ben hide something in a murder case? And what could he possibly have to hide?

Eve created a schedule for herself. She needed to time-table her upcoming work-load, her bird-watching (*or Ben-watching*, a small voice at the back of her head whispered), and any sleuthing had to fit in around these fixed items. She created a worksheet, printed it out and stuck it to the wall behind her computer. It helped to see things written down in black and white, the old-fashioned way.

Did Donna do that as well? Eve tried to remember how much or little she'd relied on an electronic calendar five years ago. Not too much, and if you wanted to keep an appointment secret, the loud pings didn't help, especially if someone else might glimpse a notification popping up. A paper diary was a lot safer.

Of course, in all likelihood Ben had gotten rid of all of Donna's belongings. Hayley might know, or at least be able to find out. Just like she might have an idea where Donna might have met a lover. Tongues wagged over nothing in small places and keeping a liaison completely under wraps would be a miracle.

Eve grabbed her purse. The charity shop woman should be her next stop. Her work stint would have to be moved to the evening.

Eve counted finding a metered parking space two doors down from "Helping Hand" as a good omen. The sun peeked through wispy clouds, and a hedgehog shaped rock propped the shop door wide open.

Eve hefted a bag filled with assorted donations out of her car boot. Some of them, like two limited edition impressionist prints bought at the Musee D'Orsay, were her own. Others were recent purchases for this occasion, including a coffee table book about Fashion in Film which she'd secretly drooled over. She hated to part with these things, but they were sacrifices in the name of a good cause. If she wanted to establish a connection with Kim Potter, she needed to give her something good to appraise. If it indeed was Kim in the shop.

A name-tag pinned to a crisp white shirt confirmed her hope.

"Hi," Eve said. "I hope you accept donations on the spot." She heaved the bag onto the spotless glass counter which doubled as a jewellery display case. "I'm Eve, by the way." She eyed a pair of art deco chandelier earrings.

"You're most welcome, Eve. I'm Kim. Shall we have a look?" She snapped on a pair of surgical gloves, emptied the bag item for item and spread them out on a folding table.

Eve admired her precision, and the sheer bliss in her face. Kim also had an enviable knack of keeping her jeans and shirt immaculate, despite dealing with used books, clothes and knick-knacks. A few sandy hairs clung at knee-height to her jeans. Kim's hair was a glossy chocolate brown, so it seemed reasonable to surmise they came from the dog.

Water and food bowl were half-filled and on display. A door at the back read "Private". Eve guessed the dog would be found behind that door.

"Are you sure you want to part with these?" Kim held up the first print. "The Star" captured Degas' love for the ballet so perfectly, Eve had fallen in love at first sight but somehow never gotten around to hanging it on her wall. The same went for van Gogh's "Starry Night over the Rhone".

She could look at them now, not with detachment, but with a kind of wonder. When she bought them, she'd thought she'd figured out a new piece of her identity, only to shelve them. If she found herself, maybe she'd stay in one place.

"Are you okay?" Kim asked.

"Memories. I definitely want to part with these things."

Eve put on a wistful look. "They were meant as gifts." Kim wouldn't ask any further questions, if Eve was any judge of character. And she'd make no more hints. This one remark should do the trick to lay the foundations. Eve estimated she'd need a few more visits to gain Kim's trust. Like fishing; she'd baited the hook, and now she needed patience to reel in her prey.

"Do the proceeds go in equal parts to the charities or how does it work?" she asked.

"Unless the donors have any specific requests, it's equally divided."

Eve fingered the brochures for the supported charities as she played through causes that might appeal to Kim personally. "If it's possible at all and you sell the stuff I brought you, I'd like the money to go to places in support of animals. And women and children."

Kim's face lit up. "I'll make sure it will."

Eve stayed for fifteen minutes, chatting about travel – Kim dreamt of exploring Italy, but wouldn't leave her dog for too long, and Eve agreed, listing places worth visiting even on a tight schedule. She left in the comforting glow of having established friendly enough terms to build on.

If traffic ran smoothly, she might catch up with Ben. She'd intended to be a little later than usual anyway. The last thing she wanted was for him to get the wrong impression as well. Whatever Hayley thought, Eve absolutely did not have a crush on Ben. Or anyone.

Yesterday's rain had made barely an impact on the soil. Only in the grassy overhung spots was the earth squishy. Eve had no problem keeping to the dry part. She'd left the borrowed throw behind. Once she'd washed it, she intended to return it to the house instead of stuffing it into her backpack. Good manners demanded it, and it would give her a good excuse to chat with Ben's father again, once she had more information.

Ben stood in his usual place. She glanced around. No rod or bucket in sight. He was simply waiting for her then. A warm fuzzy feeling spread in her stomach.

"Fish not biting after the rain, or do you have all the stock you need?" she asked.

"The pond is sorted. I wanted to make sure you survived the drenching."

"Not the tiniest sniffle. What about you?" She face-palmed. "I forgot the throw."

"No worries."

"I've never walked any further than this spot," Eve said. "What lies behind? Here be dragons?"

He laughed, a full-throated sound that brought on the fuzzy feeling again. "I think you've met most of the dangerous creatures in the area."

"The regulars at the 'Green Dragon' looked toothless, and they weren't exactly breathing fire," she said, glad about the easy banter.

"Wait until you fall afoul of the Pink Panthers."

"Why? Would they slow-bowl me to death?"

"If you make a pass at one of their menfolk. Ask Hayley."

Eve gave an elaborate shudder. "Thanks for the warning, but in that case I'm safe. I've seen the men."

He glanced at her walking shoes. "It's more forest and a ten-inch drop in the stream bed, if you can take the excitement."

"Lead me to it."

Eve decided to stay away from any probing questions, until Ben relaxed even further. He'd made it clear he didn't want anyone to dig up his past, so she'd be discreet. It almost made her glad to have no real bond with her father, if Ben got so anxious over a man who despite being disabled looked strong enough to live to a ripe old age. Unless John was a lot frailer than he appeared.

She tripped over an exposed tree root.

Ben gripped her arm. "Steady."

He let go of her arm too quickly for her liking. Something about his behaviour was off.

"Are you sure you want to walk on?" she asked. "We can always do it another day. Or I might explore on my own."

"And fall and break your leg, in the middle of nowhere?"

"I rarely make a misstep. I was distracted, and this path hardly counts as uncharted territory."

He seemed undecided.

She grinned at Ben and turned on her heels. "But you're right. I think I'll postpone my long-distance training and tackle my work instead."

She left him with a cheerful wave by the trail leading to his house.

"Eve?" he asked, an insecure tone in his voice.

She glanced back.

"Yes?"

"I'm busy tomorrow, but we could go for a drink on Thursday evening?"

"In the 'Green Dragon'?"

"There's a nice village pub, a few miles away. You need to expand your horizon."

She gave him a thumbs up.

"I'll meet you at seven, where I set you off the other day," Ben said.

"It's a - deal." Eve winced inwardly. She'd been about to say date, but thanks to Hayley's stupid ideas that would have felt awkward.

Ben waited until Eve was out of sight before he ducked between two trees onto a trail just wide enough for him. He'd established it himself, to avoid having to pass the blasted cabin.

A date. He'd asked her out on a date, something he hadn't done in an eternity. Now it would be good if he could make up his mind if he'd proposed it because he wanted to go out with Eve or to show his father, he still had a life of his own.

CHAPTER 9

*C*hris put another log on the fire as Ben arrived. John sat basking in the heat, his pale cheeks flushed pink. Ben took off his sweater.

"Hi, mate." Chris arranged a stole around John's shoulders. His demeanour was invariably cheerful, and Ben would be eternally grateful the massage therapist had stuck with them through the dark days. He'd been as shocked as Ben by the murder.

Chris could easily have cashed in on their sudden notoriety and sold his version of Ben's marriage to the tabloids, but he'd kept quiet, another point in his favour. He'd also kept his positive façade while going through his own heartbreak when his soldier girlfriend split up with him from afar, a month after Donna's death.

Ben saw Chris' gaze flicker towards the wall clock.

"Do you have to run, or would you like a drink?" Ben asked.

"I was just going to make us tea."

"I'll take care of it," Ben said.

Chris followed him into the kitchen and leant against the table. "John says you had a visitor."

"Of course he did." Ben put the kettle on and arranged the tea things on a tray. Chris had found the pottery where they bought John's cups and soup mugs. He'd devised all kinds of aids to make their life easier, so Ben should have expected John to chat to Chris, if he wanted to chat about anything. The massage therapist was a godsend for both of them, even if his cheerful manner occasionally grated on Ben's nerves. Without Chris, Ben would have no respite at all.

"I could, you know, put in a good word for the lady with John." Chris' open face showed concern.

"Thanks, but that's not necessary." Chris meant well, Ben reminded himself, despite being no loss for the diplomatic world.

"John seemed to think it's serious."

Ben spilt hot water as he filled the tea-pot. "What are you talking about? I bring home an acquaintance because we were caught in torrential rain, and you guys put together two and two and get five?"

"I'm simply saying, I'm on your side." Chris clapped him on the shoulder.

Ben spilt more hot water and scalded his hand. He swore.

John's gaze showed Chris all the fondness it lacked when he met Eve. But then Chris had experience with cantankerous patients and dealing with a man must be a lot easier than keeping the boundaries with his female patients. Or their daughters and granddaughters, if half of John's hints were true. Donna had liked him too, or at least she hadn't complained about his presence.

To be fair, if it hadn't been for his father and his work, the isolation would have driven him barmy too. Rural idyll held only so much appeal until people either fled or surrendered. He wondered how long Hayley would last. Or Eve.

Eve asked herself how long it would take for her to get restless again as she watched the regulars file into the "Green Dragon". A life regulated by routine and tradition, where people constantly measured you up to their expectations or dissected everything you did. The idea made her chest constrict painfully. This must be what being buried alive felt.

The longest she'd stayed in one place since her childhood were her university years. Variety had been her parents' mantra while her mother lived, and Eve had no intention of ever giving up her nomadic ways. They made life worthwhile. True, it could get lonely to start anew after every move, but she'd spent lonely moments with friends as well. The important bit was keeping an open mind and not getting bogged down.

Personal freedom was the greatest achievement of the women's liberation. If she made a mistake, the only person she hurt was herself, and if she was short of money, nobody else bore the brunt.

Her work. She needed to get back to her work, or she really would have to stay at it until the early hours. Another thing about personal freedom was that it also came with responsibility.

With the afternoon customers gone and the after-dinner crowd not yet in, Hayley left Dom in charge and took a tray up to her nan. Letty had lived over the pub since she had come home from a short honeymoon in the Lake District. She'd papered the walls herself, first with a creamy paper covered in rose-branches and petals, and later with funky cockatoos on a pale blue background. The rose wallpaper survived in form of matching curtains.

Hayley's rooms were next to Letty's. An old-fashioned bell system connected all the private rooms with the pub. Hayley had also decorated her rooms herself, but Letty's home-making talents had passed her by. After two failed attempts at lining up wallpaper she'd gone for ochre walls with a terracotta border. The irregular lines gave it character, she told herself, and usually she was too busy to care anyway.

Except Letty grew frailer, and Hayley would soon have to decide if she wanted to keep up the family tradition forever or sell up and leave once Letty was gone. If she still could leave by then. She would be thirty-five on her next birthday, not old, but in another five or ten years she might be stuck forever.

She knocked on her nan's door and opened it as quietly as she could. They each had an en-suite bedroom and a lounge, with a kitchen in between.

Letty's eyelids fluttered open. She heaved herself into a sitting position on the sofa. She'd been a light sleeper as long as Hayley could remember, but she never complained about noise from the pub. Hayley used to think it invigorated her nan to have the constant connection to her old life, but lately she wondered if instead it sapped Letty's energy.

"Do you mind the noise, and the cooking?" she asked as she placed the dinner tray with a reheated slice of quiche on the table.

"What are you talking about?" Letty patted the sofa next to her.

Hayley sat down. "You work so hard and it must be difficult to get a moment's peace up here."

For a second, Letty's eyes grew fearful. "I don't mind," she said. "As long as I can be useful, I'll carry on."

But how long was that?

Letty cut her quiche with her fork into bitesize pieces. "Do you regret coming back?"

"No. Of course not." It came out more forceful than Hayley intended.

"This town hasn't got much to offer you," Letty said. "The men are either married or boring as hell." She caught Hayley's surprised glance and grinned, a mischievous grin reminiscent of the young Letty still present in her photos.

"I haven't always been seventy-eight, you know," she said. "It's alright for me. I've had my life, but you shouldn't stay here forever. Just like Ben. Look at how it's turned out for him."

"I'm not going to become a murder suspect." Hayley

stroked Letty's thin mottled hand, uneasy how much her nan's thoughts echoed her own. "What did you mean when you said he knows more than he lets on?"

"He's a smart man. Always has been." Letty chewed slowly, much too slow for Hayley's liking. "He realises he'll always be the one who did it unless someone else is tried and sentenced, and even then, it might not be enough to convince most folks."

"He's trying to spare his father."

"His father is tougher than he looks. We old folks usually are. Think about it."

"John had a massive stroke when Donna was murdered," Hayley said.

"But it didn't kill him. No, if Ben doesn't want things to be cleared up it's because he has his reasons."

"But what kind?"

"Well, he dragged his wife away from London. She didn't like it here much, although for a few months before her death, she looked a lot happier." Letty ate another bite.

"He's protecting Donna, you mean? That doesn't make much sense."

"Doesn't it? He's always been a considerate man. I wouldn't wonder if he's protecting her good name, because he feels guilty for choosing his father over her."

"I never thought about that." Hayley helped herself to a morsel from Letty's plate. "When you say she looked happier, in what way?"

"Like a cat that got the cream." Letty's head shook.

"Let's get you to bed," Hayley said. "When you're rested, you can tell me more. I didn't meet Donna that often, and she used to strike me as fairly dull. Pretty, but not exactly a sparkling personality."

"Does this sudden interest have anything to do with your new friend and Ben Dryden?"

Hayley planted a kiss on Letty's forehead. "Good night."

Hayley checked pantry and freezer before she took her place behind the bar. They should be able to cope for three or four days without Letty's cooking, if she reduced the menu, but she needed to hire someone for the kitchen as soon as possible. She could kick herself for postponing the inevitable.

The Women's Institute might help. Hayley waved at Sue Littlewood, WI secretary and unofficial manager of the local grapevine. Despite it all, she could be discreet if needed. Sue came here regular as clockwork twice a week with her girlfriends. The tradition started as a subtle rebellion against the boys' night out their husbands insisted on. The wives had started an arrangement with Letty. She'd introduced burger and pint nights on the two evenings a week the men dropped by, so their spouses didn't need to cook. For their ladies' nights out, the men were left to fend for themselves, and if they dropped into another pub for a bite, it hurt no-one.

Sue and her three girlfriends giggled like teenagers. Hayley moved over to them. Bella Jones, Sue's spirited sidekick, clapped her hand over her phone screen.

"It's okay," Sue said. "I'm sure Hayley wouldn't mind getting an eyeful." Bella took away her hand.

Hayley whistled as she scrolled through a series of shirtless pictures. The ladies might be close to sixty, but they hadn't lost their interest in the acting and other talents of stars like Tom Hiddleston and Idris Elba. She paused on one shot that in itself could delay menopause.

Sue winked at her. Hayley handed back the phone. "Nice selection," she said.

"We thought if the men can ogle anything in a short skirt, we can treat ourselves too," Sue said.

"Good on you."

"Where's Letty tonight?" Bella, whose unrivalled skills as a hairdresser made her a prime source for gossip, had given Hayley her first haircut when she was knee-high, and as such counted herself as a member of the family.

"That's why I've come over," Hayley said. "Would you be able to recommend anyone I could hire for the kitchen? I want Nan to be able to slow down without having to worry."

Bella clucked her tongue. "I've told her. Again and again I've said, Letty, you're not getting any younger. Although she is the best cook in the county."

Sue said, "Would it be full time, or only the odd hour or two?"

"If possible, full time. Nan would probably want to supervise him or her in the beginning, but ideally she won't have to do anything much longer."

"Leave it with us," Sue said. "I can think of one or two who might fit the bill."

"That would be wonderful. Do I know them?"

"One of them used to do a bit of cooking and housework for the Dryden's." Sue lowered her voice. "Naturally she didn't go back after you-know-what. Her husband wouldn't have it."

"You're not thinking of Grace, are you?" Bella's lips thinned into a grim line. "I've seen her bedroom and it was not a pretty sight. I know someone who might fit the bill."

Sue nudged her and beamed at Hayley. "See? Don't you fret about a thing, love."

The brass doorbell chimed. Bella's hands went to her lavender-tinted curls to fluff them. The other ladies showed more restraint, but they too perked up.

Hayley returned to the job. A handsome man in his thirties propped an elbow on the bar. Brown curls flopped onto his forehead.

His face looked familiar, but it took her a moment to place him as John Dryden's massage therapist. He used to drop in with Ben and Donna sporadically, or on his own, so he probably lived in one of the villages close by. He'd been a huge hit with the women, she recalled, especially with an absent girlfriend, although none of them had scored. Or if she had, it all happened discreetly enough to stay secret.

"A pint of Guinness, please," he said.

"Sure." No wedding band, broad shoulders and well-defined muscles. If he were to become a regular, Hayley saw trouble ahead. Like in every other small place, there were enough single or unhappily married women to make an eligible man a prized trophy, and enough unhappily married men to dislike any competition.

She sat his glass in front of him. Chris; now she remembered the name. He wasn't her type, but she could see the appeal. Especially in comparison to her regulars. A stallion among a herd of donkeys.

She noticed him watching the room in the bar mirror.

"Looking for someone?" she asked.

He gave her a confidential grin which would have made more than a few hearts flutter. "Trying to get my bearings. Much easier to jog your memory first before I put my foot in. It's been a while."

"It has."

"I definitely remember you. Sally."

"It's Hayley."

He chuckled ruefully. "See? Slipped up already." He took a swig. "Not much change though."

"You've entered a time-warp."

"It can't be that bad. Even here people leave or arrive."

Something clicked in Hayley's head. If she guessed correctly, he'd been looking for Eve. She filed that information away in her head as she shrugged and switched her focus to one of the old-timers who leant his cane against the stool. "Your usual, Pete?"

Chris left soon after, to Bella's disappointment. She liked a bit of eye-candy, as she called it, and in her first year as a widow she'd organised the annual Women's Institute outing in form of a theatre trip. The theatre hosted an all-male dance revue. Three women resigned from the institute after their return, and ten new ones signed on.

Hayley paused, half-polished glass in her hand. Had Bella done Donna's hair? In that case she needed to have a good chin-wag. Her own hair could do with a cut. Or she could arrange an appointment for Letty. In special cases Bella offered home-visits.

Eve waited in her car until she was sure Kim had no customers.

"Hello again." Kim looked up from arranging clothes by colour on a rack. She seemed genuinely pleased. "I hope you haven't come to reclaim your donations. One of your prints is already sold."

Eve scanned the jewellery display. The chandelier earrings with their marcasite stones and the tiered fan shapes were as beautiful as she remembered.

"To be honest, I came back for these earrings," she said. "Can I have a look at them?"

Kim unlocked the display and lifted out the velvet-covered shelf.

The earrings sparkled in the light.

"They're proper period pieces," Kim said as Eve held them to her ears. "They suit you."

"I've been invited out for dinner," Eve said. "He's only ever seen me in jeans and muddy shoes, so I wanted to make a good impression."

"He's taking you somewhere fancy, I assume?"

"It sounded like it." Eve twisted a strand of hair.

"You sound nervous. Don't be." Kim held up a hand-mirror. The fans at the bottom grazed Eve's chin.

"I haven't had a first date in years. Hell, I haven't had a date in years." Now Eve had a tight knot in her stomach.

A tinge of sadness washed over Kim's face.

"I don't know if you're single or not, but why do these things get harder as we get older?" Eve asked.

"Maybe because we've got more to lose."

"True. And I'll take the earrings. If he turns out to be a loss, at least I'll have some gorgeous new jewellery."

She fished out her purse. No need to overdo the girly chat at this stage.

CHAPTER 10

*E*ve arrived at the arranged spot at a minute past seven. She'd stuck to jeans, but a blazer, the new silk blouse and the earrings carefully straddled the line between casual and dressed-up.

Ben was already waiting. He got out of the car to open the door for her. Eve climbed in, suddenly tongue-tied. She'd promised herself to steer clear of any too personal topics, and as a result was lost for words.

"How was your day?" she asked, painfully aware of how trite this question was.

"I was looking forward to the evening." He switched on the radio. 90s rock filled the car. Ben lowered the volume, so they could speak over it. Eve sat back, starting to relax.

The car park of "The Golden Slipper" was filled with

expensive sports cars and limousines. As befit the name, golden light filtered through the mosaic windows of the half-timbered Elizabethan building. The nostalgic part of Eve admired the thatched roof that made it picture perfect. Her practical side saw it as a fire hazard.

A host led them to a secluded booth close to an enormous fireplace that could easily hold a whole pig and had probably done so in the past.

Eve relaxed as no other guests paid them any attention. It must have cost Ben a lot of nerve to face down the hostility she'd witnessed in the "Green Dragon". She fought back a sudden dull pain in her chest. She'd never been that close to her father, to make such a sacrifice. Or any sacrifice at all. He hadn't wanted her to get too close after they lost her mother.

She focussed on the menu.

"You're very quiet," Ben said.

"Sorry. I was day-dreaming." She made the corners of her mouth curl up in the hope the muscle movement would transform it into a real smile. It worked.

"I need to check in with my owl again," she said after they'd both ordered salmon and white wine. "I did intend to keep a bird-watching journal, but I haven't started yet."

"It's not too late. You are taking this seriously."

"It's either that or joining one of the available clubs to get me out of the house."

"I'd choose the owl."

"My thinking exactly. Do you have any idea how long it's been living in that area, or if it's male or female?"

He shook his head. "I don't usually walk along there."

Eve touched his hand. "I didn't want to bring up the past."

"It's okay. Better than having to tiptoe around the subject. And you couldn't know."

"Know what?"

Their food arrived, intricately arranged on the plates and as delicious to eat as it looked.

Ben concentrated on his fish. "After – things happened, I cleaned out the cabin. Donna used to go there to have some privacy. She'd put in a day-bed and a few other pieces of furniture. I found a packet of antihistamines and a half-empty box of condoms in a drawer. Donna had no hay fever. She was only allergic to dogs."

"They could have been left by someone else."

"The last occupant was a farm worker who retired in 2000." He looked up to meet her concerned gaze. "It doesn't matter, Eve."

"It doesn't?"

"Our marriage had died long before that. Why should I mind if she found a bit of happiness elsewhere?"

"It could have been with the wrong person," Eve said.

"She didn't die in the cabin."

"Did the police at least talk to the man?"

"I don't think so."

"You didn't push the issue."

"My father had already had all he could take." He ate, surprisingly calm. How could he not care?

"How about your family? Do they mind that you're thousands of miles away?" he asked.

She thought about her father, and their strained conversations. "I think they're good. If I'm honest, my father seems to prefer it this way. As does the wife du jour."

"Now it's my turn to say, I'm sorry."

"It's okay. Liberating, actually. To know where I stand." She pushed her food around. "But he taught me to play pool when I was a kid. You said you've got a table."

"A family heirloom. My mother's."

"I've only inherited Mom's impatience and her jewellery. Easy to pack up."

Ben leant over and touched one of the dangling earrings. Eve could smell his musky aftershave. "Pretty," he said.

"These weren't hers. I keep those for special occasions."

"I see."

"If you invite me over to play pool, you just might." She grinned.

His mouth twitched. "Tomorrow? Or are you busy on a Friday night?"

"I haven't touched a cue in years."

"It'll come back. It's like riding a bike."

Eve held her phone on her lap as she sat on her bed. Maybe both she and her father shared the blame for their disconnect. Ben unquestioningly put his own life on hold to support his father. Hayley gave up her independence without a second thought when her grandmother needed her. And what had Eve done? Run as fast as she could when things got tough.

It had been too painful to watch her dad first retreat into his shell when her mother died, and then replace her with a long-legged blonde with expensive taste in clothes and cars and cheap taste in other men. It took him a decade to find out, or more likely, to find the courage to react. By then the bond between him and Eve had dwindled to a thread.

She checked her watch. With any luck, her father would be on his lunch break, far away from wife number three and the speakerphone.

Eve scrolled through her contacts, without success. For some inexplicable reason, this revelation hurt. How could she have left her father's phone number out when she updated the list on her new phone? She could look it up in her address book, which currently lived in a trunk-sized suitcase under her bed with a gazillion other items she intended to find a proper place for one day.

She rolled onto her back. She'd send an email instead. "Hi, Dad. Thinking of you. Talk soon? x".

She hit send before she changed her mind. It would be good to hear his voice. It hadn't mattered for so long, but now it did. She hoped for her own sake it was because she cared about him after all and not because she needed to prove to herself she wasn't a heartless bitch.

Eve swallowed her disappointment when her inbox sat empty in the morning. It had been stupid to hope for an instant reply. Instead, she'd concentrate on her work and her sleuthing. An early lunch and a chat with Hayley couldn't hurt, if she managed to catch up on her neglected translation. Technical manuals were not her favourite topics, but they put the butter on her bread and usually jam as well.

The "Green Dragon" belonged to its lunch-time regulars. The men gave Eve a brief nod as she bade them a cheerful hello. Her heart swelled with pride. They recognised her. She'd arrived.

"We've got nothing apart from sandwiches or soup today." Hayley swiped her hair behind her ears. Her accustomed beam appeared strained.

"Is everything alright?" Eve asked.

"My nan has hit a bit of a rough patch. Until I've found a chef, our menu is restricted." Hayley pulled a grimace, but Eve suspected she worried more than she let on.

"Soup is fine," she said.

"I've got to warn you. It's home-made, but I'll have to microwave it."

"No problem."

"I'll bring it to your table."

Hayley brought a sandwich for herself as well.

"If there's anything I can do to help, give me a shout." Eve tasted her thick vegetable soup. "Except for cooking. I'm useless in the kitchen."

"That's under control. I've enlisted the Women's Institute," Hayley said.

"Smart."

"Except I've got no clue how to pick the right candidate." She bit into her sandwich and pulled a face. "I forgot to put in the rocket."

"Can your nan get down the stairs?"

"With my help, yes."

"Let them cook for her. She can sit and watch, and then choose her own successor."

"Not a bad idea." Hayley let out a deep breath. "That might work."

"Have I met the Women's Institute?" Eve asked. They might be useful to chat to.

"Not yet. Or you'd find yourself with a filled out membership application form."

"Not me. Like I said, I'm not much of a joiner."

"What are you doing in a small town then? Apart from the obvious attractions."

"It's a bit like a goldfish pond, isn't it? With all these tiny ripples and undercurrents and all the inhabitants interdependent."

"Including the feeding frenzies and attacks on smaller fry going on underneath the pretty surface." Hayley finished her sandwich. "Speaking of which, I'm putting out some bait in support of your scheme."

One of the men rang the bar-bell and lifted three fingers.

"Two minutes," Hayley said in his direction.

Eve lowered her voice. "I won't keep you, but Donna had an affair. The bloke might have had hay fever. Ben found some medication."

Hayley whistled under her breath. "I'll be run off my feet this weekend, but I could pop into your place on Monday morning."

Eve folded the clean throw and set off to play pool with Ben Dryden. There was only one way from the main road to the house, but there would be a number of dirt roads or lanes leading up to the farmland.

It had rained heavily on the night in question. She needed to find out if the police discovered any unexplained tyre tracks, or if police cars and ambulance had obliterated any traces. She wouldn't ask Ben though, unless he gave her an opening.

Eve itched to have another chat with John. Why had he disliked Donna so much? Was it because he'd found out about her affair? He couldn't have been this hostile when they moved in. Ben would have seen to that. Or was it because he blamed her for her own murder and the shadow it cast over the Drydens?

Eve rolled her eyes. Now she sounded as melodramatic as one of the trashy novels Mrs Holdsworth number two left behind. Facts. She needed facts. With logic she could solve any puzzle.

She parked her Renault at the end of the driveway, in clear view from the road. She told herself she wanted to make sure the engine noise didn't disturb John in case he took a nap, but deep down she realised an edge of fear. This was a house where murder had happened, and she came here to disrupt everything.

Eve rang the doorbell, a brass circle surrounded by ivy. Someone made sure it stayed free of the intruding plant, but no more effort appeared to be spent on the maintenance.

Ben opened the door. A dim light in the hallway cast sinister shadows over his face. She instinctively took a step back. He moved closer into the remaining daylight and closed the door behind him, breaking the gothic atmosphere.

Eve handed him the throw. "I washed it," she said as he

led her to a side-wing. It was one big room, with white walls, a small fireplace, framed Hopper prints, and French doors placed to capture the day-light. A built-in bookcase, two easy chairs, a large globe, a table and a gleaming mahogany pool table with turned legs filled the room without cluttering it. A light dust film covered the bookcase. The rest sparkled.

"Can I offer you a drink?" Ben flipped the top of the globe. Inside, it held whisky, red and white wine, and matching glasses.

"Red wine, please," Eve said as she put her coat over a chair. "I'm impressed."

"It's still the way my mother left it. This was her sanctuary." *Yours too, I bet,* she thought. "Did you play with her?"

"Or read, or sit, and chat. The books were hers, too."

Eve ran her fingers over the spines. Jane Austen, Josephine Tey, Dorothy Parker, WH Auden ... An eclectic collection for a farmer's wife. "She had great taste."

"My father isn't much of a reader, but Mum fiercely guarded her private time, and that included reading. It kept their marriage happy." He poured two glasses of red wine and set them on the table.

"I used to go for walks with my mother, wherever we moved. We'd ignore the car and set off on foot. Most neighbours called her eccentric. That was in America," Eve said.

"Did she mind?"

Eve shook her head, lost in happy memories. "Why should she? She never conformed to unwritten rules she didn't like either. I think my dad was secretly proud of that." She stopped herself. "Shall we play?"

He racked up the balls.

"You break," she said as she ran her hand along the length of the cue to test it.

"They're all good," Ben said. "Mum would turn in her grave if I let you play with inferior material."

He took his leisure over his shot. Eve admired his aim, and the strategic placement of the balls. He sank four balls before he missed the pocket by a fraction of an inch.

She tried to copy him but slipped after her second shot. "I'm seriously out of shape," she said.

"May I?" Ben stepped behind her and guided her hands. Her pulse quickened. She took a deep breath.

"Relax," he said. "Plan ahead. A good player doesn't go for one ball, he lines them up for successive shots." He stood to the side.

"Okay." She closed her eyes as she visualised the set-up.

"I've got it." The next two shots brought her back into contention and she started to enjoy herself.

An hour later a bell rang in the middle of a game. Ben placed his cue in the rack and said, "That's my father. I'll need to check in with him." A troubled look came into his eyes.

Eve put her cue away as well. "Do you want me to go?"

"No. I'll be back in a few minutes." He left through the French doors. There should be a connection to the main house, Eve thought. She remembered from the newspaper reports that there had been no signs of a burglary, but these French doors could be opened with a credit card.

She ran her hands across the wall, hoping to find a hidden opening. There was none. Maybe Ben's mother had it bricked over to create a truly secluded hide-away. There were no signs of Donna. Did Ben use this room as his refuge too, while his wife went down to the cabin? She felt a new pity for both of them. What was it that held unhappy couples together long after the affection had gone? Children, she understood, and in Ben's case, economical reasons, if he really valued the family place and his father's attachment to it higher than his own and his wife's happiness. Although wouldn't that also count as an unhealthy attachment? And how could anyone leave so few traces of her personality behind?

CHAPTER 11

*B*en returned to find her settled with "The Essential Dorothy Parker". Sudden worry lines made him look older. "I'm sorry, but my father has taken a bad turn," he said.

"Not another stroke?" She touched his shoulder.

"Luckily no. He simply can't calm down. I've called his massage therapist to come over."

"On a Friday night? You're lucky."

"Very. Chris is a life-saver, and he originally started training as a nurse."

Eve took her coat. "I hope your father will feel better soon."

"Actually, if you don't mind, he'd like to say hello."

Her surprise must have showed on her face, because Ben said, "He's a pretty nice man underneath that crusty exterior. Once you give him the chance to warm to you."

John sat close to the fireplace breathing laboriously. His hand trembled, and the mottled skin was nearly translucent.

Eve squatted next to him. "Hello, Mr Dryden."

"Get your friend a chair." It cost him an effort to say it. Friend; not girlfriend, not lady friend. That was good. Much better than implying a juvenile attachment, like Hayley had.

Ben put a chair for Eve next to the wheelchair. He moved John around, so the old man could look at her without moving his head.

"You're not afraid to come here, are you?" Eve struggled to understand his slurred speech.

"Afraid? Oh. No. I believe in the police."

"Good." He sank a little deeper into himself. "They went through everything in this house. Everything. And found nothing."

"That was a long time ago," Eve said.

"Long time." His eyes were clouded with pain. "Couldn't even give away her things. Tainted. But you're right. Lot of water under the bridge."

"How many generations of your family have lived here?" Eve hoped to distract the old man until his massage therapist arrived. Ben gave her a tiny nod of encouragement.

"We go all the way back to William IV's reign." John sat a little more upright now and the trembling lessened.

"That's right before Queen Victoria, isn't it? That's impressive."

"The first Drydens raised sheep, and horses. Passed down from father to son. My father made the switch to orchards. Too few good shepherds left around to keep up the flocks." The pride in his voice was unmistakable, despite his struggle to get the words out. "We got many medals for best in show in the old days for our rams and our wool. I'd like to show you another time. They're stacked away, with all the other unused stuff."

The logs crackled, for a moment covering any other sound. Eve gave a start when she heard feet shuffling behind her back and a tall, brunette man with an open grin and the build of an athlete gripped John's wheelchair.

"Eve, I'd like you to meet Chris," Ben said.

Chris let go of the wheelchair and shook her hand. He had a good grip, firm, but not overly long, a bit like Ben. A nice, reliable man. "Pleased to meet you," he said. "Now, John, what's going on?"

Ben saw Eve to her car. She should have parked closer to the house, she thought as she saw the tyre tracks on the grass which Chris's car had left when he squeezed past her Renault.

"I probably won't have a chance to get away tomorrow," Ben said.

"I'll say hi to the owl from you. Tell your father I'd like to see those medals, if he really wants me to see them."

Ben clenched his jaw. "They're not that easy to get to. It's a bit of a jumble in the attic, with my wife's old things."

"You kept them?" Eve wished she could take back her words as she saw him flinch.

"Nobody wanted her belongings. Her parents live in Northern Ireland, and I couldn't dump her clothes and stuff in the landfill."

"Maybe if someone else donated them?" *Me, for example,* she thought. "Or Hayley. I could ask her. It might be good for your father too, to get rid of sad memories. My dad didn't keep anything of my mom's around after she died." Although that could have been the work of his next wife. Memories got muddled up in retrospect.

All Eve remembered with the sharpness of a freshly developed photograph was how naked the next house had looked, and how much her dad had changed, from a jeans and casual shirt person to golf sweaters and too tight pressed pants.

"If Hayley doesn't mind?" Ben looked relieved.

"Only one way to find out." She got into her car and waved him good-bye. Hayley would be a much better choice to rifle through Donna's affairs. She didn't have these ambiguous feelings, because although Eve pitied Donna's end, she didn't much like this woman she'd never met.

The weekend dragged on. Eve buried herself in work and when her eyes smarted, she cleaned house. If there was such a thing as euphoria to be gained from scrubbing floors and using a discarded toothbrush to remove grime from grouts, she'd still have to find it. At least her sore back and aching arms distracted her.

When Hayley arrived on Monday morning, Eve fully expected her to be astonished by the transformation of the cottage, but her hopes fell flat. Hayley must be too preoccupied with her grandmother, and their investigation. Eve put the kettle on, slightly mollified. "How's your grandmother?"

"Picking up. We're having two prospective chefs coming tomorrow for a cooking trial, and I've arranged for a hair-styling appointment for my nan to look her best." Hayley waited for a reaction.

"That's nice."

"You mean, because Bella might have done Donna's hair too, and you and me might just do a few things in Nan's apartment while she's around?" Hayley grinned.

Hayley took Eve up to have tea with her nan before the hairdresser arrived. Letty sat close to the window. Sunlight streamed over her shoulders and cast a warm glow over her face. Handmade lace doilies and a snowy-white table cloth with matching edging transformed the place into an old-fashioned living-room Eve had once seen replicated in a museum.

There was nothing old-fashioned about Letty though. The blue eyes in the wrinkled face were as sharp as a young woman's.

She didn't beat around the bush either. "My granddaughter tells me you're interested in the Dryden affair." Letty's gaze held Eve's as she waited for the answer.

Eve didn't know what to say, so she settled for the truth. "Yes."

"Why?"

Eve looked to Hayley for help, but all she got was a raised eyebrow. So, the truth again. Eve said, "Because I met Ben Dryden and his father."

"The police cleared him," Letty said.

"Not in the minds of people."

"You want to change that."

"Is that so wrong? Is it so wrong to want a murderer to be held accountable?"

Hayley passed filled cups of tea around. The part of Eve's brain which constantly observed, admired the thin china with its distinctive blue and white pattern. Wedgwood, or at least an excellent copy.

"What does Ben say?" Letty stirred two spoons of sugar into her tea.

"He doesn't know. All he cares about is saving his father more anguish."

"Noble. And stupid." Letty patted Hayley's hand. "We old people don't need protection, we need to be involved."

"Will you help?" Eve asked.

"What if you don't like what you find out?" Letty gave her a shrewd glance.

Eve was taken aback. "I don't know. Does it matter?"

"You have faith in Ben. That's good. He always was a

good boy. Too foolish to see when his loyalty wasn't deserved, but good." Letty patted her lips dry with a paper napkin Hayley handed her. The embroidered linen napkins were only for show then.

The bell from the pub rang.

"That's Bella," Letty said. "Leave her to me."

Bella's gaze focussed on Eve's hair as she said hello. She picked up a strand of Hayley's locks and tut-tutted. "We need to take off these split ends."

"But not today," Hayley said.

Bella gave Letty a resounding smack on one cheek. No air kisses for her. "Let's get started. Where's your bathroom?" she asked.

Eve and Hayley shared an exasperated glance. "Don't you need proper lighting?" Hayley asked.

"Not for washing hair." Bella gently pulled up Letty. "Here we go, love."

Eve caught an inaudible stream of chatter from the bathroom.

"Don't worry," Hayley said. "Nan's a pro." She handed Eve a feather duster. "Careful with the porcelain figures in the display case. They're heirlooms."

Eve flicked the duster over the furniture.

Hayley put a bath towel over the armchair and an overlapping layer of newspaper on the floor. She rearranged it to catch the maximum amount of sunlight through the window.

Letty shuffled over to sit down. Her wet hair fell to the nape of her neck. Underneath, her scalp shone pink. She looked like a fragile porcelain doll in that chair, Eve thought.

"Hayley told me we had a long-missed customer lately," Letty said as Bella combed through the tangles. "What was his name again? Handsome lad. And me missing him."

Bella tittered. "That Chris Ripley is still a sight for sore eyes, I can tell you that. He can massage me any old time."

"I wonder what brought him into the 'Green Dragon'."

"Sit still. Maybe he's got his eyes on Hayley, eh, girl?"

Hayley chortled. "I doubt that. He could stay away well enough before."

"Well." Bella pondered. "It must have been a bit awkward, with him and old John thick as thieves, and people saying nasty things about the Drydens. Mind, he was always nice to the girl, and to everyone else. A real keeper, that one."

The girl? Eve flicked the duster over the picture frames as she tried to melt into the background.

"You knew Donna quite well, didn't you?" Hayley flashed Eve a beam. "I'm trying to convince Eve here that she doesn't need a fancy city salon when we've got you. If you were good enough for Donna Dryden, after her London hairdressers ..."

"Stylists, my dear. She used to have a stylist. Mind you, they frazzled her hair to an inch of its life, and that brash blonde didn't suit her. She looked so much prettier when she came to me." Snip, fell another clump of hair.

"It must have done her good to have someone to talk to," Letty said. "I always say, if I need a listener, I know where to go."

"Bless you. Yes, I dare say she had her troubles. What with everything at home revolving around old John, and her being used to the city lights and all." Bella lowered her voice. "She did seem a lot happier those last, oooh, let me think, eight months or so. She went a bit more natural with her hair colour too, a nice shade of honey blonde mixed in as highlights. Her final appointment, she asked me if I'd recommend going a lot shorter for a change." Bella sniffed, as in tribute to her dead customer. "If you ask me, there was someone else in the picture."

"Another man? But where would she meet him?" Letty asked.

"At work? I've got to say, I'm not one to speak ill of the dead, and she might have had her reasons to look around, with Ben putting his father before her. I expected Ben to show his wife a bit more consideration. And then, when we found out – I never was more flabbergasted in my whole life." Bella gave a delicious shudder as she ran her comb through her customer's hair to scrutinise her cut.

"You think it was him?" Letty asked.

"Who else could it have been? My husband, may he rest in peace, was that jealous he didn't want me to take on male customers until I put my foot down." Bella pulled a hair-dryer out of her bag. "I'll put it on medium heat for you."

"What about the mystery man?" Letty asked.

"He had no reason to kill her, now did he? She was leaving Ben after all. And she was killed in her own living room."

"Maybe he was married too and needed to get rid of Donna. He never came forward," Hayley said.

"He was protecting her memory. As any gentleman would." Bella pursed her lips.

"Did you ever see her with anyone? Or did she say anything?" Letty asked.

"Chris brought her down to the pub on a few occasions,

as a favour to Ben when Ben decided his father needed him more. You could tell deep down he didn't really care much. But then Chris was nice to everyone, and with his own girl far away, in one of these Middle Eastern countries, he'd be a tad lonely. Pity they broke up. He showed her picture in uniform to me once. Beautiful black hair, all natural. He was that proud of her." Bella sighed as she gave Letty's hair a final comb-through. "Donna said to me there'd be someone new for me, if I held my eyes open. Say what you want, Donna Dryden had her airs, but she was a sweet girl at heart."

Bella held up her hair-dryer. "Shall I clean up, or is anyone else in need of my services?" She looked from Eve to Hayley, and back at Eve. "When did you have your last trim?"

"Trust her," Hayley whispered into Eve's ear before she escaped downstairs. Eve sincerely hoped she was right. A bad haircut should be considered a small price to pay for information rendered, but she liked her recent style. She'd muttered something about not taking up more of their time, and Letty's space, but was quickly overruled.

The water muffled Bella's chatter. Eve gave in to the inevitable.

She emerged with a trim that left her hopeful, and

armed Bella with innocuous information about Eve's single status, her planned length of stay and her enjoyment of her new surroundings. Eve wasn't too sure if she'd also agreed to consider joining the women's institute, but she could always cry off and claim too much work.

Hayley balked at the idea of going through Donna's stuff when Eve managed to talk to her in the pub kitchen. Eve resorted to pleading. "It's sitting there in the attic, and it might help."

"How would you feel if your dad's new wife had pawed through your mother's belongings?"

Eve gritted her teeth. "She did. She even wore my mom's favourite dress to a party soon after the wedding. Vintage Pucci. I told her it was from a thrift store."

"Your mum found a designer dress in a charity shop?"

"No. But number two couldn't get rid of it fast enough after that." Eve leaned over the counter. She kept her voice low although no-one was within ear-shot. "Please. I really think it could be good for them."

"You're not going to give in, are you?"

"Please."

Hayley heaved an exasperated sigh. "I'll do it. If you assist me."

A chill ran over Eve's body. "I can't."

"But you expect me to do it."

"Okay. I'm in. If Ben agrees."

"It is a bit gruesome to think of these things," Hayley said. "And I'm not going to read any letters, or any other personal missives. I leave that to you."

CHAPTER 12

The house was empty except for Ben. He'd taken his father to the hospital for his regular health-check. Dark smudges under his eyes made him look exhausted, and vulnerable.

He pressed a key into Hayley's hand as he led them up into the attic. Eve had expected a dark cobweb-covered space. Instead she found an airy room, with furniture covered in dusty sheets, and plush carpet.

"Everything is as she left it." Ben's voice caught in his throat. "I've given you the key to her wardrobe."

"She lived up here?" Eve asked.

"She did, for a few months. Until she'd move out." Ben surveyed the room as if he saw it for the first time. "I should have sent Donna to a hotel when she said she wanted a divorce. She might still be alive."

"How –"Eve noted Hayley's vigorous headshaking and shut up.

"We'll call you when we're done." Hayley squeezed Ben's shoulder. "Why don't you go and get some work done?"

Eve handed Hayley a pair of surgical gloves. The air in the attic smelt fresh. Ben must have opened the three narrow windows regularly, yet he couldn't bring himself to throwing out Donna's belongings despite passing them every time. That was another point towards his innocence, Eve decided. If you killed someone, you'd get rid of the constant reminders of what you'd done.

Hayley emptied the wardrobe. She dropped the clothes on their hangers onto the sheet-covered bed. Donna had good taste, Eve had to admit. She'd expected frills and an abundance of girlie colours. Instead they found tailored suits in neutral colours, cashmere sweaters and crisp cotton shirts. A few dresses displayed a more fun-loving side, but overall the wardrobe spoke of a self-assured woman, not an empty-headed pretty girl, as Eve had half hoped.

Hayley folded up the clothes into cardboard boxes lined with sheet tissue they found at the bottom of the wardrobe.

Eve sorted through the drawers. She closed her eyes as she searched among the lingerie for a diary or letters or any other clue. Nothing. She dumped the lingerie into a trash bag without so much as a glance. Looking a Donna's intimate things would have felt like a violation.

The next drawer contained boxes full of bangles and bracelets. Fashion jewellery, Eve guessed, intended to add a bit of interest to business clothes. Ben had to decide if there were any pieces of sentimental value among the lot. Silk scarves filled the rest of the drawer. Eve emptied the whole drawer into a cotton bag.

She lifted the sheet off the vanity dresser. Two small jars with high-end night cream stood on it, their lids encrusted with a brownish residue. Eve swept them into the trash bag. Donna would have kept the rest of her cosmetics in the bathroom.

She struck gold in the drawers underneath. Dried flowers, a sachet of crumbled lavender, a small, leather-bound photo album, a calendar and a stash of letters. Plus, more antihistamines.

Eve hid the letters and calendar in her handbag. She flicked through the album. A younger Ben, his arms wrapped around a blonde woman who didn't need the heavy make-up to be beautiful. They gazed at each other with the rapture of love in its early stages.

Eve moved on. More pictures, mostly of Donna on her own, posing at the beach, artfully sitting atop ruins, sipping cocktails at sunset. A few photos showed her with friends. Eve recognised Kim in one shot, and a group picture with Chris, Ben and a grim John. What a pity Donna's phone, with its presumable wealth of texts, contacts and photos was lost to Eve.

"I'm done," Hayley said. "Let's get out of here." She lifted one of the boxes. Eve took another. They carried eight boxes downstairs, plus the bulging trash bag. They'd drop the boxes off at a friend of Hayley's who worked for yet another charity.

"Ben?" Hayley called.

His steps came in staccato. He gaped at the boxes, shoulders sagging a little. From regret or relief? Eve wished she could read his face.

Hayley dropped the wardrobe key in his hand. "It's all done, mate. If you want to donate the furniture as well, I can arrange that."

"That would be great." He rubbed his forehead. "I should have done that sooner."

"My nan has a suitcase full of my grandfather's clothes under her bed. He died when I was eight. It's hard to let go." Hayley gave Ben a brief hug. He chuckled at her. For an instance, to her annoyance, Eve felt invisible. Then he turned to her and said, "Thank you. For everything."

She thought of the letters and calendar in her handbag, and what he'd think of her if he knew she'd pinched them. Her stomach lurched. They'd better contain a clue, to be worth this sickening feeling.

"How is your father?" Eve asked.

"Shaky. Not that he'd admit it. I'll pick him up tonight."

Eve spread the letters on her table. Hayley had rushed back to the pub after they'd dropped off the donations.

She'd leave them in their envelopes, unread. With any kind of luck, the calendar contained enough clues on its own. She picked it up and touched the smooth surface. Why wasn't it with the police? Or had the officers read and dismissed it? There had never been the remotest hint of another suspect apart from Ben in the newspaper reports.

Eve put the calendar down and instead searched for her own address book.

Her dad picked up after the third ring-tone. "Hello?" His voice sounded unfamiliar.

"Dad?" she asked, a little uncertain. "It's me, Eve."

"Eve. Everything okay with you, Sweetpea?"

She used to cringe at that pet name. Now she realised he'd only ever used it when nobody else listened to them. Which probably meant, he was alone now.

"Yeah, sure," she said. "But I've been thinking about you and Mum a lot lately, and I thought I should check in with you." She attempted a laugh. It rang phony in her ears. "The first signs of middle age, I assume."

"Why don't you come home for Christmas? Crystal is arranging a big party, for all her family," her dad said.

Eve shuddered. "Big gatherings aren't really my thing. How are you?"

"Well, actually, we're thinking of moving. Crystal has seen a place with a pool, and she wants me to be more active, physically. We'll still stay in Seattle though, if that's what you're wondering."

A pool. Of course. Despite the not quite Floridian climate of the Pacific north-west. They probably had a check-list with whatever status symbols mattered for Crystal. "That's a lot of work," Eve said.

"We'd get someone for the maintenance. Keep the economy pumping."

"Don't forget to give me your new address." She paused, unsure what else to say. *Screw it,* she thought. *Why not try some honesty? It would make a change.* "Dad? Are you happy?"

"Happy?" She envisaged him, blinking confused as he sat in his too young clothes in his bland home office. "What are you talking about?"

"What do you do for fun? You and Crystal? I remember you and Mum dancing in our lounge, and on the patio."

"We did? It's hard to remember." He sounded lost.

An unexpected wave of pity filled her heart. If her father had made yet another mistake, he paid dearly for it. If he was satisfied with his life, good on him. She shouldn't judge, especially from thousands of miles of physical and emotional distance away. "I've got to go. Say hi to Crystal."

"At least think about Christmas, Sweetpea. It'd be nice."

"I will."

Eve brought out a photo album labelled "Our Wedding" in gold embossing from her suitcase. There they were, Crystal and her dad, under a pink and green flower arch. He'd dyed his salt-and-pepper hair uniformly dark and ditched his spectacles for contact lenses on the bride's request. Crystal desperately tried to cling onto a faded youth with a bridal dress modelled after the latest royal wedding.

Eve turned the pages, looking for a hint of the affection Donna and Ben's early photos demonstrated. Or was that reserved for young couples, before disillusionment set it? Her dad's gaze did rest on Crystal in most of the pictures, in an expression of what seemed to be gratitude. Maybe that explained his life. Perhaps all he wanted was not to be alone, even if he'd never dance with a woman under the stars on the patio again.

It wouldn't be enough for her. It hadn't been enough for Donna either. She wondered if Ben would have had the courage to pull the plug on his marriage, if it hadn't been for the money issue.

She picked up Donna's calendar and scanned the pages. Instead of covering a year, it went on for fifteen months. The final weeks were empty.

Eve flicked back to the beginning. There were entries for Donna's days at work. Starting in April, she'd made brackets around the Wednesday work appointments. She'd also pencilled in when Ben was away for meetings. Lunch dates featured at least once a week, but she'd used abbreviations instead of writing down the full names. "Lunch @LI" appeared regularly until November. In October, Donna also lunched at TFP, which then became the only lunch spot mentioned. Donna had decorated both with scribbled flowers.

Eve's heart beat hard against her ribs. Donna had been cryptic, but not overly so. She wasn't a habitual doodler, sticking to the basic information in the other entries, so the flowers had special meaning.

Eve tapped her fingers on the table. A married woman living in a small town might easily meet her lover in a remote cabin while her husband was gone. If she wanted to meet another man in public without the affair becoming common knowledge, a lunch date in another town was one of her few options.

Eve read through the entries again. All the lunch dates coincided with Donna's work days. The days marked in brackets also showed love hearts and exclamation marks.

TFP and LI had to be within walking distance from the boutique, to fit in with Donna's lunch hour. She and her colleagues would take turns, Eve assumed. Which made it safe enough for Donna to meet her lover.

She took the first of the letters. They were all addressed by hand, with the ink faded. Eve peered at the date stamp. It was too smudged to decipher. She turned the envelope around. No name, only an address in Northern Ireland. Donna's parents, presumably. No love letter from Ben, then. She breathed easier, relieved not to poke her nose in his most intimate thoughts.

The letter covered a scant page. Health news, gossip about neighbours, questions about work, and John's health. Perfectly innocent and useless for Eve's purposes. The one interesting fact was the date. The letter was written four weeks before Donna's death. She hadn't told her parents about her plans to divorce Ben and move out. Why?

Eve skim-read another letter from the parents. The same pattern, eerily echoing her own thoughts about her dad.

She had her answer. Donna's parents weren't close enough to their daughter for Donna to confide in them.

One letter bore a different handwriting, and no stamp or sender's address. Inside, written in spiky letters slanting to the right, Elizabeth Barrett Browning's sonnet brought back memories of Eve's high school days. *"How do I love thee? Let me count the ways …"* She whispered the words. A single tear rolled down her cheek as she finished with the line that never failed to tug at her heartstrings. *"I love thee with the breath, smiles, tears, of all my life; and, if God choose, I shall but love thee better after death."*

How on earth could a love like this fade away? If Ben wrote this, he must have wanted to win Donna back, desperately. The letter couldn't be old, the ink looked fresher than on the other envelopes. An icy hand grabbed Eve's heart. Donna wasn't a hoarder who held on to things of sentimental value. Her belongings proved that beyond a doubt. This allowed only one conclusion. Donna had kept the letter with the poem because it held meaning for her too.

Eve needed a sample of Ben's handwriting to be sure, but if he penned this, he'd lied about his relationship with his wife. What else had he been untruthful about?

Eve piled up the other letters. She'd ask Ben what she should do with them. The poem, she'd keep. And the calendar. The staff at Donna's lunch venues wouldn't remember after five years, but the places themselves might offer more clues about her and her mystery man.

She slipped the letter in her sock drawer.

What if the rumours were right, and her own husband had slain Donna Dryden in a fit of passion and jealousy?

CHAPTER 13

*E*ve found Kim restocking vinyl records at the back of the charity shop.

"Well, hello again," Kim said. Her eyes twinkled. "Do you need more jewellery for another hot date, or what brings you here?"

Eve winced. "Not very likely."

"Didn't it work out? That's too bad."

Eve grimaced. "I'm trying to salvage another relationship instead. Before I've ruined that too." Eve took out her dad's wedding picture. "I'm looking for something quintessentially British for her. Something that screams old and inherited status."

"Ouch. That awful?"

Eve had another look at the photo. Crystal did hover

over her husband, and she lacked sophistication or brain, judging by the handful of occasions they'd been together. But was she really as much of a monster as she'd become in Eve's head? "I have no idea, to be honest," she said. "I had this preconceived notion of her the moment my Dad told me her real name was Christa, but she went by Crystal."

"That's not a crime," Kim said. "A bit new age hippy, but we have a lot of those around here as well."

"That's why I'm here, to give our relationship a chance. Maybe she's exactly what my dad needs, and I'm the bad guy."

"How old is Crystal?" Kim asked.

"Officially, forty-five. Since at least a decade."

They settled on a delicate cameo carved out of Whitby jet, dating back to the end of Queen Victoria's reign. A tiny chip at the bottom explained why it ended up at the "Helping Hand". It came with an embossed and wax-sealed certificate which in itself made it worth the price tag of one hundred pounds.

Kim produced an antique velvet case for it. Eve's hand trembled.

"Do you want to sit down?" Kim asked. "You look like a ghost."

"Thank you. It must be nerves, I suppose. Weird."

"Stress does that."

Kim flipped the sign over to 'Closed' and locked the door. "I live upstairs, if you'd like a bit of a rest."

She settled Eve on a cardinal red tub chair. The complete room was furnished with 1960s pieces in bright colours. A pair of gigantic false lashes framed the peephole in the door, reminiscent of her mom's favourite TV heroine of the period, Emma Peel in the classic show "The Avengers". Eve had bought the box-set to watch whenever she was in serious need of an emotional pick-me up. Sometimes, if she tried hard, she could almost sense her mother's presence.

"Tea?" Kim asked. "I'd offer you brandy, but I assume you have to drive."

"The classic British remedy. I'd appreciate a cup of tea."

The tea was hot, strong and sweet, and soothing. The British were on to something with it. Eve chuckled.

"What's so funny?" Kim asked.

"I just realised how often I switch personas without even thinking about it. One day I'm fiercely British, thanks to my mother's side, the next I'm an outsider clucking my tongue over local foibles."

"Perfectly normal. You should hear the locals complain about the folks in London, or Wales, or up North. Unless the same people do something fabulous and we fall over ourselves to claim them as ours."

Eve drained her cup and got up. "I'd better run along. This was exactly what I needed."

"I'm glad you feel better."

"I do. In many ways."

On her way out, she glimpsed a series of photographs in a triptych frame. Kim as a teenager, hand in hand with a blonde woman pictured from the back, and Kim with a dog.

True enough, Eve heard a faint bark from the back room as she left through the shop.

"Why don't you come to see me one evening?" Kim asked. "The doorbell on the top is for the flat. I'm free most nights. I'd like to know how your relationship rescue works out."

"I'll keep you updated," Eve said.

Eve went in search of the nearest post office. She'd scribbled a short note to Crystal, saying "Happy Anniversary". Number three – no, she must stop calling her that – Crystal and her dad had tons of anniversaries, from first glimpse to first date and first sushi class. There would be a suitable occasion Crystal would think of. The price was a bit steep, but then they'd never exchanged Christmas gifts.

She found a corner shop with a post office counter a short stroll away, tucked in between a tea room and a ristorante called "Little Italy." Her pulse quickened. The initials fit Donna's calendar entry, and the distance fit as well.

Eve posted the jewellery and ambled into the restaurant. A big main room with ochre walls and prints of Italian landscapes gave way to a number of alcoves, made for clandestine meetings. Her heels clicked on the black and white floor. The décor was upscale, with a blend of authentic and chic that would have appealed to Donna. She'd found the place.

Eve peered around in a vague manner, implying she searched for a friend. The waiter politely stood back instead of pestering her; another good sign.

Under normal circumstances she'd have wanted to come back here and sit in one of the alcoves with Ben. Her stomach flipped. She'd managed not to think of him in hours, or of the sonnet she'd found. "*How do I love thee?*"Apparently until death.

Ben took the furniture in the attic apart. Like a coward,

he'd ignored confronting Donna's personal belongings. They seemed to accuse him, for not loving her enough or in the wrong way and letting her down. She'd be alive without him, they seemed to say.

He'd sat in his office while Hayley and Eve did his dirty work, staring at the wall and loathing himself. What kind of man didn't even clean up his own mess?

Now the bed and dresser, the wardrobe and the velvet ottoman Donna loved to recline on with a fashion magazine would finally go. Hayley had arranged for a collection the next day. The house would be finally free of Donna's memory.

His father rang his bell as Ben loosened the back panel of the wardrobe. He let it slide to the ground without a second thought. Duty called, now and for the rest of John's natural life. On good days, it hardly felt like a punishment any longer.

John lay in his bed, a sunken old man. Only his eyes blazed with new-found vigour. "Have you not finished with the trollop's stuff yet? I want you to bring down the medals."

Ben stiffened. "Donna wasn't a trollop, and I remember, you used to like her for quite a while."

John sneered, if one could call it that with his half-frozen face. "I tried to be nice to her, for your sake." He coughed, gasping for breath.

Ben gave in, like he always did when his father became upset. "I'll bring you the medals, and the records."

"She'll be interested to see them, your lady-friend." John had to rest his voice for a few moments. "See to it she doesn't meddle in our affairs. Females tend to stick their nose into everything, and Americans have no natural shame."

"She won't." Ben saved his breath when it came to John's views of women. His father wouldn't change, he simply got upset when lectured. The doctors said he needed a calm, nurturing environment, whatever that meant.

"Good. Just promise me you'll be very, very careful." John dozed off.

Ben climbed up into the attic. He had every intention of keeping the family secrets under lock and key.

A battle raged in the kitchen of the "Green Dragon". Grace Archer and Heather Miller, both in their late forties and normally of cheerful demeanour, eyed each other like duellists over a scrubbed oak table strewn with scales, flour, mounds of vegetables, and cuts of meat. Pots with stew and broth simmered.

Letty presided over them. She sat serenely in a high-backed

chair in a corner. Her sweet smile and her newly fluffed white hair made her the epitome of a lovable grandmother. But, and Grace and Heather knew this, in this kitchen she was the supreme ruler, and the battle for succession would be won with blood and sweat and the tastiest pies.

Letty had resisted the temptation of giving out her recipes. Any halfway decent cook could follow instructions. She needed someone with an eye on costs and a flair for innovation. She hadn't told Hayley, but she'd been relieved when her granddaughter told her she wanted to find her an assistant. For Letty wasn't simply looking for a chef, she had an eye out on someone capable of taking over the reins.

Hayley might not think about her own future, but Letty did. The "Green Dragon" had been the ideal solution when Hayley found herself at loose ends when her job as an HR assistant and a relationship ended simultaneously. Letty would see to it that Hayley got her freedom back at her own terms before she ended in a rut.

Grace folded another quarter cup of flour into her dough.

Heather watched her rival like a hawk and with a flourish, added more spices to her stew. They had half an hour to go.

Letty decided to crank up the pressure, to see who could cope better. She'd make it up to them afterwards.

"Fancy me missing Ben Dryden's visit," she said, sniffing the fragrant air appreciatively.

Heather banged the jar with her own spice-mix on the table and gaped. "He never."

Grace shuddered. "It gives me the creeps to think of him. I always said, he had a shifty look, even as a teenager. You can't hide a nasty temper, say what you will."

"That fancy wife of his gave him enough reason, if you ask me, and you didn't seem to mind cleaning and cooking for them until it happened." Heather screwed the lid onto the jar. "My friend went into that boutique on one of Donna's regular days, and you know what? She'd cut down from three days to two without anyone the wiser. Otherwise why would they get you to come in for all three days? Unless you didn't tell us."

Grace's eyes bulged. Her pastry was all but forgotten. "Why would she do that? They never cut my hours, and she went, same as usual."

"We'll never know for sure, but I have my ideas. That's all I'm saying." Heather popped a tray with bread rolls into the oven, a self-satisfied smirk on her face.

"What did the police say?" Letty asked.

"Nothing. They never asked me, and it wasn't my place to

say, was it?" A smug look spread over Heather's face. "Another ten minutes, and I'm done."

"Drat." Grace attacked her pastry with the rolling pin.

"Two days instead of three?" Eve pulled out the stolen calendar.

"Heather's positive," Hayley said. She dropped in at Ivy Cottage as soon as Letty shared the revelation with her. "She's our new kitchen assistant, by the way. And the woman who used to cook for John when Donna was at work didn't have a clue. Any other questions you have, let my nan ask them. Heather's well-meaning, but her mouth runs a mile a minute."

"She's a gossip."

"But a reliable one and trusting." Hayley grinned at Eve. "So, anything else you need wheedled out of her?"

Eve had thought about that. She asked, "Did the helper have a key? I wish I could see the police report, to see how they think the killer got in."

"They focussed on Ben."

"Who would have had enough sense to fake a break-in," Eve said.

"In a premeditated case, yes. But if it was a crime of passion?"

"That wouldn't explain the petrol station receipt. Or why he didn't turn himself in," Eve said without conviction.

"And leave his father after a bad stroke? Not likely that he'd done that. But I thought we operated on the premise of his innocence."

"We do. Except ..."

"We can always stop." Hayley gave her a swift and unexpected hug. Eve let herself go limp. She'd hardly noticed how tightly wound she'd become.

"No. Whatever the outcome, I want to find out what really happened to that poor woman," Eve said. "Your nan said pretty much the same thing."

Hayley nodded in agreement. "I'll put my feelers out. After I've figured out how to rearrange the kitchen to both my nan's and Heather's liking. And you can think of ideas where Donna might have gone every Thursday from June onwards."

Eve made a list of entries for the Thursdays. They were the ones in brackets. It was a satisfying start, to see part of the puzzle fall into place. She could think of two places where Donna would go: her lover's home and the cabin.

Eve found her birdwatching binoculars underneath a

stack of towels. Her lack of house-keeping skills became more pronounced with every relocation. She needed to fix that. Maybe Donna was the same. A woman who left condoms in a place her husband might enter unannounced might have dropped another clue. Eve intended to search for it.

The cabin lay deserted. Eve caught a glimpse of feathers in the tree hollow, but the only sounds were her breathing and a slight rustle of leaves in the undergrowth.

She sneaked around the cabin and tried the door. It was locked. Eve felt under the eaves for a key. Nothing. She lifted rocks. One was suspiciously rubbery. She probed it with her fingers and found an opening with a key inside.

As she slipped inside the cabin, she kept an eye on the windows, to watch for movement. Her mouth went dry. This couldn't be fear, she told herself. There was nothing to be afraid of. If Ben discovered her snooping, she'd admit to having been curious. That would be embarrassing, but nothing else.

The cabin was fully furnished. Eve remembered a farm assistant used to live here. Ben would have checked all the obvious places. Otherwise the condoms and antihistamines would have stayed undiscovered.

The bed had been stripped of its mattress. Eve switched her small torch on and shone the light through the bed slats. There was something in a corner. She groped for the object. The dust made her sneeze as she lifted out her find. A piece of a wrapper, too small to tell where it came from. Not that it mattered. It probably had been dropped years ago and overlooked during the clean-up. The dust under the bed spoke of neglect, whereas the film on the floor was thin enough to make her hope her footprints would go unnoticed.

She waved her torch around, for good measure. But there was nothing else to see.

Outside, Eve patted down her clothes and crept towards the path.

"Hi there." Ben's voice made her almost jump out of her skin.

"I didn't expect to see you today," she said.

"I got that impression. Birdwatching?"

"That was the plan. Routines are hard to develop, so I need to keep at it. And you?"

"I was looking for you. I wanted to thank you and Hayley. For the clean-out."

"You're welcome," she said.

"And invite you out as a sign of my appreciation."

"Oh." A few days ago, she'd have leapt at the idea of spending another private evening with him. Now, everything was in doubt. "No written RSVP?" she asked, hoping her flippancy masked her real emotions.

"Do you have any idea when Hayley's free?" Ben asked in return.

A date for three; great. On the other hand, there was safety in numbers. She wanted to trust him again, but Elizabeth Barrett Browning's poem stopped her. "I'll ask her," she said.

"Would you like to see the fish pond I've been stocking?"

Ophelia's image formed in her mind. Long, blonde hair drifting among the water lilies. She suppressed a groan. Now she was getting melodramatic on top of everything else. *Get a grip, woman.*

To Eve's relief, they took another, longer way, away from the cabin and past fields with cherry and apple trees. Their blossoms perfumed the air. "Are these all yours?"

"We leased one half and sold the other when my father had to give up. I'm not much of an agricultural man."

"What's going to happen? Long-term, I mean?"

He shrugged. "We'll see."

The garden behind the house was fenced off, with a wrought-iron gate big enough to let a car through. The killer could easily have taken this path, Eve thought. Unless he had no need for a stealthy approach because he lived here.

A garden bench stood next to an irregular pond with the water lilies she'd imagined. Fish darted back and forth, causing the silvery water to ripple. A large oak cast its shadow over John's wheelchair. He snored gently.

Chris came out of the house. He gave Eve an appreciative look that managed to be both flattering and inoffensive. She smiled at him. Objectively speaking, he was the handsomer of the two men, and he came without the baggage. If she'd met him first, she might have been interested to get to know him better. As it was, she enjoyed looking at his body, in a detached way. What a pity he didn't set her pulse racing.

John stirred.

"We found some letters," Eve said, low enough for only Ben to hear. "With a Northern Ireland sender. I can bring them."

"No. Do me a favour and burn them." He held her gaze for an infinitesimal moment, and butterflies stirred in her tummy. The siren call of the bad boy had been pretty hard to resist in her youth, and here it was again. Even if the only bad boy thing about Ben was his reputation. She must have been crazy to doubt him.

Chris studiously ignored them, in a clumsy attempt at giving them privacy.

"I'd better get back to my desk," Eve said.

"I'll walk with you." They took the shorter path, leading up to the cabin. Eve's heart beat harder. Had she put the fake rock in its proper spot? What if Ben looked into the window and saw her footprints in the dust?

"I can take it from here," she said as casually as she could manage, one hundred metres from the cabin. "I don't want to startle the owl."

His cheek brushed against hers as she gave him a friendly hug. Her breath grew irregular.

"Does Hayley have your number?" Eve asked.

He shook his head. "I'll text you."

Eve held the letters into a candle flame, one by one. She dropped the burning paper into a galvanised bucket. All, except for one. She wished she'd never found it. Now it had become impossible to ignore the evidence of her own eyes as long as she didn't know for sure Ben hadn't written it.

he main room of the "Green Dragon" lay in serene peace. Three of the old boys who to Eve seemed interchangeable with their gummy grins, sinewy hands and inevitable pints of ale hovered at one end of the bar. A fortyish woman with a too tight blouse unbuttoned too wide and a nervous look on her face polished glasses. Hayley sat at the other end, observing them. She raised two fingers at the woman and said, "Lemonade for my friend and me."

They sat down in Eve's usual spot. "I'd take you upstairs, but I need to keep an eye on Grace," Hayley said. "She was crushed to not snag the kitchen job, so I offered her this instead. She even bought a bar maid's outfit." She glanced down at her own white shirt and black tailored pants. "Or what she thinks of as one. I can't bring myself to tell her to do up another button."

"Your customers appear to enjoy it."

"As they should. It's the most flesh they'll get to see without paying." Hayley gave Grace an encouraging thumbs up as her new bar maid poured a shot of rum. "Anyway, I've discovered who wrote the police report in question."

"Can I meet him?"

"It's a her, and no, you can't. She's only talking to me because we go way back. She used to date the brother of my friend."

"At least it's something," Eve said, swallowing her disappointment. She'd envisaged herself in full Miss Marple mode, except younger and irresistible to the cop who'd be bowled over by her personality and the uncanny way in which she solved a cold case. Or perhaps she wanted to interrogate the police officer because she needed to quiet that niggling doubt in her head once and for all.

There was after all a reason the case had grown stale. Apart from Ben, who could have wanted Donna dead?

"It's a lot more than something, thank you very much." Hayley caught Grace's intimidated glance as three more regulars planted their bottoms on their bar stools, ready for a few sociable hours. "Give me a list with your questions and I'll see what I can do."

Eve agonised half the night over her list. The most important clue still was, how did the killer gain access? Had Donna opened the door, or were there any signs of a break-in?

If she opened the door herself, she could have expected that person. Fingerprints on the door handle should show who opened it last. If the crime scene staff had secured the prints.

Were there any muddy or wet footprints on the floor? It had rained hard on the day in question. But Ben might have obliterated every other print as he stumbled upon the scene.

Eve counted herself lucky the newspapers had not printed any pictures of the body. She tried hard not to imagine Ben finding his wife, her blonde hair turned crimson, and a bloodied brick next to her.

Who drugged John and where did the sleeping-pills come from? She needed to know if the police had pinpointed the time John took those pills, and in what form they'd been administered. If Donna had expected someone, she didn't want her father-in-law to see, it would have made sense for her to ensure her privacy and drug the old man. But then Ben was supposed to come home a lot sooner.

Eve rubbed her sore eyes. Nothing made sense.

Eve dropped off her short questionnaire with Hayley the next morning. She'd expected to find her in her apartment, but Hayley obviously liked an early start. She'd spotted Eve through the window as she watered the potted plant on the windowsill.

"I'll meet my source later," Hayley said as she scanned the sheet of paper. "Breakfast tomorrow?"

"Great. And Ben wants to take us both out for dinner one day."

Hayley mulled this over. "I need to get Grace trained before I can leave her and Dom to fend for themselves."

Eve nodded. "I'm sure Ben will understand."

"Why don't you cook for us?" Hayley gave her an innocent look. "It's much easier to chat in private, and I could pop back here if I'm needed."

This came unexpected. Did Eve want to have Ben visit her cottage? But she had nobody but herself to blame. If she hadn't snooped in the private correspondence of someone she'd never met, she'd feel unwavering support for Ben Dryden.

"Good idea," she said, before the pause dragged on too long. "Just say when."

"Any day except for the weekend suits me. My nan will be delighted to supervise the staff."

Ben replied to Eve's text before she had a chance to regret the invitation. He'd be free the day after tomorrow.

To distract herself, Eve threw herself into her work. When her phone rang, she cursed the interruption. "Hello?"

"Eve, honey?" Eve almost dropped her phone. Dulcet tones from Crystal were nothing out of the ordinary. Heartfelt sweetness was.

"Hi, Crystal, how are you?"

"That necklace you sent me, well I don't hardly know what to say." Crystal sounded close to tears.

"I'm glad you like it."

"Like it! Oh, honey. Your dad insisted on taking me out to dinner to show it off. Would you like to talk to him? Now, where is that man?"

"Don't worry. I've got to go anyway, but thanks for calling."

"You won't forget about Christmas, will you? Or Thanksgiving. Please. We haven't seen you in ages."

"I won't. Bye, Crystal." Eve ended the call with a sensation of light-headedness. Possibly she had done the poor woman an injustice. Failing to fulfil Eve's expectations of the kind of woman who could successfully take her mother's place did not automatically make her a bad person. If Eve's dad was happy, what more could she ask for? Especially when she secretly conceded that, objectively speaking, he might not be the greatest catch himself.

Her alarm pinged. She'd set it, so she prevented too much eye-strain from staring at the screen. Painful experience taught her that lesson.

If Crystal loved the Whitby jet cameo so much, it would be worth asking Kim to keep an eye out for matching pieces.

Eve needed a break anyway. She examined her sparse bar, which consisted of a bottle of medicinal brandy, a bottle of Merlot and a six-pack of beer she'd bought on a whim a week ago. She'd justified it with the thought that Hayley, or another visitor, might like it. Because Eve definitely didn't.

She rang the bell to Kim's flat.

"Hello?" Kim's voice echoed through the loudspeaker. Eve gave a start.

"It's me. Eve. You said to come by."

The door catch released. Eve clutched the wine bottle and made her way up to the landing where Kim waited. Behind her, a small dog sat back on his haunches and watched Eve.

Eve held up the wine. "I've come to thank you."

They settled in the living room. Kim produced two wine glasses. The dog sighed as if he felt excluded.

"Do you mind Laika's company?" Kim asked as she served the drinks.

"If he doesn't object to me, how could I?"

"What do we celebrate?"

"A family reconciliation. Of sorts."

Kim lifted her glass. "I'll drink to that."

"Me too. I was wondering if you have any more of that kind of jewellery. Crystal adores it."

For a moment Eve imagined she saw pain flicker in Kim's eyes.

Her new friend squatted and fondled the dog's ears. "I've got a few boxes with trinkets in my bedroom. I don't like to leave them in the stockroom until I'm sure they're not worth a fortune."

"Have you ever had any break-ins?"

"Only petty theft, but at least up here I've got a video camera connected to the entrance area."

"I always think I should upgrade my security, as a single woman, but then I tend to forget," Eve admitted.

"I'd do it. Now. You may feel safe, but believe me, you're not." The pain in Kim's voice was raw. It made Eve feel horribly insensitive, although her remark had not been planned as a way to bring up Donna. If only she'd met Kim without a hidden agenda. They could have been real friends. As things stood, Eve had too much to hide to properly engage. She wished she could come clean. Why shouldn't she? *Simply mention you are acquainted with Ben Dryden,* her inner voice said. *Bring it up naturally. See what happens.*

No. The timing was wrong.

"I didn't mean to scare you." Kim twisted the glass in her hand. The wine swirled around and ran down the sides in blood-red rivulets.

"When I grew up and my mother told me of her childhood or she gave me all these old books, England seemed so bucolic and peaceful," Eve said.

"Are you disappointed?" Kim asked.

"Strangely enough, no. It helps to be free to come and go."

Laika gave a sharp woof. "I'll be back in a minute," Kim

said. "His dinner is overdue. If you would like to have a browse in the boxes, be my guest."

Eve marvelled at the breadth of donations. In between tacky costume jewellery made of rusting metal and plastic, she found a silver bracelet with jadeite inlays, and two pairs of dangling Whitby jet earrings. She set all three pieces aside.

"Found anything?" Kim returned alone. Happy munching sounds from the kitchen betrayed Laika's whereabouts.

Eve showed her what she'd discovered.

"I can price them up for you in a few days, if you can wait," Kim said.

"I'm not planning on leaving in the near future, so, yes, that would be fantastic."

"It must be scary to start over and over again. You must miss home."

"I miss a few places, and people. Mostly people."

"But not so much you'd stick around for them."

Eve forbade herself to think of names, when she said, "I might, if it's the right kind of person. What about you? Are you here for good?"

"I was going to travel the world, but things change. Luck

changes, and this is as good a place for memories as any other. Besides, I've got Laika to consider."

"I'm sorry. I didn't mean to dredge up painful stuff."

"It's okay. We weren't public yet," Kim said.

But the mood was spoilt. Eve promised to return for the jewellery and drove home, with a bad aftertaste in her mouth.

CHAPTER 15

*H*ayley knocked loud enough on the door to wake Eve from a heavy sleep. She hurried to throw her trench-coat over her pyjamas, in case anyone else watched. She could imagine the rumours flying if the newcomer showed herself at nine o'clock in the morning still in her night clothes. The trench-coat might just cover enough for her to escape detection.

"Breakfast." Hayley put a bag with oven-warm bread rolls onto the table. "I'll make coffee while you get dressed."

Eve splashed cold water on her face and ran a comb through her hair.

Hayley's coffee jolted her awake. She reached for her second caffeine-shot when a text arrived on her phone.

She read it twice before it hit home. "Tonight. Ben says he's free tonight."

"Suits me." Hayley reached for a bread-roll and sniffed it while feeling the texture. "Let me know what you think."

Eve's mind reeled. "Think of what?"

"The food. These are Heather's own recipe." She broke off a piece and chewed it slowly.

Eve took a bite. "It's fine. But what do I do about tonight?"

"Cook. Or reheat ready-meals. Whatever you prefer. Ben comes for our company, and since you aren't interested in him beyond a purely platonic friendship, what does it matter if you're not a domestic goddess?"

"You're right." Eve took a deep breath. "I'm not used to entertaining, that's all."

"Relax. I thought you'd grill me over my sleuthing, but we can discuss menus instead."

The questionnaire had momentarily fled Eve's mind. She needed to focus.

"And? What did your source say?" she asked.

"First you need to promise to keep this secret. I'm not getting her in trouble," Hayley said.

"Fine. I swear it on my mother's grave."

Hayley lowered her voice. "No signs of a break-in, and the top fingerprints on the door handle inside belonged to Ben. Donna apparently stayed at home, without a visitor. The killer must have had a key, unless the door stayed unlocked."

"Did Ben leave it like that when he left?"

"He says no. Which was another point in his favour. He could easily have said yes, anybody could have entered the house."

"Your friend's opinion, or the official police train of thought?" *Please, let it be absolutely clear that he was framed. Stop these doubts in my head,* Eve thought.

"Mostly mine," Hayley said. "I told her that I had a few worries, because my nan is so frail, and while I am convinced Ben is innocent, I needed to be sure before I could let him visit her."

"That's clever." Eve reached for a second bread-roll.

"That's either a back-handed compliment or an insult."

"It was meant as a compliment."

Hayley graciously accepted it with an incline of her head. "Next. John's tea contained diazepam. The correct amount is unknown, but he usually had his tea at half past three to four-ish. It stood ready for him in the kitchen. He and Donna weren't on the friendliest of terms back then, so they kept each other company as possible."

"Had they been fighting long?" Eve asked.

"Ben said their relationship hit rock bottom when Donna said she'd make sure she'd get every single penny she was entitled to in the divorce, and the estate be damned."

"What did John say?" Eve's curiosity was piqued.

"He suffered a bad stroke before the police could question him. His speech took a while to come back. He confirmed Ben's statement eventually."

"He would. Okay, was there any evidence on Ben's clothes or shoes? Droplets of blood perhaps." Eve swallowed. "Or brain matter?"

"That's a ghoulish thought. There were traces of Donna's blood on his shoe soles, but nothing on his clothes or the shoe leather. Although he could have changed and burnt the things he'd worn if he'd killed her."

The idea caught Eve like a vicious punch. Could Ben be this cold-blooded and conniving? "The police would have asked the people he saw about his dress," she said in his defence.

"A grey business suit. You've seen one, you've seen them all, unless you're heavily into fashion."

Hayley's phone tinkled. "I'll see you at seven. That should be enough time for you to come up with ideas on how to pump Ben for information without letting him know what you're after."

"Do you remember his handwriting?"

"What do you mean?"

"Only a question." Eve gave a dismissive shrug, unwilling to mention the sonnet yet.

"I'm not sure I'd recognise anyone's handwriting. I type everything in my phone."

"Handwriting's safer," Eve said. "Paper can be destroyed. Electronic evidence stays in the cloud."

"I'll remember that if I ever plan a crime." Hayley gave Eve a reassuring grin. "It'll be fine. Wait and see."

"Last question. Did your source say anything about Donna's lover?"

"That was the interesting part. She didn't mention it with a single word." They shared a baffled glance.

Eve pushed her trolley through the supermarket aisles, stressed out already. She could cook to a certain degree, but her skills were nothing to write home about. Would paper napkins do? She dimly remembered wife number two creating elaborate shapes out of starched linen napkins, or maybe having them created. That woman had a catering service on speed-dial. At least Crystal did a few things around the house herself.

A message from Hayley saved Eve as she stood transfixed in the frozen dinner section. "I'll bring the food. You supply the rest," it read. Simple enough. An assortment of wine and non-alcoholic drinks should do. She already had beer, and while Hayley could walk home, Ben had to drive.

Hayley arrived first, laden with casseroles and side dishes. She told a grateful Eve she'd accept reimbursement for the ingredients, but not a penny more. "These are all Heather's experiments. If I didn't know better I'd say she's fattening us up for slaughter."

Eve placed a newly purchased potted plant in the centre of the dining table. She'd read that Aloe Vera improved the air, and it gave the kitchen a homely touch.

Hayley peeled the price tag off the pot. "Someone here is trying to impress."

"Someone here is trying to not freak out." Eve rearranged the cutlery on the paper napkins. She'd already put a set of cotton napkins into her trolley when she remembered they should be washed first; not that she ever did. Anyway, this should be fine for an informal evening among friends.

"Nervous?" Hayley put the dishes in the oven, to keep them warm.

"What if Ben finds out I'm meddling and that's the end of it?"

"The question is, why do you care? For yourself or for his benefit?" Hayley asked. "If it's for your entertainment, stop sticking your nose in. If you do it to clear up a bad situation and help a man we presume to be innocent, that's a good enough reason in my book."

To Eve's relief, Ben arrived before they could dive into a deep philosophical discussion.

He carried a bunch of anemones and a bottle of wine.

Hayley greeted him with a peck on the cheek. Eve lingered, making sure her hands were full because she was not sure what terms they were really on. Or what she felt about him.

"Hi," she said, more sensing than seeing Hayley's amused eye-roll.

"Sorry we had to drag you here," Hayley said to Ben. "I need to stay close while my nan's under the weather."

"How is Letty?" he asked.

"It's just old age and too much work." Hayley crossed her

fingers. "I hope once Heather's allowed to do the cooking unsupervised, I can send my nan away on a holiday. One where she is pampered and doesn't have to lift a finger."

Hayley ushered Ben towards the kitchen, with Eve trailing behind. "You can see for yourself if her cooking's up to scratch. The dinner's courtesy of our new chef. Letty has decided cook sounds unprofessional when we pay for the service."

The food was excellent. The stew was rich, the meat tender and the vegetable and roast potatoes crispy. Eve thankfully concentrated on her meal and listened to Hayley's stories about her grandmother.

"How's your father?" Eve asked during a lull.

"Hanging in there." Ben gave Eve a resigned glance. "I wish he had outside interests like Letty, but all of his life has revolved around the land."

"He must do something to keep himself occupied." Hayley sounded horrified.

"He watches TV, and I try to spend some quality time with him every day. But apart from Chris, there's no-one else left of his old mates. Which is kind of understandable, given our situation."

"That's awful," Eve said. The poor man, sitting in a wheelchair, with nothing to keep him busy but his memories. No wonder he'd treated her coldly. Any person in Ben's life must be a threat for his son's attention, romantic involvement or not.

"We should send him and my nan to a spa together." Hayley pushed her empty plate away. "Not in September though. Heather and Bella are planning a cruise. Bella's hoping to bag a man as a souvenir. Good on her, if you ask me. She's been widowed forever."

Ben broke into loud laughter. "Is the local talent not enough for her?"

"Bella says, these days she expects a bit of sophistication. Like a guy who knows the difference between ice-cream and gelato."

"Which is?" Eve asked, intrigued.

"According to Bella, about one quid per scoop."

"Some people never change." Ben chuckled.

"Luckily they don't. She's responsible for Eve's new hairstyle, by the way. Looks good, doesn't it?" Hayley winked at Eve who instantly felt self-conscious again.

"What about you?" she asked Hayley. "When are you going to see Bella? She'll probably need every customer to finance her cruise."

Hayley ignored the question. "You should visit my nan," she told Ben. "She'd love to see you."

"I might. If you don't think it would be bad for her. Or taint your reputation."

Eve glanced at the empty dishes. "Shall we go to the living room?"

"What about the dinner things?" Ben stacked the plates in swift, efficient movements.

"They can wait." Eve nudged her guests towards the sofa and casually said, "You should write down your contact details for Letty." She pushed a notepad and pen towards Ben. Her spirits soared as he picked them up.

"There's no need," Hayley said.

Eve kicked her.

Hayley shut up.

Blast. He'd written down his mobile number, not his name. Eve needed letters to compare the writing.

Hayley's phone buzzed. She checked it and frowned. "Sorry, guys, I've got to run."

"Is everything okay?" Ben got up with Hayley. "If you need my help ..."

"Gosh, no. A staff issue I need to sort. I'll see you another time."

Eve accompanied Hayley to the door. Hayley whispered, "Good luck. We'll talk tomorrow."

An awkward silence filled the room. Eve tucked her hair behind her ears. "Music?" she asked.

Ben looked around the room, with its chintz curtains and old-fashioned wallpaper. "I didn't see you living in a time-capsule."

"It may not be my taste, but it'll do for a while. Now I think of it, it saves me the trouble of figuring out what exactly my taste is." She frowned. "It's like I catch glimpses of a picture, but they change when I move on." They sat down on chairs, an arm's length apart.

"A rolling stone," he said.

"Not quite as bad, I hope. What about you? Your home doesn't strike me as a replica of your personality either."

Ben rubbed his chin. "I'm with you on that one. Maybe because it still feels mostly like my father's place."

"Your wife must have loved that." Eve could have slapped herself. Hadn't she promised herself to stay away from that subject at least for a little longer?

Ben didn't appear to mind. "At first we thought we'd stay a short while, so the décor didn't matter, and when our moving in became permanent, she no longer cared enough to make huge changes."

"That's sad," Eve said.

"Nothing to be done about that in retrospect."

"I think a holiday for your father is an excellent idea."

"It'd take dynamite to budge him."

"What do you do when you need a break?"

He gave her a wry smile. "I take my fishing rod."

"My father and his wife have asked me to see them for Christmas, or Thanksgiving," Eve heard herself say.

"So, you're going?"

"I don't know. I might do it."

"You should. I've learned the hard way not to put off things, because you never know how long your chances last."

Eve drew in her breath. *Was he talking about his wife, or his lost freedom?* "I'll think about it," she said. "I've got months and months to decide." She looked around. "You're right. That wallpaper really is hideous. I never really noticed."

"Perhaps you should take someone along to viewings before your next move."

"Maybe I should."

"I should be on my way too," he said, but he stayed in his spot.

"Would you like some coffee?"

"Another time." He picked up the paper with his phone number. Hayley had forgotten to take it. "Can you give this to Letty for me?"

"Sure, if you don't want to do it yourself."

"Letty's an old woman. I don't want to cause her any trouble, and you've seen for yourself, I'm not exactly welcome in public."

"Are you planning to hide forever?"

"I'll stick around as long as my father needs me to." His face told her he considered this subject closed.

"What a pity he didn't remarry," she said nevertheless.

"Spoken from experience?" He gave her a wry smile.

"Well, my dad had the excellent taste to originally marry my mother, so I might be willing to overlook one or two later lapses in judgment."

"Or he realised your mother was impossible to replace and he settled for a compromise."

Eve nodded in appreciation. "That sounds much nicer than my theory. Can I borrow that quote?"

"It's all yours. You can also have, 'Beware of dinner guests who saddle you with the dirty dishes'."

His cheek rested for a moment on hers as he said good-bye.

She closed the door behind him and leant against it. What had she learnt? Not a damn thing when it came to the poem or his true feelings for Donna, she admitted to herself. But another issue had become clear. Hayley had been right all along. She did have a massive crush, and if she wanted to have a fighting chance with Ben, she needed to officially clear his name.

She went to bed with a notepad on her nightstand. If inspiration struck, she had to be prepared.

A faint clink from downstairs registered at the back of her mind as she dozed off.

CHAPTER 16

*E*ve stared at the brick in her hand. It had smashed a hole in a window. She'd swept up the shards and vacuumed twice before it sank in what happened. Scrawled with a black permanent marker on the brick was the word Murderer.

The glazier had promised to send out a man within the hour to replace the broken pane, to Eve's relief. She'd expected a long wait. She weighed the brick in her hand. It would have been useless to call the police and have it finger-printed, and she also intended to leave the insurance company out of it.

No doubt the vandal wanted to call attention to Ben and stir up more trouble. She wouldn't tell Ben either, because he'd use this vandalism as another reason to stay away. Hayley would have to know though. The pub would be secured, and the CCTV camera was in plain sight, but anyone intent on hurting Ben might not think clearly.

Eve put the brick in a kitchen drawer and went to do yesterday's dishes, all the while fighting the niggling feeling all her movements might be watched. That's what the nightly visitor wanted, to stir paranoia. In a small town he might get away with stalking her cottage in the middle of the night. In broad daylight, there was always someone who watched your movements.

When did she hear the clink? She remembered checking her alarm clock a few minutes before one. Ben had left around 9.30pm. That gave the vandal a few hours to spot Ben, get a brick and wait until the neighbourhood was asleep.

The glazier accepted Eve's explanation about accidentally hitting a rock while digging in her garden without batting an eyelid. All he cared about was her cheque.

"Why would anyone target you?" Hayley asked in a sombre mood. "It would make more sense to smash in Ben's windows, or his car."

Eve had given this question a lot of thought as well. "Because he'd shrug it off if someone hurls a brick through his window? Or because his house is remote and might have hidden security cameras installed?"

"Or your visitor wanted to make sure Ben stays isolated," Hayley said. "Unless – what if it's a warning? To stay away from a murderer?"

"I thought we'd agreed he's innocent." Eve's left eye twitched.

"But we're the only ones who think so. Still, it's a bit extreme to smash in your window all because Ben visited once. After five years, people really should move on." Hayley glanced at her mid-morning regulars, nursing their pints. The low music shielded their conversation from prying ears. "Do you think it was personal? That your visitor was close to Donna?"

"The secret lover," Eve said. "You would have heard if she formed any open friendships in town, but if they were careful enough, they would be able to keep it secret."

"And he wants to punish Ben by driving you away." Hayley's eyes lit up. "In which case he must be a local guy, who knew that Ben had reappeared and who also saw him enter or leave Ivy Cottage."

One of the regulars whistled for Hayley's attention. "What does a body have to do to get a drop in his glass?"

"How about asking nicely, Bob?" Hayley strolled over to the bar, nodding towards the kitchen door and miming scribbling. Eve relaxed. Hayley would discreetly pump Heather for information, and then she'd write down the results.

⁓

Eve typed furiously to make up for a lost morning. She had no intention of giving up her planned walk. When the phone received a new message, she groaned in frustration. Why couldn't people leave her in peace?

She perked up as she read the message. John had renewed his interest in showing Eve the medals, Ben wrote.

She replied, *"Would love to visit. 4pm okay?"*

She twirled twice on her swivel chair before she concentrated on her task again.

⁓

Eve kept an eye on the rear-view mirror. Sweat slicked her palms as she gripped the steering wheel unnecessarily tight. She deliberately took a detour along minor roads to see if another car followed her, but so far, she seemed to be alone. She pulled into a side road and switched off the engine. Nobody came past. Her pulse slowed until it reached its normal pace. Her nerves had frayed more than she'd expected. She started the car again and drove on.

Ben kept his greeting casual. Eve hoped his detachment was a show he put on for John. The old man sat on the patio, his eyes half-closed, but Eve could swear he registered every tiny change in the atmosphere.

"Hello, Mr Dryden," she said. "Thanks for inviting me over."

"Call me John." He lifted his left hand agonisingly slow until it reached higher than his head.

Chris came out of the house, towelling his hands dry. The sun glistened on his skin, and his rolled-up sleeves exposed well-defined muscles. His shirt had the top four buttons undone.

Eve wondered if he showed off his looks for her benefit, until she noticed he seemed taken aback to see her. The subtle preening came natural to him, then.

She saw Chris dart a glance at Ben, whose slender physique was no match for his own muscle tone. A friendly competition would explain it.

"Hi Chris," she said.

"Nice surprise to see you again." His smile exposed white teeth that were saved from boring perfection by a crooked incisor.

"Eve is my visitor. Ben!" John might be physically frail, but he could still show himself in command.

Ben rolled a trolley up to his father. What appeared to be books wrapped in cloth and a wooden box sat on the lower tier. On the upper tier, he'd placed tea and biscuits.

Ben pulled up a couple of chairs, so he and Eve could sit close enough to his father and still reach the trolley. His hand brushed her neck as she sat down. A thrill rushed through her body and sent a faint blush to her cheeks. She hoped John and Chris missed that.

"The box." John held out a shaking hand.

Ben opened the lid. Inside, vintage medals and ribbons rested on velvet trays faded with age.

John's finger pointed at one. "Queen Victoria herself visited the show when Jonathan Dryden received this medal for his prized ram. Three years in a row 'Best in Show.'"

"That's amazing." Eve leant over the tray. "It must have been hard to give up sheep farming."

"Things change. Cheap imports, that's what it was. Cheap meat and wool from the colonies. Still, we didn't do too badly, did we?"

Ben closed the box. "We still don't."

"That's true. You can deal a Dryden a blow, but we

always bounce back, right, Chris?"

John's massage therapist grinned at him, an easy, infectious smile that crinkled the corners of his eyes.

Bella's image appeared in Eve's mind. Chris must be a hit with older women.

"I can definitely attest to that," he said, directing the full force of his beam at Eve. "Do you need anything else from me?"

John shook his head. "I'll see you later, as usual."

An hour later, Eve's head whirled with information about the family tree, the lineage of animals, dead for over a century, and anything else documented in three thick folios. John had to rest his voice in between, and then Ben took over. He showed less obvious pride and enthusiasm, but then he wasn't a farmer. Still, together they formed the picture of a dedicated family.

Had Eve and her dad ever shared close moments like this? If yes, she'd forgotten. All she did remember was her mother, tucking her in, reading bedtime stories and letting her chestnut hair fall over Eve's face and tickle her. No wonder Ben didn't leave. Some bonds were too precious.

"Eve?" Ben's voice brought her back to the present. She pulled herself together. She must stop reading meaning into everything she saw, or thought she saw.

"Sorry, you were saying?"

"I was asking if you'd like more tea."

"I'm good. And I'm sorry if my mind wandered off." She touched John's arm. "Thanks for showing me the medals. My father's wife would love them. Most Americans are overwhelmed with the idea of all this history."

"I almost forget you're American." Was there a note of disapproval in his tone?

"On my father's side. Hence my hopefully slight accent. My mother met him when he was working in the London office of his company for a year."

"You're a Brit then."

She chose to smile for an answer.

"Nothing wrong with freshening up bloodlines," John said to her surprise. "Any farmer knows that."

His head sunk closer to his chest.

"You're tired," Ben said.

"Nonsense."

"Well, I need to crack on with my work," Eve said. "But I hope I'll see you again soon."

On her way home, she wondered why John had really invited her. Did he want to chat to keep himself entertained, or did he want to suss her out? The old man was sharp. She'd love to find out how much he knew about Donna's private life. He might talk to Hayley, or better still, to her grandmother, if they could find a way to make a visit appear natural.

Eve spent a nervous night. The wind ruffled the ivy that covered almost the whole front of the cottage, and a climbing rose scrabbled over the bedroom window, interrupting her sleep. She needed a security system. Kim would be able to advise her with that.

The thought still occupied her mind over breakfast. She pushed it aside. As much as she ached to go out for advice straight away, her laptop told her to stay put, unless she wanted to default on her deadlines. Her new-found paranoia, and her interest in Ben's case, would have to take a backseat until she dug herself out of this self-created hole. It was one thing to devote her spare hours to a cause, and a whole other ballgame to risk her best client. Her bank account was never in the red, by sheer dint of effort. But jewellery purchases and window repair meant she needed the next payment, especially if she wanted to invest in security equipment as well.

Eve toyed with the idea of a mock camera, only to rule it

out. It had to be convincing for the news to spread through the local grapevine. But first, work.

Her tongue stuck to the roof of her mouth. Eve felt lightheaded from lack of water and food. She'd silenced her phone and put it in her bedroom to be undisturbed. That also meant she'd missed her usual breaks and other little things like lunch, dinner, or messages. Still, she'd almost caught up with her translations.

A glance at the wall clock told her it would be useless to drop into the "Green Dragon". The kitchen would be closed before she got there, and the bar would be buzzing. Ten years in merry old England, and she nevertheless struggled with the concept of social drinking night after night. Neither her liver nor her finances would stand for it.

Eve checked her phone for messages. One from Hayley, promising to catch up tomorrow. Nothing from Ben. He obviously hadn't missed her. Which was perfectly fine. Crush or not, she couldn't picture herself getting all hot and bothered with him in a house where his crippled father and dead wife haunted the atmosphere. Or have him over at her place where the thought of malevolent watchers would definitely cramp her style. At thirty-two she was too old to make out in a car, so that option was out as well. Apart from the fact that he obviously only saw her as a friend without any romantic attraction.

Considering that she wouldn't stick around forever, not getting entangled was all for the best, anyway. Discussion over.

She searched her refrigerator for leftovers. A few eggs, cream cheese and a squishy tomato she could use for an omelette. Eve mentally slapped herself that she hadn't stocked up her groceries at the supermarket, because she hadn't thought past their dinner for three. It served her right for becoming single-minded.

Eve broke the eggs into a bowl and stirred them viciously. From now on she'd channel her attraction to Ben, which after all was nothing but a matter of hormones, as an incentive to look her best, but nothing else. A bit of self-love went a long way.

Ben checked his phone for messages. Nothing. John was finally asleep after a fretful day. Ben was unsure if Eve's visit had caused it, but his father kept him busy with his restlessness whenever he took a break from his work. He wished John would tell him what bothered him. Although, if he did, Ben was almost certain it was something he did not want to hear. Ever. The truth might set one of them free. The other one would face hell.

CHAPTER 17

*W*onderful, what a clear head could do. Eve's fingers danced over her keyboard. She'd changed out of her pyjamas, brushed her hair and swiped on a layer of mascara. Instead of feeling like a frazzled, stressed-out frump, she had her life and her work under control. Only five more pages to go, and she could afford to pop out for groceries and take the whole, glorious afternoon off.

Hayley caught her as Eve unlocked her car. "How are you?" she asked. "No nightmares?"

"I'll feel better once I have a security camera installed," Eve admitted.

"It does make a lot of difference. Do you have any idea what you're looking for?"

Eve thought of Kim. "I need to ask someone about her camera, but the answer is yes. I think so, at least."

"Good. But what are you going to do in the meantime?"

"I was wondering if you could put the word out that my cottage is protected. Single woman and a stranger and all that."

Hayley's eyes twinkled. "I'll do you one better. I'll whisper a few words in Heather's ears and let her do her magic."

"How come you're not at work?" Eve asked, touched by Hayley's concern.

"My nan's keeping an eye on the ladies. She told me to get out from under their feet, because I seem to make Grace nervous. Which means. I've got a little bit of freedom on my hands."

"Damn. I'm on my way to the shops."

"Pity." Hayley waved a piece of paper under Eve's nose.

Eve gave in and locked her car again. "I could go out later. Coffee?"

The paper was blank. Eve was puzzled.

"Interesting, isn't it?" Hayley said. "Heather could think

of only two people who'd tried to get close to Donna. One is Sue Littlewood, which makes sense. She's always on the hunt for new blood for the Women's Institute. Preposterous idea to think of her as your vandal though."

Eve reached for her watering can, to top up the Aloe plant.

Hayley stopped her. "What are you doing? Haven't you read the instructions? You'll drown the poor plant."

Eve put the watering can away.

"Sue asked me when she should drop by to see, you by the way," Hayley said.

Eve pulled a face.

Hayley patted her hand, in an annoyingly patronising way. "Don't worry, I've told her to catch you at the 'Green Dragon'. That woman is a lot wilier than she appears, and you're no match for her on your own. Unless you desperately want to see yourself roped in to the sisterhood of the Women's Institute."

"Good grief, no. Who's the other one?"

"You're going to like this. It's Dom's older brother, Harry. Used to fancy himself as a bit of a ladies' man. Heather swears to high heaven he had his sights set on Donna."

Eve's pulse quickened. "Could he have been her secret

lover? I'm sure she was planning on moving in with him."

Hayley's wrinkled her nose. "That, I'm afraid to admit it, is where Harry drops out of the picture. During the period in question, he'd moved back in with his parents after his divorce, and I can't see any woman willing to shack up in a spare room above a garage."

"He could have rented a flat," Eve said.

"He could, but I'm sure that Heather would have heard. Give that woman enough time, and she can tell you the colour of your underwear and where you bought it."

"Is this Harry attractive enough to have been Donna's type?" Eve asked.

"Intellectually he was no Ben, but a lot of women wouldn't have minded his company." Hayley caught on to Eve's surprise. She sighed. "Not me, if that's what you were wondering. Like Bella, I prefer my men to be slightly more sophisticated. And not from around these parts. But Harry has the six-pack and the swagger, and he does scrub up well."

Eve decided against prying. "Can you picture him as the brick-thrower?"

"That's the second snag. He got engaged two months ago and moved in with his fiancée. That's why he's too busy to show his face in the 'Green Dragon'. He might have heard about Ben resurfacing, but it's all speculation."

"What about a motive for murder? Maybe Donna told him she wanted something better than to live with Harry's parents, especially since she expected a nice bit of cash as divorce settlement. He might have felt insulted, or belittled."

"I might at a very long stretch see Harry lash out in a rage, but drugging John means premeditation. Plus, the killer needed a key to get inside."

"And Donna wouldn't have given him a spare key to the house. She used the cabin for her trysts." Eve drummed her fingertips on the table. It helped her concentrate. "What about Grace? She used to work for the Drydens. Did she possess a key that Harry or someone else might have swiped to get a copy made?"

"That's another dead end. Ben offered her one, but she'd walked in on another elderly client once, doing naked yoga, and declined." They broke into a giggle.

"This is hopeless," Eve said after they composed themselves. "We're getting nowhere."

"I wouldn't say that. At least you have a lot of information about what didn't happen. What's left – ", Hayley glanced at the clock. "Speaking of leaving, I have to get back to the pub. Will I see you there tonight?"

"I'll try."

Eve followed Hayley out of the door, before she forgot about groceries again.

With her fridge full to bursting, Eve concentrated on her final stretch of work. Hayley's words popped into her mind. *"What's left."*

What was left, apart from a handful of pesky sentences unwilling to form into smooth constructs?

Eve switched on the television, hoping the background noise would drown out her thoughts while she made sense of the words in front of her and definitely would not digress.

The second she'd switched off her laptop, Eve clasped her backpack and fled the house. She needed fresh air to clear her brain. Her feet took her along her usual path, without any conscious thought.

Eve stared at the roof of the cabin, willing the owl to appear and impart some of the wisdom it was supposed to possess. After all, without the bird she wouldn't have met Ben. Which meant, the owl caused this whole messy situation.

She stuck out her lower lip. A sensible person would have walked straight away instead of involving herself in the life of a man who would not appreciate any of her efforts.

Soft footsteps made her turn around, to see Ben.

"It's in the tree hole," he said.

"What is?" Her heart beat ridiculously fast. How young could one have a heart attack? And why should she be frightened at all? Nobody but Hayley and Letty knew she was snooping around, and she posed no threat to the killer. Unfortunately, thanks to her lack of insights.

"The owl," Ben said. "You're looking for it, right?"

"Of course. Is it nesting?" She smoothed her curls, a bad habit to cover up nervousness.

"Probably."

"Then we'd better leave it in peace."

They walked towards the river, their steps in easy synchronicity.

"I didn't realise you had no security cameras," Ben said.

Her step faltered. How did he know?

"Careful," he said. "Hayley called me, to warn me against visiting Letty."

"I see."

"You should have told me what happened."

"It was only a brick. No big deal." Every nerve in her body was aware of his presence, the way his eyes crinkled when he laughed, the scent of his after-shave. Blood rushed into her face.

"What if you'd been awake and been hit?" he asked.

"It won't happen again. I'll have the cottage secured. End of story."

"I would install the equipment for you, but your neighbours could take offence if I show myself again."

"Five years. They need to get a life," Eve said.

"People have a long memory."

"I don't understand why you're still here. I get why you're looking after John, but he should see what that is costing you." She deliberately kept her gaze on the horizon.

"I told you how much the land means to him," Ben said.

"More than his own son? Especially when he's practically house-bound?"

"I promised I'd take care of everything, on my mother's grave."

"That's a noble oath. Did you take a chastity vow as well?" Eve bit her tongue. She didn't even know where those words came from. "Sorry," she said. "I was trying to be funny."

Ben stepped in front of her. Their gaze met. He reached out a hand as if to touch her cheek, only to halt half an inch from her face. He let the arm drop.

"You weren't. And the answer is no. I just don't want things to get more complicated than they already are." The ghost of a regretful smile flitted over his face.

Warmth spread through her body. She moistened her suddenly dry lips. A rumble over her head made her look up. As if on cue, the blue sky had turned leaden, with dark clouds moving towards them.

"You should hurry if you want to get home dry," Ben said. "I would offer to drive you, but it might take us as long to even reach my car."

"And you don't want to be seen around Ivy Cottage." She pushed herself up on her tiptoes, brushed his cheek with her mouth and ran off without looking back.

CHAPTER 18

*N*o complications. Ben stared at Eve's retreating back. He'd promised himself to stay clear of any more problems as long as he had to. He should never have brought Eve home and let John meet her. She'd disturbed the balance of their carefully crafted life together and he had no idea where it might lead. For all of them.

Chris and John played a game of chess when Ben returned. They were evenly matched, Ben thought as he watched them from the doorway. John was the better player, but his concentration flagged halfway through, whereas Chris' foresight never reached further than the next three or four moves.

John grunted as he moved a pawn.

Chris looked up from the board and spotted Ben. "You're back," he said, as he rose and slapped him on the back in a chipper, manful manner.

Usually Ben played along, to keep peace. Today, it grated on Ben's nerves. "Looks like it."

"Had a good walk?" John gave him a sly glance.

Ben bristled at the interrogation. "Why are you asking?"

Chris gave John a small shrug. "A massage might help Mr Grumpy get rid of his tensions."

"A less juvenile choice of words might help as well." Ben gritted his teeth.

John struggled to wheel his chair around, away from Ben. Chris grabbed the handles and pushed the wheelchair towards the hallway.

"Wait," Ben said. "I'm sorry." Except he wasn't. He meant every word.

John grunted. Chris kept going, a more pronounced swagger in his step.

Chris knocked on Ben's office. He came out and closed the door behind him. "I've come to apologise if I caused trouble," Chris said. His face registered remorse. "I only meant to lighten the mood."

"I appreciate that."

"Let me know if there's anything I can do to make things easier. With your girlfriend too."

Ben found himself cooling towards Chris again. "She's not my girlfriend, and I'd be grateful if you remember that, especially when it comes to my father."

"Shame. She's got great legs."

"If that's all?"

Chris laid a brotherly hand on Ben's shoulder. "I'm sure John would come around. Eventually."

"Well, there is no need. At all." He wanted to slam the office door in Chris's face, but that wouldn't have accomplished anything. Also, the door opened inwards.

Kim's windows were dark. Eve strolled around for a few minutes and checked if she could see the cameras covering the back entrance to shop and flat. She spotted one tiny lens embedded in the frame of the door-bell. There would be more but they were too well-hidden for her to spot. This kind of security system was exactly what she needed. Where was Kim? Out on a date, presumably. Or walking Laika.

Eve passed by "Little Italy". Inside, Dean Martin sang "That's Amore", and the tantalising smell of herbs and garlic wafted by her nose.

Her stomach rumbled. She'd try Kim's place one more time and then head home.

The flat still lay in darkness. Eve sighed. She'd hoped not solely for advice, but also for company. Self-love and self-reliance were all well and good, but that did not mean she had to spend her all of her evenings alone. Especially if it prevented her from overthinking that stupid kiss and Ben's total lack of reaction to it. At least she still had the "Green Dragon".

Hayley had her hands full with the bar, while Dom served the Pink Panthers at the tables. He moved with a languid grace he must have practiced in front of a mirror. A few more gin and tonics or wine spritzers in, and Eve wouldn't have bet on his safety from his female audience.

For now, the ladies were happy with giggling and slipping tips into his rapidly filling shirt pocket.

Bella and Sue sat at another table. Bella waved at Eve and beckoned her to join them.

Eve stopped Dom on her way over. "Can I have a cheeseburger and chips?"

"No worries." He gave her a cheeky grin that would have made her heart flutter fifteen years ago. Now, it made her feel like patting him on the back and telling him to flirt with girls his own age.

Bella took a strand of Eve's hair and rubbed it between her fingers. "So much better," she said and patted the strand back in place.

"How are you finding our town?" Sue inched close to Eve, a calculating gleam in her eyes. "Not too lonely, I hope. We wouldn't like to feel we're not welcoming enough."

Eve inwardly thanked Hayley for the warning about Sue's agenda, or she might have fallen into the trap. "Not at all." She beamed at Sue and Bella. "I'm much too busy for loneliness, and everybody is so friendly. I do wish I had more leisure."

"I see. But if you should ever find yourself at a loose end, you know where to find us. Our doors are always open." Sue slid a business card for the Women's Institute over to Eve.

"Absolutely. I'll remember that."

Dom placed a ginger ale and a bowl of chips in front of Bella. She winked at him lasciviously. "Thanks, cupcake."

He flushed slightly, a response seemingly at odds with his flirtatious manner but, to Eve, it was endearing.

Bella burst into laughter as he strode off. "Bless his heart," she said. "Nice little bum though."

"How old is he?" Eve asked.

"Nineteen. Old enough to know how to use his charms, and too young to keep those gals in check." Bella said as one of the Pink Panthers fondled Dom's biceps. A withering glare from Hayley made the woman take her hand off the young man.

"Nothing wrong with that boy though," Sue said. "He's a nice lad. Saving up for university."

"Brains and brawns," Eve said, annoyed with herself for being surprised.

"Oh yes." Bella nodded with enough vigour to make her chin wobble. "Raking in twice as much as he did since I gave him my 'Magic Mike' DVD. Not that he's going to strip, mind you, but look at the moves this boy's got. Gives you that nice fuzzy feeling, if you get my drift. Now we only need the Panthers to remember, they're only allowed to ogle, not grope."

"How do the men like it?" Eve asked.

Bella snorted. "He's a sports hero, love. And he doesn't strut his stuff when the old blokes are around."

Sue leant in on Eve. "Lots more to the Women's Institute than you'd think."

A sudden lull in the Panther's giggling made Eve and Bella look towards the door. Chris stood in the frame, lingering for a moment as he spied the bowling team. Then he noticed Eve and entered.

Half a dozen eyes mustered him from the Panther's tables, and what had appeared slightly raucous but harmless in Dom's case, now looked predatory to Eve.

"Someone has bagged herself an admirer," Sue whispered audibly in Bella's ear and motioned towards Eve. Eve glared at her.

Chris stopped by the bar and pulled up a stool.

Dom brought Eve's cheeseburger. She enjoyed it less than she would have without the sly glances towards her and Chris. He seemed oblivious to them, engrossed in easy banter with Hayley.

As soon as Eve finished her food, Bella nudged her. "Go and talk to him," she said. "If the Panthers' get their paws on him, he'll run a mile a minute and there goes your chance."

Eve opened her mouth to claim her lack of interest, to

snap it shut again. If anyone knew the Drydens, it was Chris.

She sauntered to the bar and ordered a glass of Merlot.

Hayley gave her an encouraging nod. "Sit down and talk to us," she said.

"If I'm not interrupting?"

"Not at all." Chris flashed Eve a grin. His chin had a marked dimple she hadn't noticed before. With that face and body, he wouldn't look out of place on a firefighter's calendar.

Hayley put Eve's glass in front of her. "We were just talking about how little things change in places like this."

"To be honest, I feel like a coward for staying away so long. It simply felt kind of disloyal to John and Ben." Chris made a sheepish face.

"It must have been tough to stick by them." Hayley mixed another couple of pink gin and tonics and set them on a tray for Dom. "Did you ever doubt Ben's innocence?"

"Good grief, no." Chris was aghast. "He's a good guy. He has a bit of a temper on him, when it comes to his dad, but then what kind of man doesn't fight for his family?"

Eve found herself liking Chris more and more. "Who do you think did it?" she asked.

"A burglar. I'd bet on it. A rich looking place, no car outside because Donna's Audi was in the shop that week, he must have been surprised to see her." Chris's voice left no room for doubt.

"But how did a burglar get in? The police would have found traces of a break-in." Hayley propped her chin into her hands as she leant on the bar.

"Ben probably left the door unlocked. I mean, he'd just had a fight with Donna. The way I see it, he slammed the door shut behind him and huffed off. A mate told me, burglars try the door knob first. You'd be amazed how many people leave their doors open or have the alarm switched off."

"Crazy, right?" Hayley said. "I'm glad Eve finally got around to having a security system. You're still adding to it, you told me?"

Hayley's eyes beseeched Eve to take up the cue. "Totally," she said. "What I have now covers the bases but give me a week and Fort Knox has nothing on me."

Chris furrowed his brows. "That sound serious, Is there any particular reason?"

Eve slowly shook her head, unsure what to say.

"Unless you count kids playing a prank." Hayley took a tray full of dirty glasses from Dom.

"Anyway," Chris said, "I wanted to tell you, the old man's

a tad grumpy in the beginning, but he'll get used to you, Eve."

"Understandable he's a bit wary of strangers," Eve said. "I would too, in his situation."

"Was he close to Donna?" Hayley asked.

"Who? John? She was his daughter-in-law."

"Being married to someone who puts his blood relatives first can be tough. Or the other way around," Eve said.

"She was a bit too citified for John's taste, I reckon. But he liked her well enough when they moved in." Chris bit his lip. "I should not gossip about them. They're my friends."

"I'm sure the Drydens appreciate that," Eve said.

"Ben's worth putting up with John for, if you want my advice." Chris tuned his empty glass in his hands.

"We're friends, that's all," Eve said, an edge creeping into her tone.

"Too bad. He deserves a bit of happiness."

"How about yourself?" Hayley asked.

A shutter came down in Chris's face. "Me and my work, that's all these days."

"Let's drink to that. We're a band of happy singles." Hayley smiled.

Eve clinked her glass against Chris'. "Happy singles."

Eve read the latest pages through for one final edit before she hit the send button. There'd be at least one typo she'd overlooked. There always was. Among writers, translators, proof-readers and editors the last elusive typo was a truth universally acknowledged. She'd learned to live with that, and she'd learned to let go. All that mattered at this stage was the invoice, and her new freedom.

Kim helped two customers as Eve arrived. She noticed with pleasure that her own donations all had gone.

"Have you come for the jewellery? I've kept it upstairs. It's a bit pricey, I'm afraid. One-ten for all of it," Kim said when they were alone.

Eve scratched her nose. "Can I make a deposit until I get paid?"

"Sure." Kim put the 'Closed' sign on the door. "Shall we go upstairs? It's my lunchtime now."

Laika rubbed his head on Kim's legs as they entered the flat. "Good boy," she said and stroked him.

The jewellery sat in a velvet box. "You don't have to take it," Kim said.

Eve touched the pieces. "They're beautiful. Crystal will go crazy over them."

"As long as you don't go overboard. Or she might expect expensive gifts all the time."

"I'll keep these until I visit them. I haven't had a family Thanksgiving since I left for college," Eve said.

"I can't imagine not seeing my family for years. They keep me sane when the shit hits the fan." Kim sounded wistful.

"Can I ask you something?"

"Sure," Kim said.

As Eve had hoped, a similar security system to Kim's should be easy to handle, and it came at a just about affordable price.

She put her notebook with a contact address away. "Can I take you out for lunch, as a thank-you for all your help?"

Kim led her to her favourite café, in a tucked-away alley. It lived off locals, Kim explained as Eve gaped at the full tables. Perennials cascaded from hanging baskets, and blooming miniature roses formed the centrepiece of every table, explaining how 'The Flower Pot' got its name.

"Wow," Eve said as the realisation hit her. 'The Flower Pot,' aka TFP. This had to be the place where Donna met her swain for lunch.

"Shall we go into the garden?" Kim ordered two jacket potatoes with sour cream and salad.

A man-high, ivy-covered wall separated the garden from the road. A profusion of flowers crept over arches, forming secret nooks. The clientele was with one exception female. Despite the privacy of the nooks, a man in Donna's company must have stood out, Eve thought.

The food was simple, but delicious, and came in record time.

"Your landlords should pay for the security system," Kim said as she drenched her salad in home-made dressing.

"They probably would, but I don't want any delays while the estate agent gets in touch with them."

"Why, do you have a problem?"

It couldn't hurt to tell Kim, if she left out a few details, Eve decided. "It could have been a prank," she said, "or somebody in my new neighbourhood is averse to foreigners. Whatever the reason, somebody broke my window."

"That's awful. What did the police say?"

"I decided against notifying them. They're understaffed enough, and a minor act of vandalism isn't worth the hassle," Eve said.

"Are you sure you don't want to file a complaint? Lots of crimes start small."

"Cameras will be enough." Eve thought of Ben. "I probably positioned myself as a target."

"Promise me, if anything feels threatening in the slightest, call for help." Kim covered Eve's left hand with hers. "There's a lot of scary people out there." The pain in her eyes was unmistakable.

"Something happened," Eve said. "Something bad?"

"We were going to spend the rest of our life together," Kim said. "Instead, my partner was killed before we even had a chance to take our relationship public."

"I'm so sorry," Eve said. "I didn't mean to bring back painful memories."

"It's okay. I haven't talked about it for a long time." Kim wiped away a tear.

The security system company promised installation in three days. That should also restore her sleep, Eve hoped. She'd woken up again at the smallest noise, and the dark rings under her eyes threatened to become permanent.

Eve pushed the coffee table aside, clearing as much floor space as she could, and stepped into its centre. She closed her eyes, concentrated on her breathing and kicked out. It almost threw her off balance. She needed a refresher course in karate, she thought. She'd practiced self-defence as a student, but she'd never had any reason to use it in real life.

Eve punched the air and kicked out again. And again. That was better.

She pushed back the chair and sat in it, slightly out of breath.

The door-bell rang. A chirpy middle-aged woman stood on Eve's step, a small square parcel in her hand. "Great evening wasn't it?" she said. "Sign here please."

She handed Eve a clunky device and a stylo. It took Eve a moment to take it, and to mentally place the post woman. "You're a member of the bowling team," she said, proud of her observation. After all, she'd barely watched the Pink Panthers.

"County championship finalists, two years running," the woman said with audible pride. "We're always on the lookout for new talent, if you're interested."

Eve took her parcel and beat a retreat. "I'm really too busy."

The parcel bore her father's handwriting. Eve tore off the paper. Inside, a baseball sat in layers of bubble-wrap in a cardboard box. She lifted it out with a reverence that surprised her herself. She hadn't seen this baseball since her mother died. She'd suspected wife number two to have sold it as a collector's piece. It carried the signature of June Peppas, left-handed first base pitcher and two-time member of the All-Star Team in the All-American Girls Professional Baseball League.

Eve's mother had thrown herself whole-heartedly into all things American after her wedding, but she put her own slant of things. Instead of cheering for the modern male teams, like the rest of the neighbourhood, she developed a passion for the women's league which had filled the gap left by the soldiers during World War 2 and in the following years.

She'd queued for two hours in the rain to get June Peppas' to sign this ball. Eve wished her mother had lived to see her heroine being inducted into the National Women's Baseball Hall of Fame.

A note accompanied the ball. "Crystal found this tucked away. We thought you might want it."

Eve gently placed the baseball in her own backpack. Her

mother used to carry it around for luck. She'd do the same.

"Thank you, Crystal," she said to the empty room. "I appreciate the gesture."

Hayley drove as gently as she could, to avoid the potholes on the road. Letty clasped her hands around a cake tin. She'd baked the marble cake herself, despite Heather's offers to help. Making a visit empty-handed was rude, Letty said, and it had to be her own work. Otherwise she might as well lower herself to offering store-bought fare.

Letty hummed to herself. She looked forward to getting away from the 'Green Dragon' for a change, and Hayley suspected she enjoyed her chance to snoop around. They'd rehearsed a few points of inquiry, and with her fluffy white hair and innocent smile, Letty looked the role of Miss Marple too.

The car hit a bump. "Are you okay?" Hayley asked.

"I'm fine. You worry too much." Letty picked up her humming, a melody from an old song she used to sing to a small Hayley at sleep-overs. "Que sera, sera."

Hayley frowned. She'd be happier if she knew in advance what would be. If she lost Letty, or gave up the

'Green Dragon', she would be adrift. In Eve's company, the idea of freedom to come and go held a lot of appeal. Without Eve around, the thought of having no roots scared the hell out of her.

She blew out her breath. Plan B could wait. For the moment, they had another task at hand.

Ben came outside as soon as he heard the car. "Thank you for coming to see us," he said. He tucked Letty's arm under his and led her towards the house. "You haven't changed at all, my dear."

"Flatterer. But it's true what they say, it helps to keep busy, and to have young people around. I'm sure your dad will agree on that."

John basked in the sunshine on the wind-still patio. He tried to sit up straighter when they approached him.

"Look who's here," he said. "You're still a sight to behold, Letty, and young Hayley as well."

"Not so young anymore, I'm afraid." Hayley pulled a playful face. He'd kept up well, she thought, despite the stroke. She'd been afraid to find him a wreck, but his eyes were as sharp as ever.

"Fiddlesticks. You've got your whole life ahead. Not like us old-timers." He glanced at the cake tin. "Why don't you and my boy get the tea ready, while your nan and I catch up?"

"Your dad's in a great mood," Hayley said as she helped Ben prepare the tea.

"Surprisingly so." Ben placed sugar and milk on the trolley. "He usually prefers it if no-one apart from Chris darkens our doorstep."

"Well, he and my nan have known each other forever."

"I know, but he turned his back on all his old cronies when things got bad."

"Could be he didn't want them to see him in a wheelchair," Hayley said.

"That's possible."

"I've promised Letty we'd sit by the pond," John said as they returned.

Ben dutifully pushed the wheelchair onto the flagged path running through the lawn all the way to the water. Hayley took charge of the tea trolley after she'd made sure the pathway was well-kept. She had a deep-seated fear of Letty falling and breaking her hip.

The upper tier of the trolley had fold-away boards which turned it into a table.

Ben supplied picnic chairs and gallantly lowered Letty into the most comfortable one, with cushions for her head and back.

They chatted about the weather and the upkeep of the pond with its fish and water-lilies while they enjoyed their tea.

"Why don't you young folk go for a walk and take a peek at the fish?" John said. "I haven't seen my Golden Orfes in a while. The heron might've had them as a snack."

Ben gave Hayley a resigned glance as they rose to stroll around the pond.

"They make a nice pair," John said when the two were out of earshot. "I didn't see a ring on your Hayley's finger."

Letty tittered. "She's a bit too independent and headstrong for most men, I'm afraid. Most blokes like their women pliant. And that last man of hers. Well." She shook her head sadly. "I could have told her straight away he was wrong for her. Too demanding by half. But they don't want to listen to us, do they?"

"Same with my Ben. I knew it when I clapped eyes on the gal it wouldn't work out. But no, he had to marry her." John reached for his special cup. A droplet of tea ran down his chin. Letty patted it swiftly away with a napkin.

"Your daughter-in-law did seem a bit out of place to me," she said.

"I shouldn't have let the boy come home. Not with her anyway. My mistake."

"You couldn't know that. Mind you, I sometimes wonder if I did the right thing with my Hayley, when she decided to return. Not exactly a lively place for young people, is it?"

"We found enough entertainment in our days. Now it's all just technology and foreign trips and out with the old," John said.

"Your Ben seems happy enough with you."

"He has to make the best of it. It's not as if he could up and leave."

Letty massaged her neck, to work out a kink. "I thought he stays because of you. It's nice to see my Hayley's not the only one devoted to family."

"What you need is a massage," John said as Letty gingerly turned her neck. "I don't know what I'd do without Chris. A week without him when he's on holiday, and my whole body aches. Funny thing, muscles. You should think mine'd be numb, but now. But no. Give me merry hell, they do."

"It must be a great comfort, and a relief for Ben to have Chris around. I'm so glad Hayley finally saw fit to hire more bar staff, and Heather's shaping up nicely in the kitchen. We can't have the children tied up forever." Letty broke off a small piece of cake and nibbled on it, satisfied with the direction their chat took.

John would bristle at being told the blunt truth, but it couldn't hurt to seed a few ideas. She showed her dimples. "I've been telling my granddaughter to go on a holiday and meet new people. Ben and his wife should have done that."

"Donna went off on her own for a few days. That worked well." John grunted. "Came back, she did, bold as brass, and told him to put her stuff in the attic."

"Poor Ben. He must have been distraught." Letty's tone showed just the right amount of commiseration, she thought, without being overtly curious.

"If you ask me, he was glad. Donna wanted it kept secret, of course. Told the cleaner not to tidy the bedroom anymore." Anger blazed in John's eyes.

"How long did she live up there?" Letty asked.

"Six weeks or thereabouts."

"And she already told him she wanted a divorce?" Letty sadly shook her head.

"About halfway through. When she'd totalled how much money she could squeeze out of my boy. A schemer, that's who she was, with all her simpering and fancy clothes."

Letty gasped. "I made Hayley promise me she won't let anybody touch what's hers when I signed over the 'Green Dragon'. You hear about so many bad things happening when people break up."

"I should have kept the farm in my name, but I wanted to do the right thing by the lad when he put in all his money to keep all this afloat. That's why I added his name to the deed." His good hand shook. He gripped the armrest of his wheelchair.

"It is nice though to see you're both still here. Traditions matter, don't they?"

"When I leave, it'll be feet first." An obstinate look came into John's eyes.

"You have a good span ahead of you. We're a tough lot, our generations." She chuckled softly. "I'm glad my Hayley's found a new friend. It's good to have things shaken up once in a while, and Eve is just the sort my girl needs."

John grunted again.

Letty said, "But of course, you've met her. Nice girl. Good head on her shoulders, too."

"She seemed alright." John moved his wheelchair a few degrees.

Letty suspected that he was a lot less dependent on Ben's constant support than his son realised. Maybe she should tell the boy to stop clucking over John like a brooding hen.

He looked across the pond, at Ben and Hayley who were laughing together. "Much better to stick with someone you know," John said. "Trust is what matters. New is all very well, but it's relying on another that's important in the end."

"I can't see Hayley with any of our regulars," Letty said. "Although your Chris is making a habit of dropping in again."

"In that case Ben'd better get a move on, before he's outshone in Hayley's eyes."

For an instant, Letty was surprised to hear John contemplating a relationship for Ben. But then matchmaking for his son would still put him in a position of power. She decided to probe further. "Chris might come in to see Eve."

John perked up. "She'd be good for him. Chris could do with a bit of fun. He's been single too long. How anyone could choose the army over settling down with a good solid lad like him is beyond me."

"He looked fine to me, not heartbroken at all. He must have to fend off some of his patients with a stick. Or their daughters." Letty smiled.

John laughed, a short, wheezing sound that struggled to come out. "If you could hear half the stories he's telling me. Not always suitable for female ears."

He'd be surprised if he could hear half the stories she'd heard over the years in the "Green Dragon", she thought. "He must have a knack," she said.

"The one person who got a word out of my daughter-in-law when she had one of her moods. Treated her like a patient."

Letty rolled her head again from side to side.

"I'll ask him to have a look at you," John said. "Or you could come on one of the evenings he babysits me."

"That would be lovely. I don't want Hayley to worry unnecessarily." Letty waved across the water. "I hate to run off, but we shouldn't leave Grace and Heather on their own for too long. It's a lot of responsibility, taking care of the whole pub."

John lifted his good hand and touched Letty's cheek. "It's good to see you again. Have a proper chat with a mature person."

"I'll be back," she said.

Hayley insisted on Letty having a rest before Eve came

over. She left her nan resting on the sofa, Letty's body at peace and her mind churning away.

Eve struggled to temper her impatience. Luckily, Letty didn't keep her in suspense.

"John Dryden is hiding something, and I believe it's about money, or another reason why he can't afford to let Ben go his own way." The old lady shook her head in resignation.

"What makes you think that?" Eve asked.

"He said as much. And he wants Ben to get a girlfriend." Letty's eyes gleamed.

Eve's cheeks grew warm. "Pardon?"

"He does." Letty patted the seat next to her. Hayley, torn between curiosity and the urge to check on her staff, sat down.

Letty stroked Hayley's arm. "And it's you, my darling, John's set his sights on for his son."

"What?" Hayley and Eve said in unison.

"That's crazy," Hayley said.

"Is it?" Letty asked. "Look at it from John's point of view. He's known you since you went to secondary school, he can be sure you're not after whatever money there may be left, and you look after me as much as Ben looks after him."

"Ben likes Eve. John must have noticed." Hayley spoke as much to herself as to Eve.

"He has. That's why he's so keen to set you up with Ben, before his boy gets any ideas of running off with Eve." Letty chuckled. "You won't miss out on romance either, Eve. For you, John has his eye on Chris."

"That's the most stupid thing I've heard," Eve said.

"Is it? I think it's nice to have a parent who cares about your happiness," Letty said.

The bell from the pub rang. Hayley jumped off the sofa. She said, "Isn't it just? Because Ben always used to be the apple of John's eye. Why then would he try to steer Ben away from Eve?"

"Maybe because you're all wrong." It hurt Eve to say it out loud. "Ben's not exactly shown any kind of interest in me, and I have tried. Subtly."

Hayley gave her a pitying look. "The local ideas of subtle are pretty much one step away from flinging yourself on his lap. You said yourself, he'll shy away from you until he's cleared. I've seen him and you. He is more than interested."

"What about you?" Eve asked.

"Me? And Ben? Are you kidding? You see the strong, brooding guy, manfully masking his wounds. I see a gangly youth who swapped packed lunches with me.

He'd written his name in computer code on his lunch box. Hopeless."

Hayley blew Letty a kiss and flew off.

Eve took the spot next to Letty. "What should I do?"

"Go on with what you've started. One thing I've been wondering about." Letty's head drooped a little. She needed rest, Eve thought, as music erupted from the pub and startled them. Letty's head shot up. She pressed a button on a remote, and a minute later the music died down enough for them to hear nothing but a faint baseline.

"What is it? The fact that Ben kept Donna's affair secret from the police?" Eve mulled it over for the umpteenth time.

"That too, although he would do anything to spare his father. John hated to be the subject of gossip."

"But it would have been in their own interest to deflect suspicion."

"Ben had his alibi. No." Letty stifled a yawn. "My question is, how did the sleeping pills get into John's tea?"

CHAPTER 19

The words reverberated in Eve's mind as she tried to sleep. Even if the door had been unlocked and the killer found easy access, the drugged tea threw everything into confusion. Unless – she sat upright in her bed and grabbed her notepad – Donna had been the mastermind. She could easily have ground up a few of John's pills and put them into his teapot, ready to dissolve when the hot water was filled in.

She could have given her lover a spare key and drugged John to keep him out of the way for her rendezvous. They could have planned to steal a few heavy, valuable items while Ben was gone. He wouldn't be able to stop them, and if Donna disliked the Drydens as much as Ben told Eve, it would have made perfect sense.

It would also explain why there were no signs of a

struggle. Poor Donna had trusted her killer. As for his motive, they could have argued about money, or a lack of affection, or any number of things. Wife number two used to fly into a rage whenever one of her fake nails broke.

Eve put the notepad away and snuggled back under the duvet. Her theory needed a few more details to bolster it up, but that shouldn't be too difficult, and then Hayley could run it by her police source if they got stuck with identifying the lover.

Ben sauntered into the 'Green Dragon' the next Monday. Grace's eyes popped as she saw her former employer, but she managed a weak smile. The two men at the bar beat a sulking retreat. News about Hayley's threats of banishment for any customer spoiling for a fight must have travelled, Eve thought. She stayed in her spot at the table in the back. If Ben wanted to join her, he had to make the first move.

Instead, he established himself at the bar.

"Quiet tonight," Ben said to Hayley.

"That's why I called you." She handed him a bottled beer. "Drink's on the house."

Grace moved close enough to overhear them. As did Eve,

who'd brought her empty glass as an excuse to eavesdrop.

"My nan could do with your tech advice, if you can spare a moment." Hayley came around from behind the bar and clasped his arm. "She's worried about vandalism, with everything going on in the news."

"Sure." Ben followed her, the bottle in his hand.

"She's asked you to join us, Eve. She's interested in your new security measures."

Eve could sense a wave of dislike rolling towards Ben. Unless it was aimed at her as well. She stiffened her neck and trailed her friends.

"Hello, Letty." Ben kissed the old lady on both cheeks. Letty coloured slightly, testament to Ben's appeal. He hadn't kissed Eve. Or taken her hand.

"What can I do for you?" he asked.

"Sit down and relax." Hayley pulled up a chair for him. "We only wanted to send a message not to mess with Nan and me, or Eve, or you."

"I can't stay too long," Ben said, but he accepted a beer.

Letty patted his hand. "It'll do your father good to grow up a bit. Give him an emergency button to summon aid and become a little independent. Or John will run your life for you, if you like it or not." She glanced at Eve who sat as far away from Ben as she could without it being obvious.

"It's complicated." Ben stared at his bottle without drinking.

"Looks simple enough to me," Hayley chimed in. "Do you want to still be hanging around him every waking minute when you're fifty?"

"Good heavens." Ben ruffled his hair. "I'm doing what I have to, to take care of him. One day –"

"One day he'll be dead, and you'll be a lonely old sod, shuffling around in carpet-shoes and saggy cardigans in that bloody manor," Hayley said.

"Thanks for that lovely picture." He inched closer to Eve. "Do you agree with Hayley?"

"I don't know the situation well enough to say anything."

Hayley gave her nan a small signal.

"You do realise that John is convinced you need female company?" Letty's sweet smile showed off a dimple.

"He does?" Ben's glance wandered to Eve, only to be redirected at Hayley, and Letty.

"He told me himself. He also thinks Eve should find a

partner." Letty twinkled. "Your father wants her to get together with his nice massage therapist."

Ben caught his beer bottle before it crashed on the floor. The liquid sloshed over the side and onto his jeans. He hastily mopped it up with a tissue.

"Of course, it's nice to see him take an active interest in other people again. I've got my share of company, but your father's alone too much," Letty said.

"You just told me to leave him on his own more often," Ben said.

"Only so he'll stop seeing you as a caregiver and start seeing you as a person again. That's a different kettle of fish." Letty twinkled at Hayley, who gave her a quick squeeze.

Ben didn't seem convinced.

Eve wasn't surprised, only slightly disappointed. He'd always put his father's needs first, she thought. Which was silly and sad and simultaneously sweet.

She took her bag. "I'll walk you home," he said, "unless you'd rather not be seen with me in public."

"Not at all."

Hayley gave her discreet thumbs-up as they all walked downstairs. At the bar, she waved them off in a display of enthusiasm. Hayley might as well have flipped her customers the bird.

Ben took a close look at the visible camera. "Good work."

"Fast too," Eve said. "And the work crew cleaned up their mess without being prompted." She had four cameras altogether, covering front and back. They instantly recorded any movement and sent an audible signal to her phone.

"I'm glad you feel safe again."

"It wasn't that bad," she lied. If she told him how much the word murderer and the hate behind it had spooked her, he'd bolt.

"Would you like to come inside?"

"Next time." He held up his phone, grimacing wryly. He'd missed two messages from his father.

"Had a nice evening?" John watched Ben with an unusual intensity.

"It's always good to help out," Ben said. "I don't want Letty to get ripped off by any smug salesman."

"Hayley would take care of that, don't you think?" John's mouth curled up into a lopsided grin. "Great girl, that."

"Ready for bed?"

"It's still early. No need for you to rush home."

Ben held his phone under John's nose. "That wasn't the impression your messages gave me."

"Don't mind me. Chris told me off, for being a troublesome old codger." John's mouth slackened.

"I didn't know he was coming."

"He only dropped in for a few minutes. He'd forgotten something or other." John gave Ben a sly glance. "Good-looking bloke."

Ben said nothing.

"The ladies like him too, I've been told," John said.

"Nice for him. Now if you excuse me, I've got things to do."

Ben proved to be elusive again. Eve fought against the impulse to call him. If he wanted to see her, he knew where to find her.

Nevertheless, she did return to her owl-watch routine. If she was honest, the cabin intrigued her more than the bird. She had the odd feeling if she stared long and hard enough, it would reveal a hitherto missed clue. Where had the man come from, when he met Donna?

Any trampled path leading through one of the fields would have become overgrown within a short span, so it was useless to search for it. Eve wished she had any reasonable idea about horticulture. Sold or leased, the orchards and meadows must have been worked at intervals. The police were unaware of an affair and thus had no reason to question the helpers. She made a mental note to ask Hayley if farmers here hired locals or used cheap seasonal labour from Eastern Europe. In that case, it was hopeless to search for an answer.

Ben stood on the river path, casually waving at her.

She gave him a mock salute. "Fancy meeting you here."

"Busy week. I needed to get a break from my desk for a while."

"How's your father?"

"Meddlesome."

"There's a surprise." She drew circles with her toes in the soil.

"I understand I must seem like a coward to you, but I have my reasons to worry about him," Ben said.

"Which is absolutely your right, and also absolutely your business."

"Eve." He held out his hand.

She took a step back.

"Are we having a fight?" he asked.

"No. Why should we?"

"In that case, will you go out with me for dinner tonight?"

Eve opened her mouth to say no but thought better of it. "With or without Hayley?"

"I thought, the two of us. Unless you want her to come as well. But I warn you. I'm not taking Chris."

A germ of an idea formed in her head. "I'll pick you up," she said.

"Fine. It's not very gentlemanly of me, but probably safer for your reputation."

"Meet me at seven at your gate. We don't want to upset your father." She tried to keep the bitterness out of her voice. A brittle smile accompanied her little act.

"I'll be there," he said.

This time she refrained from kissing him good-bye or touching him at all. Instead she waved and left him standing.

Hayley promised to make discreet enquiries about any farm workers who might have been toiling on Dryden land. "If my nan doesn't know, Heather will," she said.

"I assume you don't want to join us for dinner."

"Tempting, but I'll pass. I'll come over for breakfast, and I expect a detailed report, unless it's too risqué."

Eve harrumphed. "Not bloody likely, is it?"

"Use your charms, woman. Unless you'd rather try your luck with one of our regulars."

"Thanks, but no thanks. Which reminds me. Dom's brother, the one you thought might have had a fling with Donna."

"The one we ruled out," Hayley said.

"Almost ruled out. It's still a possibility. Do you have a picture of him? Yearbooks, social media?"

"He plays rugby for our local team. Not as successfully as his brother, but they have a club newsletter. I'll get hold of it," Hayley said.

"Great. If you find anyone who's seen a man around the cabin, the year before Donna's death, perhaps they'll recognise him."

Ben leant against one of the pillars which held the gate. It stood wide open. Eve stopped outside and let him step into the car without cutting the engine.

"Where are we going?" he asked.

"That depends on your curfew."

"Chris is staying for a while, but I've told my father not to wait up."

"No wonder the poor bloke needs your father to play cupid, if he's always at your beck and call."

"It's not constantly, and he should do alright when he's elsewhere. Nice to hear you're concerned about him." His voice said otherwise.

Eve allowed herself a smug moment. "I am a kind person. That's why I'm taking you out tonight."

She parked the car a short walk away from "Little Italy". "I've asked a few people for recommendations," she said, as she took his arm. She hoped it looked casual to him, and not as if she wanted to check his physical reactions when he saw their destination. Although she was ninety percent sure Ben was not Donna's lunch date, it would be nice to be certain.

"Do you know this place?" she asked and motioned towards the restaurant.

"No, but you can't go wrong with Italian food." They peeked inside. The place was packed.

"Or we could see what else there is." Eve pulled Ben away.

His physical proximity raised her heartbeat. He smelt good, too, like a faint mix of suede and lemon, she thought.

"The Flower Pot" was closed, like most cafés in the evening. Eve faked disappointment. "I've heard great things about this place. Have you been here before?"

He shook his head. "You've already seen my favourite restaurant. Both, if you count the 'Green Dragon.'"

They headed back to "Little Italy". The waiter found them a secluded place in one of the booths Eve had originally earmarked as ideal for lovers.

They kept the conversation neutral during salad and pasta. Ben regaled Eve with wisdom about owls, and local customs. She heard with disbelief that Hayley once dated a Morris dancer, although the relationship died after his first public display.

"I've never seen Morris dancers in action," Eve said. "I've read about them, but that's all."

"That's easily fixed. I can take you to one of the events. They're usually on in May and June. How could you miss that?"

He sounded suspiciously enthusiastic. "Don't tell me you tie bells around your legs and jump up and down with brooms and swords," she said.

"More likely sticks and hankies, and you'd better respect our ancient ways." He signalled the waiter. "Coffee?"

"Cappuccino."

"Two cappuccinos, please." He laughed. "My maternal grandfather was a dancer, and they used to drop into the 'Green Dragon' after practice. Legend has it, one hour's dancing equalled five hour's drinking."

"It must have been a popular sport, then."

"Before the advent of television, and computers. What about your hometown?"

"We've moved around quite a bit, so I'm not sure what really counts as my hometown, and I wasn't really into folklore. I could ask my dad and Crystal." The name came over her lips with a surprising easy. She'd make it up to the hitherto much maligned woman, she thought. It couldn't have been easy to be saddled with a judgmental person like Eve when you tied the knot with a biddable man.

Ben peeked at his phone, probably making sure he hadn't missed a summons from his father. Eve's hackles rose. She had enough of the shilly-shallying.

"What are you afraid of?" she asked.

"What do you mean?"

"You're wasting your life, and what for? I get it if you feel unready for a new relationship, although five years is taking it a bit far."

He opened his mouth to interrupt her.

She put a finger over his lips. "I'm still talking. Like I said, I understand that. But this whole running after your father and putting up with his every whim? What's so difficult about telling him you're not romantically interested in Hayley, and to stay out of your private affairs? You know, it's no wonder people look at you in a funny way when you don't seem to give a damn about anyone. Not even your wife, and I don't care what she did to you, doesn't she deserve better?"

A vein throbbed on his temple. "Think what you want."

"Thanks, I will." She signalled the waiter for the bill.

"You have no idea what you're talking about."

"Then enlighten me," she said.

"Fine. You want everything to be black or white. Let me tell you this. Once in a while, when he's pushed too far, my father flies into a rage. A proper, blood pressure to the ceiling kind of anger, which causes another massive stroke. He's in a wheelchair because I was suspected of murder. The doctors say the next one, which could be triggered by another outburst, would most likely be fatal.

I'm not killing my father to please you or anyone else. And I don't give a shit about what you or the rest of the world think of me." He crossed his arms over his chest.

"Fair enough." Her anger deflated. "You've made your point. But you have to understand how demeaning it is for me to have you sneak off behind your father's back to meet with me. Like you're the lord of the manor and you're slumming it with the milkmaid. Although in that case John would probably cheer you on."

"The milkmaid?"

"Yes. Or the kitchen help." She shoved a handful of banknotes inside the leather folder with the bill.

"I'm sorry if you feel that way."

She shrugged.

"I understand if you don't want to see me again." Ben's voice betrayed no emotion, which made it worse.

"I didn't say that." Eve blinked away a sudden dampness in her eyes. "I just want you to think about what you're actually doing."

They drove back in silence.

Eve stopped the car on the grass verge outside the gate.

Ben lingered. "I shouldn't keep you," he said.

"No."

"Okay." The emotional distance between them widened with every breath. Eve's chest constricted.

He played with his seat-belt. "We should talk another day."

"If there is anything to say. Without having your father's blood on our hands."

He left without another word.

She watched him move away. His shoulders hunched forwards.

Eve slammed the steering wheel with both hands until the pain became unbearable.

CHAPTER 20

"Good job. That stupid bugger needs tough love." Hayley enveloped Eve in a rib-crushing hug. She'd refrained from commenting on Eve's red-rimmed eyes and the mad hair.

"I don't know. It feels as if I've cut off my finger to cure a hangnail." Eve slumped onto a kitchen chair.

"You need food, and coffee, and Auntie Hayley's signature good cheer." Hayley waved a muffin under Eve's nose. "If you eat this like a good girl, I might tell you something you'll like."

Eve broke the pastry into pieces and pushed them around on her plate.

"Do you go all tragic after every little lovers' tiff?" Hayley clucked her tongue. "You must have been a joy to be around in college."

"I stuck with one boyfriend during that period, and this wasn't a lovers' tiff. Ben pretty much told me to get lost, because the thought of him and me together would outrage John so much he'd have another stroke and die."

"That's emotional blackmail."

"Tell him that."

Eve tried a morsel. And another one. Hayley was right, food did help. "That's also why he isn't remotely interested in finding out the truth," she said. "All Ben Dryden cares about is his precious father."

"I can understand protecting your family," Hayley said. "I'd protect my nan, but I wouldn't ruin my life for her. She wouldn't thank me for that."

"That's because you're not stuck in a toxic, unhealthy relationship like the Drydens. No wonder Donna wanted out so badly."

Hayley winced. "It's over, then?"

"There wasn't anything, but hypothetically speaking, if there had been, it would be finished, snuffed, kaput." Eve ran a finger across her throat for good measure.

"Does that also go for our investigation?" Hayley asked.

"No. It's simply become impersonal."

Hayley gave her an amused look. "If you say so."

"You said you were going to cheer me up."

"And I shall."

Like the majority of workers in agriculture and horticulture, most helpers came for the season and left as soon as they were no longer needed. But one man, a Pole, had stayed, and married a local girl. He earned a living doing gardening and odd jobs, and he remembered the Drydens, and the cabin.

Hayley paused and helped herself to another muffin. Eve snatched it out of her hand. "Go on."

"He saw a man a couple of times, coming up from the public footpath by the stream."

Eve leant forward, spellbound.

"It was during the summer and late autumn before she died." Hayley took back the muffin and nibbled on it. She usually was in a hurry, but for this revelation she seemed to have infinite time.

Eve counted to ten under her breath. "What else did he say?"

"Not a lot. He thinks the man was youngish. Late twenties, early thirties, with brown hair."

"Harry?"

"I showed him the picture in the club newsletter, but he wasn't sure. He said the hairstyle's wrong, and he

doesn't remember any tattoos on the man's arms."
Hayley pushed the rugby club leaflet over to Eve. A
group of men in their thirties and forties in two rows,
dressed in shorts and sleeveless tops. The front row
squatted, and they all had their naked arms crossed
across their chest.

Eve read the names in the caption, but she'd recognised
Harry from his likeness to his much younger sibling. His
left arm was covered in what Eve took to be a colourful
depiction of George and the Dragon which would be
hard to overlook. "How old is the tattoo?"

"Too old for your purpose. And he's worn his hair
shoulder-length even longer."

"But how much would your witness truly remember?"

"Enough to say where the man came from, and that it
wasn't Harry."

"Which leads us nowhere. That's not cheering me up."

Eve regretted coming to the 'Green Dragon' when she
saw Bella and Sue waving at her. There went her hope of
a good meal and a chance to mope in silence outside her
own four walls. She forced herself to beam.

Hayley winked at her. "Your usual?"

Was Eve becoming that predictable? She'd see to that. "What's today's special?"

"Curry," Bella said before Hayley could answer. "Hotter than that admirer of yours and just as juicy."

Eve shook herself. Curry was an acquired taste, one she didn't intend to master. As were Bella's jokes.

Hayley took pity on her. "Mac and cheese?"

The ultimate comfort food. Heather had put her stamp on the menu. Eve nodded in agreement.

Bella expected her to squeeze in next to them despite an empty table. Eve gave in. One of the joys of small-town life meant somebody would always take an interest in your doings. Although today Eve counted it as a major drawback.

A grizzled man came closer. His slightly unsteady walk and beer breath made Eve shrink back.

He steadied himself on their table. If Eve remembered correctly, his name was Bob. He pushed his face close to hers. "You," he said and pointed an accusing finger at her. "You shouldn't hang out with that bastard."

"Bob. How dare you?" Sue glowered at him.

"You too, Sue Littlewood. I'm warning you all. Nothing good ever came from Ben sodding Dryden. He should be rotting in prison." His eyes were glassy, but he kept his steady at Eve. "A friendly word here. Before you regret it."

"That's enough." Hayley yanked him away by his grimy collar. "Go home, sleep it off, and then you can apologise to the ladies. And to Ben Dryden."

Bob spat on the floor. One signal from Hayley, and Dom left the bar, hauled the drunk man across the floor and pushed him outside.

Hayley addressed her stunned customers. "Is there anyone else who wants to get something off his chest?"

"Why are you defending the bastard?" Another regular stood up to confront her.

"Because this is a public bar, and every patron is welcome as long as he or she behaves himself."

"The tosser killed his wife." The man planted his feet wide to steady himself.

Hayley took a step closer. He sucked in his breath.

"If you've got proof, I'm sure the police will welcome it," she said. "Otherwise, shut up or drink somewhere else." He slunk back to his spot at the bar, grumbling under his breath.

Bella's eyes gleamed. "Ben Dryden," she said to no one in particular.

Eve kept her mouth shut.

"Now he's a looker, too, but my money's on that lovely Chris to give you a good work-out," Bella said.

"Stop it." Sue gave her friend a playful slap. "You're old enough to be their mother."

"But not too old to appreciate fine optics." Bella laughed. "Relax, you two. I'm only trying to tell Eve to ignore these old codgers. They're jealous."

"That may be." Sue moved her drink aside to make room for Eve's food. "But as they say, there is no smoke without fire."

"Only we don't know which direction it's drifting from."

"Did anyone watch 'Eastenders' last night?" Eve said, in a desperate attempt to stop them before she screamed. The long-running soap was one of her staples when it came to changing topics. That, the weather and the royal family. They had never failed her yet.

Bella launched in an enthusiastic scene-by-scene. Eve let out a deep breath. The hairdresser might be a bit tactless, but she liked her enthusiasm for life.

Ben spent the evening in his office. He and John shared their meals, but apart from that Ben kept to himself for a change. He stared at his computer, trying to make sense of the code, but his mind drifted off. Ten hours, and he'd managed twenty minutes' work, if that.

He could drive over to Eve as soon as his father was asleep, to apologise. John had taken half a diazepam and would be out for the count.

The only problem was, he'd meant everything he said. She didn't understand, couldn't understand, because there were things he kept buried away in his mind. Dragging them out in the open would be the end of everything.

Eve decided to take her afternoon stroll in the opposite direction from her usual path. Along the meandering way, bird-houses hung from oaks and beeches. The splitting wood and fading paint established their age, so the local avian population should be used to them. It would be easy to find another animal to transfer her interest to. Eve hoped her owl would miss the human who used to drop by, but who was she kidding? She could be gone, and in six weeks she'd be forgotten by pretty much everyone. She used to prefer it that way, but now it felt lonely.

As soon as she returned to Ivy Cottage, she'd book her flight to see her father and Crystal. She could make it a long vacation, two weeks at least. The thought of getting to know her dad again, and his wife for the first time, cheered her up.

Eve whistled an unrecognisable tune. One of the perks of her solitary status. She could sing or whistle as tone-deaf as she wanted, and nobody told her to shut up.

It wasn't as if she'd asked Ben for a serious commitment, she told herself. She simply objected to being treated like an embarrassing secret. The human equivalent of smelly feet.

She'd solve the mystery, admittedly with help from her friends. Then she'd present him with the solution and sail off into the sunset, although unfortunately not literally. Her rental agreement was in place for another ten months.

She envisaged herself, smiling vaguely at Ben, as she strolled past with a gorgeous man at her side. She'd used a dating site before, as a dare with a friend from college, and finding someone to go out with would be easy enough for an attractive, young, and unattached woman. That would teach him. Not that she cared about his opinion.

Eve sauntered back, her cheerful mood restored for the moment.

Her cottage looked drab and spinsterish as she opened the door. She needed a change of scenery.

The sun was still up when she rang on Kim's door. A few moments later, she climbed up the stairs.

"I hope I'm not disturbing you," she said. "I should have called first."

Kim switched off the television. "That's fine. I've got nothing planned for tonight."

"Would you like to go out with me for a drink?" Eve fussed with her hair, an old habit when she got restless.

"Okay. Where shall we go?"

"You're the local. Surprise me."

They ended up in a wine bar that doubled as art gallery. A pianist and a singer in a vintage dress and a curly black bob reminiscent of pre-war Hollywood presented classic swing. Eve found herself swaying to the sultry music.

In London, this bar would have been packed with trendy people who came to be seen and heard. Here, the audience came to see, and to listen.

The singer hit the last melancholy note of "One for my Baby" and put the microphone on the piano, standing still in the soft spotlight.

Eve applauded until her palms hurt.

The singer blew kisses into the audience, her scarlet lipstick glistening.

"She's amazing," Eve said. "Why isn't she somewhere on the big stage?"

"Andrea used to tour the States, but she became homesick. And she owns this bar."

"Do you come here often?"

"It's a good place to remember. And to forget." Kim signalled the waiter for another glass of wine. Eve declined a second drink, regretfully, because she had to drive home.

"What happened to that date of yours? Any progress?" Kim savoured the fruity bouquet of her Chardonnay.

"It's over. That is, it was never really on. Just one of those butterfly moments." Eve pulled a face.

"That's a pity," Kim said.

"Not all all. It's much better this way. I think I was getting caught up in this whole, mysterious stranger thing, and I felt a little lonely as a newcomer."

"I thought you're used to that," Kim said.

"I am, but once in a blue moon I have this idea that I'm on the wrong track. It never lasts long." Eve glanced towards the singer, who launched into "Voodoo". "How about you?"

"No. No-one since Donna. I miss her every single day."

CHAPTER 21

Kim's words hit Eve like a punch in the stomach. She gulped, glad the music drowned out the sound. How could she have been so blind? The pictures of the blonde woman who seemed vaguely familiar, anti-histamine medication for a woman who was allergic to dog hairs, the fact that Kim had given Laika away for a few horrible weeks.

Eve touched Kim's hand. "That's tough. You must have loved each other very much."

"She came into the shop one morning in May, carrying a blue coat with a gash in the lining over her arm. The sun caught the window at an angle that created a halo over her head. I don't know why, but I couldn't breathe."

She paused, gazing blindly into the distance. Eve waited

for her to continue, ashamed how much Kim's bombshell excited her.

Nothing had happened for a while, Kim said after an eternity. "We became friends, that's all. We clicked. She wasn't happy at home, I knew that much." Kim cupped her chin and lost herself in a distant memory. "It's hard to break free, even if there's no love left, if it ever existed at all."

"Did she have children?" Eve hated herself for misleading Kim, even in the best of causes. She'd come close to forgetting the original reason why she sought her out.

"No, only a father in law who disliked her. Well, the feeling was mutual. And her husband."

"And then she fell in love with you."

Kim's lips curled up into the hint of a smile. "It took her forever. We'd been out for lunch, at 'The Flower Pot'. We always met there."

"The same place for every date?" What about the diary entries about "Little Italy"?

"The table closest to the wall. It was like our private hideaway. A lush, evergreen paradise far removed from the outside world."

They'd talked about work. Donna complained about a rude customer, and Kim gave her a gift, an Italian pendant shaped like a twisted silver horn, which would ward off the evil eye.

"It was a joke between us," Kim said. "She told me her father-in-law was giving her the evil eye."

Donna attached the pendant to her chain necklace and leant over the table to give Kim a thank-you kiss.

Kim touched her lips, lost in the memory. "She used to kiss me hello, and good-bye, but this kiss landed on my mouth. She stared at me, with a kind of wondering gaze, and then she kissed me again. That was all it took for us to fall in love."

"How long did you have?" Eve asked.

"Five months, three weeks and two days."

"That's terribly short. What happened? An accident?" Eve's stomach revolted at her falsehood, but she ploughed ahead. The truth mattered more than her newly discovered sensibilities.

Kim gulped down her wine. Her hand shook. "She was – Donna was killed. Murdered."

"Oh my God. I hope they sent the person responsible away for life."

"They never got him."

"How horrible. Not even a suspect? What was it, robbery?"

Kim stared at the ground. "Nobody knows the reason. The husband had an alibi, and there was nobody else who could have a motive to hurt her."

Eve handed Kim a tissue to wipe away a tear. "We don't have to talk about Donna."

"It's good to get it out of my system. For years, I've been lying awake, wracking my brain. It's the not knowing which is the worst part. I could walk along a street, or push a trolley in the supermarket, and run into the person who took away her life."

Eve shivered. "You believe in the husband's alibi."

"Why should he kill her?" Kim asked. "She told me he was relieved when she told him she'd file for divorce."

"Some people hide their jealousy well. Or it's about money."

"We'll probably never know. The case is done with, and that's all there is to it."

"But you need closure."

"We all need a few things. Doesn't mean we're going to get them." Kim slammed the table, only to give Eve a rueful look. "I didn't mean to dump my misery on you."

"It's okay," Eve said. "It really is. We all need a listener."

"Let's make it a more cheerful evening on our next visit."

"Deal."

~

Donna and Kim were lovers. Eve could barely begin to imagine the hell of losing the person one cared most about and having to hide the grief and pain. Kim had said they hadn't been out in the open yet. Donna's death made it impossible to change that.

She could picture the gossip, and the accusations which would condemn Donna and Kim as quickly and possibly with more relish than Ben had experienced. Greed, or jealousy made a good story. But a lesbian love-triangle and a spurned husband would take the crown any day.

If Ben preferred to play the innocent victim, he only had himself to blame. Eve eased her car into a space next to the kerb, glad to be alone with her thoughts. Her visit, only intended to keep her distracted, had yielded unexpected results. Clearing Ben's name no longer claimed the top spot on her priority list. Instead, she'd make sure Kim got the closure she needed.

Nice piece of reasoning, her inner voice whispered. *Nothing's changed, but you can fool yourself into believing it's not still all about a man who doesn't want you.*

Speaking of man – Kim's story explained where Donna intended to go, but it shed no light on the man Donna had been seeing before. Her diary was proof of another secret, and so were the condoms. Donna had no need for contraceptives with Kim.

Hayley tallied their weekly, and monthly accounts. They looked slightly worse than she'd expected, not even counting the increased expenses thanks to Heather and Grace.

"Is anything wrong?" Letty peered at her.

"We're a few quid down on the takings, that's all." Compared to the rest of the year, they'd made close to a hundred less per week. If it was a fluke, they could easily weather it. If it turned into a trend, she might have to let Grace go.

"So much for healthy economy and growing wages," she said.

"Is it the drinks or the food side?" Letty stood up from her sofa and sat next to Hayley at the table. She'd kept the books until Hayley decided she needed to learn, and if a number held a secret, Letty got to the bottom of it with the same ease she'd run the business with, until age caught up with her.

Hayley went through the stack of hand-written orders. The bar staff keyed in every request on the bar computer, but Letty and Hayley insisted on ordinary pen and paper duplicates. Technology could glitch, and books needed to be precise to a penny.

Letty leafed through them. "Heather's cooking is popular."

"Customers still miss your food," Hayley said.

"I don't. It's nice to prepare a stew or a pie for the two of us, but I've had my share of twenty litre pots." Letty held the notes close to her eyes. Her annual vision test was overdue. Hayley chided herself for neglecting her nan's needs because she got swept away with Eve and Ben on top of her regular work.

"It's the drinks," Letty said. "Lager and the guest ales have sold less." They offered a changing selection of small brewers' beers.

"That's weird. They used to be wildly popular when we started before Christmas. Perhaps the novelty has worn off." Hayley paused. An image of a group of wiry blokes came to her mind, all drinking whatever sort was chalked up on the blackboard. The same group of men who'd itched for a fight with Ben.

"It's me, isn't it?" Hayley said. "I drove our customers away. With standing up for Ben and threatening to send them packing."

"A few of them, and good riddance." Letty put her hand

on top of Hayley's. "They'll return soon enough, don't you fret. You did the right thing."

Hayley traced the numbers with her finger. "The sooner all of this is over, the better," she said.

"I quite enjoy the excitement," Letty said to Hayley's surprise. "It's good to have an interest outside the 'Green Dragon'."

"Sleuthing as therapy?"

"Would you rather I shut down like John?"

"Impossible." Hayley planted a kiss on Letty's cheek.

Ben's head sank to his chest. His fingers touched the keyboard, and a beep brought him to his senses. After two o'clock in the morning. He needed sleep, and a clear head, instead of letting his thoughts run in circles, following the same grooves they had for five years.

It was all Eve's fault, he repeated to himself. He'd said that straight away, as soon as she inveigled herself into his life and into affairs that were solely a Dryden matter.

Ben avoided any prolonged sessions with John. He had

too much work ahead, he told himself, because tomorrow he'd have to leave for a two day business trip.

John put on a brave face too, keeping out of Ben's way. Maybe Letty's talk had shown results, or the fact that Ben would also be away from Eve. Whatever it was, John only mentioned that Chris would come over for breakfast. Since Ben's annual trip had been planned since January, arranging dates for him to look after John had been easy. If Chris ever left, they'd be doomed, Ben thought as he ticked items off his to-do list.

He toyed with the notion of dropping in at the "Green Dragon" on his way but decided against it.

Hayley (and through her, Eve) would laugh if he started to inform her about every little absence of his.

He put his weekender-bag on his bed and packed.

To make up for his trip, he suffered through an evening of "Carry On" television comedy which only John considered funny.

His father caught Ben glancing at his phone. "If there's anything you'd rather do, I won't keep you."

"No. We're good."

His forced jollity made his jaw ache. John quietly nodded his head, satisfied he'd got his way.

Ben breathed easier. They both deserved a break from each other.

Ben grabbed bag and briefcase as soon as Chris took over the reins in the morning.

"You're in a hurry," Chris said.

"I'd rather be prepared for traffic delays. The joy of the British motorway."

"I told you to take the train." John watched from the living room.

"Horrible suggestion. They're always delayed or cancelled. The car is the only sensible way to travel." Chris winked at Ben. "And there's no need to rush back if you have something planned with what's-her-name? Eve?"

John's face turned darker, a sign for a brewing storm. Ben stifled a groan. Couldn't Chris see he only made matters worse?

"Nice offer," Ben said, "but I'll be home as soon as I can."

"I'm just saying, John and I will be fine."

Ben managed to get through a full day's meeting without sparing a single thought for his private dilemmas. If he'd mastered anything at all in those last years, it was the fine art of compartmentalisation. Otherwise he'd be in the loony-bin by now.

He dined alone, in the hotel restaurant, and afterwards prepared for tomorrow's meeting. The good thing about being on your own was that you also were the only person you could let down.

Eve found herself mindlessly strolling towards the cabin. She squared her shoulders. This was a public right of way, and she had as much justification to be here as the rest of the population.

A tiny sense of unease lingered. What if she ran into Ben and he thought she was stalking him? Which she wasn't. Far from it. If anything, he was stalking her. After all she'd begun her owl-watch before she even met him, and he knew about her interest in the bird.

If they met, she'd point out to him that he was the one who could easily avoid her.

They did not meet. Nor did Ben appear the next day.

"Anything wrong?" Hayley asked as Eve ordered tea and crumpets after her second day without spotting the owl or Ben.

Eve pouted. "I feel stupid, that's all."

"Why don't you go up and see my nan? I'll bring afternoon tea." Hayley slid a warning glance towards the Pink Panthers who sauntered through the door.

"Thank you," Eve said.

Letty snored gently on the sofa.

"Hello?" Eve poked her head through the door.

Letty gave a tiny start. "Did I doze off?"

"I didn't mean to wake you."

"I'm glad you came to visit. Would you like a cup of tea?"

"It's all under control, Nan." Hayley pushed the door closed with her elbow and sat a laden tray on the table. "The Panthers will pace themselves until Dom's shift begins and Grace should be fine until then."

She spread lashings of golden butter on the hot crumpets.

The dough oozed with it as Eve took a bite.

"What's going on with you?" Letty asked. "Hayley tells me Ben got cold feet?"

"I probably should have waited in best Victorian manner until the head of the family gives up his resistance." Eve shrugged it off. "I always thought tyrannical parents went out with girdles and petticoats. Or Ben uses his father's ill health as an excuse, so he won't hurt my feelings."

"Men," Letty said, as if that one word explained every fallacy. "Can't see further than their own nose, on a clear day."

Hayley giggled.

"It's true. Your own grandad, bless his soul, took six months to ask me out. He thought him standing in line to run the pub would make him wrong for me. The poor daft man came close to tying the knot with the barmaid, all the while being keen on me."

"What did you do?" Eve asked.

"Put on my best dress and flirted with the most handsome man at the local May fair. A black-haired rogue with a roving eye. I wouldn't have wanted him for all the tea in China, but it spurred my Tony into action."

Hayley took a framed photo and showed it to Eve. A young Letty nestled in the arms of a broad-shouldered man with Hayley's infectious smile. "It's a picture from their honeymoon."

"It was easier in those days," Letty said. "You got married, and then you had to make it work."

"That doesn't sound easier to me. I like to have the option to go when it's wrong," Hayley said.

"Me too," Eve said. "I don't believe people were happier in the old days, they simply kept more bad things hidden away."

Her phone rang. An unknown US number. "Excuse me for a moment," she said as she accepted the call with mounting trepidation. What if her Dad had an accident, and this was the hospital? Or he and Crystal both sat in the car, and now Eve had to deal with two people in a coma? Or funerals?

"Hello?" Her voice wobbled. Letty and Hayley gave her a worried glance.

"Eve, honey," Crystal said.

Eve gripped the armrest of her chair. "Is anything wrong with Dad?"

Crystal laughed, a tinkling noise that reverberated in Eve's ear. "Oh, honey, of course not. I just wanted to tell you how excited he'd be to see you."

Eve's breath whooshed out in relief. "I'm definitely coming over for Thanksgiving."

"That's wonderful." Crystal lowered her voice. "And if you want to bring a special someone, we'd be happy to pay for the ticket. Or for yours as well."

"No. I mean, that's incredibly generous, but there is no special someone."

"There might be by Thanksgiving. I only figured out I was sweet on your daddy when I kept bringing up his name all the time." Her laughter tinkled again.

Eve fell silent.

"Hello," Crystal said.

"I'll book my ticket this week and I'll give you the dates. Promise."

Crystal blew her a kiss through the phone.

"Bye," Eve said. "Say hi to Dad."

Eve put away her phone and chortled.

"Well?" Hayley took the last crumpet.

"Dad's wife made a pertinent observation. Remember that crush stage, when you can't stop mentioning whoever you've set your heart on?"

"Like talking about Ben?"

"That's different." Eve glared at Hayley. "Anyway, you also kind of knew you weren't that much into a guy when you kept quiet about him?"

"I remember that," Letty said to their surprise. "Come on, you two. Did you think I sat on a shelf until my knight in shining armour picked me up and dusted me off? I also had a son, and boys are much the same, only louder and more obvious. And then there's you, my darling Hayley. You were the same"

"Then how is it possible Donna kept her mouth zipped about lover-boy?" Eve asked.

"Discreet? Practice?" Letty looked at Eve.

Don't ask me, Eve thought. *I don't want to lie in your face.*

Hayley wiped a few crumbs off her lap.

Letty pointed at a small table vacuum in form of a ladybird.

Hayley obediently ran it over the crumbs.

"I think she used him for a fling, and she was never serious about him," Eve said. It was the best she could come up with, without giving Kim's secret away.

"Which would give him a motive when she broke it off." Hayley frowned. "That doesn't add up. She was going to move out, and she had no apartment lined up."

"Because she was going to stay with a girlfriend." That

sounded vague enough. Kim hadn't asked for Eve's silence, but it was implied.

"The key and the sleeping pills?" Hayley asked.

"Donna could have given her lover a duplicate. Just because they used to shag in the cabin doesn't exclude the occasional tryst in the house, when Ben was away, and John was asleep. Especially if she wanted to spite her husband." Eve was sure she hit the truth.

"She would have been able to figure out how much diazepam it took to knock out her father-in-law," Letty said.

"Lover-boy visits, she tells him she's going to live with a friend, he gets angry, picks up one of the convenient bricks from the floor and, wham, good-bye, uncaring girlfriend." Eve liked the chain of events. They were simple, logical, and fit all the circumstances.

"There is no shred of proof." Hayley put her finger on the weak spot. "No name, no face, nothing."

"Which means he's clever," Eve said.

"I'd put my money on Donna being the brains of the affair," Letty said with an air of finality. "She had to fool John, and he's as shrewd as they come. If he got wind of her cheating, he'd have kicked Donna out, no matter if he'd signed over the property to Ben."

"How do we find the elusive guy?" Eve pushed out her lower lip. It was all such a tangled mess.

"I could tell my police contact about Donna having an affair," Hayley said.

"Which is another thing we can't prove," Eve said.

"True enough." Hayley walked towards the door. "We'll simply have to muddle through, until something pops up."

Eve followed Hayley downstairs.

The Pink Panthers were onto their third bottle of prosecco, and Dom's shirt pocket bulged with tips. His smile had an air of fearfulness.

One of the Panthers leant forward to pinch his bottom.

Hayley whistled shrilly.

Everybody froze.

"Hands off my staff," she said. "If you want to behave like you're on a hen-night, I can recommend a few places where you can hire a gigolo."

The Panthers gasped.

"If on the other hand you behave yourself, Dom will go on waiting on your tables." Hayley showed her teeth, inwardly wondering if this incident cost her more customers. Nevertheless, if the Panthers got frisky with Dom before sundown, the teenager needed protection.

Ben's last meeting ended early. The clients had been happy, he'd signed another contract to convert a games idea into software, and he was free to go home. If he called that freedom.

On a whim he steered his car towards a car park close to the stream. From here, a twenty-minute walk would take him to Eve's door, without his car causing more gossip.

All he wanted to do was talk, and then walk out of her life.

He smoothed back his hair. The business suit and polished brogues gave him a salesman look that suited city meetings, but not strolls in the countryside. A thin film of dust settled in his shoes.

They needed rain. While his father was still in charge of the farm land, he used to keep a rain diary. This weather would have given him into another stroke, had their livelihood depended on it.

He approached Ivy Cottage slowly, facing the camera with deliberation. If Eve preferred not to see him again in person, at least she could decide to ignore the doorbell.

She didn't. She stood barefoot on the wooden floor, with water dripping from her hair and a bathrobe wrapped around her body.

"May I come in?" he asked.

"If you want to. You could put the kettle on while I get dressed." She stomped off, still in a decidedly frosty mood.

When she reappeared, her mood had mellowed. Carefully applied make-up and a business suit for her as well made them look like a couple of insurance agents.

She waited for him to speak, her hands folded in her lap in perfect hostess-manner.

Ben's brain came up empty.

Eve broke the silence. "Did you watch 'EastEnders' last night?"

"Should I watch it?" He seemed dumbstruck.

"Don't you have a set of safe topics, when you've got nothing to say?"

He shook his head.

She glared at him. "Then what do you want to talk about? Or, to be precise, what do you want, full stop?"

Ben stretched out a finger to touch her lips. She caught his hand in the air.

"There's a piece of fluff," he said.

She dropped his hand and pressed a tissue on her painted mouth. "Thank you."

He looked different in his suit, and his new-found insecurity turned him into a stranger. Eve shook her head at herself that she had pined for this man. Short-lived as her infatuation had been, it was pathetic. Perhaps she should try life in a big city next, where eligible partners counted more than one, or zero.

"I wish circumstances could have been different," he said.

She made a haughty face. "It's perfectly alright. You made your position very clear, and we can still be friendly should we bump into each other."

Her still wet hair dripped onto the shoulders of her jacket. "Excuse me," she said and ran off.

She returned jacket-less, with a towel wrapped around her hair and patting dry her shirt with a kitchen towel.

Ben stared at her, with a forlorn look in his blue eyes.

She stood in front of him, arms across her chest. "Anything you want to add? Otherwise –"

"Did you keep the brick?"

Her mouth formed a surprised o. "What? Oh." She opened a box and lifted it out.

He took the brick from her and examined the writing. "Murderer. Nice sentiment." Anger built up in inside him, but he'd keep it bottled up. He had enough practice.

"Who cares?"

"I do," he said.

"About what? I'm old enough to take care of myself."

He stepped up to her, the physical distance between them shrinking alarmingly. "Are you?"

"Absolutely. Brick-throwers, unexpected visitors, and everyone else included."

He pushed a strand of her out of her eyes. And then his lips were on hers, and she didn't think anything apart from a triumphant yes.

CHAPTER 22

*E*ve stretched herself luxuriously in her bed and rolled on her side, blissfully aware she'd been right all along. Ben was in love with her, and now she knew how to deal with the situation.

She smiled. He kissed the tip of her nose. "I could stay."

"No. You don't want to leave your father waiting."

"Eve." He pulled her close.

She wriggled free and grasped her clothes. "It's okay," she said. "This was a one-off, and it doesn't have to mean anything. Easy as that. You go home and do what whatever it is you've got to do. No complications, remember?"

"You don't mean that."

"It's the best for everyone, at least for now. And don't

think of bringing up that brick incident. That, it seems, was a one-off too."

She watched under lowered lashes as he got dressed. A woman could enjoy the finer details of a one-evening-stand.

He reached for her as she opened the door for him.

"Don't. The neighbours might see us," she said.

"This isn't the end."

She gave him an enigmatic little smile. For one horrible second, she'd feared he'd mention the cabin for undisturbed love-making. And that she might be tempted.

She closed the door behind him, ran into the bedroom and pressed the pillow against her nose. His smell lingered on the fabric. Now that she was no longer chasing him, he'd have to come up with a plan to woo her. In the last three hours he hadn't made the impression he was keen on another eternity of a celibate lifestyle.

Ben stopped the car on the grass five hundred metres from his gate. He banged his head on his hands. He hadn't intended to fall into bed with Eve, although he'd been on the brink a couple of times.

She was right to send him away. What sane woman wanted to be entangled with a man who couldn't show his face with her in public? John wasn't the only obstacle between them. Whether she was willing to accept it or not, the brick was worse.

Eve had seen it as a warning, or intimidation. Ben had another perspective. To him, it was a threat. After five years, one would have to be obsessed to remember exactly how Donna was killed. The brick looked like the ones he'd used for that cursed fireplace. Whoever hurled it through Eve's window had put a lot of thought into it. It might as well have been her head.

"I'll push off," Chris said as Ben put his suitcase down. "See you tomorrow."

Ben handed him a cheque, which included a hefty tip. "Thanks," he said.

"You're late," John said.

"Traffic." Two nights away, and it already was as if Ben had never left. Barring another stroke, his father easily had another twenty years left, the doctors said. Two decades of being ruled by consideration and guilt. He must be a glutton for self-punishment.

He walked past John, to put his suitcase away.

His father sniffed the air. "Traffic, eh? Smells more like perfume to me."

Eve's scent, of course. "Female managers still wear it." He gave his father a smile that consisted mainly of baring his teeth at him. "Now if you'll excuse me?"

Eve deliberately stayed at home the next day, busying herself with housework. She'd stripped her bed and washed sheet and duvet cover. The pillow case lay folded in her bedside drawer. She wanted to preserve the remnants of Ben's smell as long as she could.

Had Kim done the same with Donna's lingering fragrance?

Eve took out the diary again. Working back through the dates and the two places where Donna met her lovers, there appeared a two month overlap. It made sense. If Kim was the first woman she'd slept with, she would have wanted to make sure it was more than a phase. Dumping a male lover, who gave her the exquisite satisfaction of avenging herself on her husband and probably as much on her father-in-law, would have waited until she made up her mind for good.

This meant, after over three months without meeting him for lunch and maybe a quickie, she'd agreed to see him on the day she died. Either they arranged the date for some unknown reason after a long period of separation, or they'd stayed on friendly terms, making it easy for him to come up with a reason why he had to see her. In any case, she hadn't been afraid. The break-up had to have been on good terms.

What did Eve know about the man? He had to live locally, or at least he used to, to be able to make all these lunch dates. Donna either knew him before they left London, in which case Ben might have been acquainted with him as well. Hayley could find out if any old friends had resurfaced.

The alternative was, she met him after their move. In that case, "Paula's Parlour" would be the logical place. Brothers, fathers and sons might accompany a woman on a shopping trip. Donna's colleagues hadn't mentioned anything though, and they'd seen the man she met with. Not very likely they'd forget if she'd picked him up in the shop. Alternatively, she could have met him online, or started a fling with one of the workmen who did repairs to the house.

John spent a chunk of his time in his own room, and he used to be mobile. It would have been easy for John and Donna to avoid each other, giving her the freedom to flirt with any eligible man who visited the house.

The Polish farm helper said he'd seen a brown-haired man coming from the public path along the stream.

Depending on the light, dark blonde hair also looked brown.

Hayley should be able to establish if a man of that description who worked in the same town as Donna lived in the neighbourhood.

She mulled the facts over in her mind as she had a quick lunch. No wonder it was a cold case after Ben was out of the picture. An unimportant woman, by all standards, cared for by a few people and mourned only by one, who'd died without any obvious reason.

Five years! The murderer could live on the other side of the world by now, except for one tiny thing. She hadn't mentioned it to Ben, because of the gruesome connotation, but she no longer believed the brick was meant to warn her. The vandal wanted to hurt Ben, by scaring her away and cutting him off from the world again.

Donna's murderer had been cold-blooded enough to plan the crime and to leave no traces. Only Ben's unexpectedly late return and the receipt and CCTV picture from the petrol station had saved his neck. Otherwise, there would have been nothing to prove his innocence. Ben Dryden was supposed to be the scapegoat, and the brick through her window might well have been thrown by the one person who hated to see him free.

If her vandal and Donna's murderer were one and the same, Ben had to be kept in the dark. Or he might ruin any chance Eve had with laying a trap.

Of course, there was the second small snag, apart from needing Ben's unwitting cooperation. Eve had no idea what form a trap could take.

Hayley declared herself stumped as well. "Unless you want the word to be spread that you've discovered the truth and set yourself up as a target?" she asked.

"I might, if we could be sure when the murderer would strike and have a couple of burly constables hiding in my wardrobe."

"You'd also need a bullet-proof vest. Shooting accidents happen."

A chill crept over Eve's body. "Not a funny joke."

"It wasn't meant to be one."

They stood on the landing above the pub, to stop anyone else from eavesdropping.

Hayley said, "I hope you realise you could stir up a lot of danger if you're not careful."

Eve had woken up bathed in sweat when the same

apprehension first sank into her conscious mind. "That's why we're all careful, right?"

"Nan and I are. But there's a difference between a few innocent questions aimed at unsuspecting people and putting yourself out there as bait."

"Which is exactly what I'm not going to do," Eve said. "I'm not reckless, or naïve."

"Speaking of which, how did your evening with Ben go?"

A blush spread over Eve's face. "How did you hear?"

Hayley patted her arm. "Relax. Sue spotted him return to the car park by the woods when she took her dog for a walk. I told her he'd probably picked up something for his father, like usual."

"Did she believe you?"

"She had no reason not to. I have a reputation for being charmingly blunt in my honesty."

"He's not coming back. It was just something we had to get out of our systems," Eve said.

Hayley sniggered but didn't comment. "Anything else you want ferreted out, Sherlock?"

"Did any of the confirmed singles give off the impression of being jilted about three months before the murder?"

"Heather or Bella should have an idea about that. But why?"

Eve bit her lip. "Promise this won't go any further."

Hayley crossed her heart and mimed zipping her lips.

"Donna fell in love with another person. Truly in love," Eve said.

"Which explains the unexpected change in hair colour and style. Okay, but why not look for the new man?"

"Because he was a she, and she was at work, blissfully counting the hours until Donna shacked up with her."

Hayley whistled. "I wonder if Ben had any inkling."

"Why should he?"

CHAPTER 23

The owl peered unblinkingly at Eve, its yellow eyes bright disks in the mottled plumage.

Eve shaded her eyes against the sun. If the bird had a shred of the wisdom subscribed to its species, it would stay well away from human dwellings.

She wondered how long it had used the cabin roof as its private perch.

She searched for the fake rock with the key. The door opened silently, and she saw with satisfaction that her earlier footprints had disappeared. Although the cabin was deserted, wind and sand crept in through tiny gaps in the walls. She locked it again and pocketed the key, with the dim idea of using the fact Donna and her lover used to meet in the cabin.

If a rumour went around, about a strange, unspecified

find in the cabin, or the police interested in retrieving the condoms and fingerprinting them, her quarry might be tempted to come and destroy the purported evidence. He wouldn't know Ben threw out the contraceptives, and she could easily plant a new pack. Better still, she didn't have to. It would be enough to lure the murderer into the cabin. His footprints would be visible in the dust for at least a day or two until the dust obliterated them. The police could work wonders with the imprints of soles.

Eve congratulated herself on this stroke of genius. Even better, if she could get a camera with a trigger wire installed in a tree. Didn't proper birdwatchers use all kinds of technology?

All she needed was a photograph of whoever entered the cabin. Once the police force had a name and face, they could piece the evidence together. Donna's colleagues would be able to identify the man.

She winked at the owl. Wise or not, it had helped.

Eve returned to the shop where she purchased her birdwatching binoculars. The shop assistant recognised her, which she attributed to the fact she was half the age of his normal crowd, and that she'd proved herself to be utterly clueless when she asked him for advice. This visit was no different.

As soon as he'd stopped reeling off pixel numbers, trigger times, audio boosting and angles, they decided she needed a simple video camera. It needed to be small and easy to camouflage, but swiftness of response wasn't priority, whereas a clear picture was. Humans moved slower than most animals.

"I'm branching out into mammals," Eve explained.

"Don't underestimate them," the shop assistant said. "Those critters can be fast too. Is it more squirrels, dormice, foxes, or what is it you're interested in?"

"Does that make such a big difference?"

He tut-tutted. "I'm thinking about the angle. A fox stays on the ground. Dormice and squirrels are both climbers."

"I see. Squirrels. My stepmother adores them." Her choice of words surprised herself, as did the realisation she dragged Crystal into a perfectly normal situation at all.

That's what a guilty conscience did. After years of turning the poor woman into a monument of greed and bad taste, she had developed a certain liking for her father's wife. "Go figure," she said to herself.

The shop assistant piled up half a dozen cameras. "Now these are all excellent models for your needs."

"Can you programme it for me, so all I need to do is hide it?"

"No problem."

They settled on a chunky camera in a camouflage body. It set her back two hundred pounds. This would be the absolute last investment she made for the case. Ben Dryden had turned out to be an expensive hobby.

"And you turn it just so, and fix it like this ..." He demonstrated again how she could adjust the angle. "I'd advise a trial run, and when you check the video recording you'll see if you've covered the correct field of vision."

"Excellent." Eve beamed at him. "Spare batteries, and then I should be done."

"Exciting," he said.

"You have no idea."

In the evenings, her footpath belonged to joggers and dog-walkers, but installing the camera could wait.

She stroked the cardboard box. Once her plan was fully formed, she'd be ready to restore Kim's peace of mind. As for Ben – she closed her eyes, a wide grin on her face. He'd be dumbstruck by her ingenuity. She'd point out

Hayley and Letty's contribution, modesty demanded it, but as for the rest…

Funny to think how one stroll had changed all their lives. Despite all the little frights and annoyances along the way, and the rapid depletion of her funds, at least she couldn't complain about boredom.

Ben wished his father would stop brooding. Any son in his right mind would have cut his losses long before.

After a silent dinner, with John's eyes fixed on him with an intense stare, he pushed back his chair. "Go on," Ben said. "Say your piece."

"You promised. No more chasing after a skirt and landing us in a mess."

"I told you before, there will be no repetition. You used to be keen on having a grandson, to carry on the name and the tradition."

"The price is too high."

"What do you expect from me? To live like a monk?"

John's breath grew harder. "Hayley would do fine. There would be none of this other business."

"She doesn't give a toss about me, and rightly so." He touched his father's shoulder. Under his hand he felt the bones and muscles. The massage and physical exercises

Chris performed with his father worked well on the good side of his body.

Up close, Ben saw something else in John's eyes, something that took his breath away; fear. He softened.

"I promise you there's nothing to worry about." For a heartbeat, they shared a moment of unspoken affection.

Eve formed a camera with her hands in front of her eyes as she dashed around from one tree to the next. She needed to establish the perfect shot of the door area.

The key was back in its hiding place, and she kept a copy in her backpack.

The undergrowth rustled. Her heart skipped a beat until she saw a small bird dart away, a twig in its beak. Clandestine work tested her nerves to breaking point.

She settled on a large chestnut. The camera fit perfectly into the fork between two thick branches, and the wide leaves covered everything but the lens. If she made sure to keep it that way, she could monitor the comings and goings in the cabin.

Eve wished she could get a notification on her phone, similar to her private security system, but it really made no difference if she retrieved any information straight away or with a delay of a day or two. If she fussed with the video camera too often, Ben might catch her red-handed, forcing her to lie even more to him.

She stepped back and admired her handiwork. The camera was almost invisible, and the camouflage body blended in with the bark and the leaves. She mentally congratulated herself as she strolled home, a happy little spring in her step.

Eve gave her troops, as she'd come to regard Hayley and Letty, a spirited report of her preparation for the plan. They rewarded it with the enthusiasm it deserved.

"It could work," Hayley said. "You've really hit on something, Eve."

"I know, and best of all, nobody will be in danger at all. If the camera does its trick and I've got the angle and everything right, we're onto a home run."

Letty appeared confused.

"It's a sports term," Eve said. "We're in for the win. All that's left is for us to come up with a bait the murderer can't resist."

CHAPTER 24

*E*ve performed a few wobbly twirls in the privacy of her cottage. Her elation survived even another urgent work assignment requested over the phone. Her bank account sorely needed an infusion of cash and dealing with boring technical details on a translation would keep her hands and her conscious mind busy, while her subconsciousness whirred away in the background and hopefully came up with a stroke of genius.

She switched on her laptop. A reminder pinged onto the screen. Her flight tickets; she'd promised she'd book them as soon as possible.

How long should she stay, if she seriously intended to mend fences with her dad and get properly acquainted with his wife? Two weeks in Seattle should do it, she decided. Long enough to chat and do things together, short enough to afford a hotel if the visit went wrong.

Twenty minutes later she was officially down to a three-figure sum in her account and had committed herself to spending the longest period with her dad since she finished school. In grey and wet November, of all months. Eve emailed a copy of her flight schedule to her dad. "What could possibly go wrong?" she asked herself. The answer was a depressingly long list.

Eve rose at the crack of dawn. So far, her subconscious had let her down, possibly because she was too tense. More work might do the trick. At worst, it would get her assignment out of the way.

Her wrists ached, and her foot was numb from sitting on it when she paused for a snack. Her unladylike posture at her desk had been on the top of her things-to-change-asap-list for a decade, without success. She rolled her shoulders to relieve the tension. Better, but still painful, like stabs with a blunt needle.

Eve grabbed her backpack. She deserved a break, and with any luck, the video camera had recorded test footage of some two-winged or four-legged visitor passing the entrance to the cabin.

She trotted along the path with a sense of exhilaration

tempered by the pain in her muscles. Too much sitting took its toll on her body since she'd hit thirty.

The cabin lay deserted in the midday sun. Reaching the camera and taking it down took less than a minute.

Eve squatted behind a tree, in case Ben appeared out of the blue. Her pulse quickened at the thought, but that was because she needed to be undisturbed, not because she missed him. Which she didn't, much.

The camera had 87 seconds of recorded footage. Eve tried to remember how to play it back. Luckily, she'd had the foresight to keep the instruction manual in her pocket. She pressed three buttons and was rewarded with the sight of a furry animal bolting across the path. A rabbit. At the top of the screen, the door was cut-off about a metre from the ground. She'd need to adjust that. Showing a pair of legs and a bum would hardly allow a reliable identification.

Eve fumbled with the settings. The shop assistant had made it all look deceptively easy.

Her palms were sweaty as she put the camera back in its hiding spot.

Back on the path, she had the eerie sensation someone was watching her. She stiffened her back and trudged on, willing herself to resist the temptation of looking back.

"That's unexpected." Hayley came face to face with Ben at the back entrance to the pub. It had been well-used once upon a time, when late-night revellers beat a hasty retreat from the local copper after hours, or from their wives.

Beer barrels still were transported along this way, if with less frequency than in the last century. The flagstones sagged in the middle and moss sprouted in between the grouts, another job for her to tackle soon.

"Come in," she said and took him upstairs.

Her nan's face lit up. "What a nice surprise."

"That's not something I hear very often," Ben said. "Are you sure I'm not in the way?"

"I'll leave you to it." Hayley ran downstairs. Her nan could be relied upon to give her a blow-by-blow account later. Bloody pub, she thought. Maybe she really should consider handing it over to a manager. Selling was out of the question, at least while her nan was alive. It would have been different if Hayley had a child, but since she had no plans to procreate ever, succession was a moot point. The Trowbridge bloodline would end with her.

"I'd like your advice," Ben said.

"I'll be glad to be of help, my dear boy." Letty offered him the biscuit tin. He declined.

"It's about my father," he said.

"Yes?"

Ben blew out his breath. "I'm stuck about what to do. We're stuck. At the moment, Chris is enough, but how much longer until my father needs more care?"

Letty said, "There are excellent retirement villages, with doctors and nurses on call. He'd have some independence left, and you'd have peace of mind. I've been considering moving into one myself, while I still can."

"You?" Ben stared at her in amazement.

"It's not fair on Hayley to expect her to give up her life for me," Letty said with a calm that surprised him. "I know she says she likes things the way they are, but she hardly has a choice, and neither do you."

"My father would never agree to leave the house of his ancestors. He's like a tree. When you uproot him, he'll die."

"Could you afford daily or live-in help?"

"I'd intended to sell the leased orchards to the man who

works them. He wants them. That will give me the money, but who would take the job? Nobody local."

"Eve is right," Letty said. "You need to get out from under that cloud."

"Eve has been chatting about this?" A steely glare came into his eyes. "That's interesting."

"Only in private. She cares about you." Letty's gentle voice held a biting undertone. "There's nothing wrong with that."

"My father thinks otherwise, and I'm not having him being upset again. Donna was enough."

"You could advertise further away for a helper."

Ben was grateful to Letty for changing a painful subject.

"Hire a male nurse, a young man. Then John can put his mind to rest about your love life, and he'd have a new companion. If you ask me, its unhealthy to live like a hermit. For both of you."

"That's not a bad idea. I'll think about it," he said.

"How about a cruise?"

"Pardon?"

Letty opened a drawer and took out a stash of brochures. "Bella's given me these. A week or two in the sunshine, and they have doctors and masseurs and what have you on board. Some of the ships are floating spas for us oldies these days. It would do him a power of good, give him a few interests."

Ben took the brochures, but he doubted John would even look at them.

"If you see Eve, tell her to come and visit." Letty's blue eyes were guileless.

"I will. If I happen to run into her." He prided himself on his inscrutable face. At least she had kept quiet about their private affairs. Or, the notion hurt him more than he'd expected, she was ashamed of having slept with him.

The mail landed with a soft thud on Eve's floor. She ignored it. She received nothing but advertising material or invoices on ninety-nine out of a hundred occasions. Both were not worth interrupting her work flow, or anything else.

She read her translation out aloud. She'd tried a software, to have it read to her, but its ignorance of any but the most basic foreign words made the pronunciation both hilarious and disruptive.

Dusk washed the sky with an orange and pink tinge. Eve considered going down to the "Green Dragon". On a Friday evening, the pub would by now be three-deep in customers, with conversations reaching dangerously high decibels, perfect for losing herself in a mindless crowd.

She picked up a handful of envelopes and flyers and put them on her table, to be opened later.

The "Green Dragon" presented itself exactly the way she'd expected. Hayley and Dom had their hands full with pulling pints for the men and mixing gin and tonics for Bella and Sue. Eve shook off the impression of having been watched along the way. Her imagination ran away with her lately.

Grace flitted around, collecting empty glasses and darting through the swing door to the kitchen without so much as a second's break. She'd found her rhythm.

Hayley greeted Eve with a nod. "House red?"

"Lime soda. Take your time."

One of the men made space for Eve at the bar. She squeezed in between him and his mate, both weather-beaten old age pensioners with callused hands and a huge capacity for beer.

"Yoo-hoo," Bella called out.

Eve signalled she'd soon be over. Music washed over her,

a few bars rising above the general din. She liked the noise in British pubs, and the banter between regulars and staff. The men next to her started to talk about sheep, and football. She took her drink and weaved her way through the throng to Bella's table.

Bella sniffed at her lime soda. "Grace, another glass." She lifted a half-empty bottle of Prosecco out of a cooler.

Grace obeyed. Bella filled the glass to the brim, without a single spilt drop. "We're celebrating."

She touched Sue and Eve's glass with her.

"Congratulations. What's the occasion?"

Bella pulled a rolled-up community newspaper out of her voluminous bag. "I'm in the paper. Page three."

"You should have received our copy yesterday," Sue said with a disapproving frown. "If you haven't, I'll let them know."

"It's sitting on my table. I was too busy to look at it," Eve said.

Eve opened the paper to page three, and the headline, "Let's Hair It For Bella – Local stylist makes the final cut in competition" over a suspiciously unlined picture of the hairdresser.

"That's fantastic," Eve said with conviction.

"People have been ringing the salon non-stop," Bella

said. "If I win I'll get a nice trophy too. That'll look good on my new dating profile. Bella – a cut above."

"I'll drink to that." Eve joint in the giggles.

Eve stumbled through her front door at midnight, a little light-headed from the noise and the alcohol.

She'd read the paper tomorrow. Who knew what other excitement she might have missed about her neighbours?

The next morning the pile of mail sat where she'd left it. She rifled through it. Take-away menus, intriguingly all for food to be delivered and not picked up, a garden service, her weekly offer to save money when switching broadband providers, and a plain envelope with her name printed in black block letters.

She helped herself to coffee and slit the letter open with her butter knife. A moment later, the hot liquid dripped down her leg and the mug rolled on the floor. Eve stared uncomprehendingly on the piece of paper in her hand. On it, words cut out from the newspaper she'd just read, said, "Stay Away From Him". The paper itself was pale blue, with a white cloud covering most of it. She'd seen it before.

Eve ran to the bathroom and retched until her stomach sat empty. She splashed cold water over her face. Her hands trembled, and her head pounded. "No," she whispered. "No."

She tore off the drenched jeans. Something was wrong with her eyes as she searched in her wardrobe for another pair. Everything was fuzzy, as if she was caught in a bad dream.

She picked the letter of the floor and shoved it in her backpack. Hayley would help her make sense of this.

"Eve?"

She suppressed a scream as Ben loomed in front of her on the cottage's doorstep.

"What are you doing here?" The words came out barely audible.

"I wanted to see you. Are you okay?"

He wouldn't hurt her, Eve thought, not in public, and not in broad daylight. She should send him away and run for her friends.

"Can I come inside?" His face had a concerned look.

She forced herself to stay calm. "Hayley is expecting me."

"Five minutes. Please." He stepped through the still open door. She followed him, her heart beating painfully against her ribs.

They sat down in the living room. "Tell me what's bothering you," he said. "You know you can trust me."

"You killed her," Eve said before she could stop herself. "I trusted you, and you lied to me. I don't know how you did, if you hired a man, or hired someone to use your car and your credit card." Every breath hurt, but she didn't care. "If you kill me too, you won't get away with it."

"What are you talking about?" Under Ben's tan, his skin drained of all colour.

"He sent me a warning. Your father sent me a warning letter, to stay away from you. He knows what you've done."

"Eve." He reached for her. She shrank back, repulsed and scared.

"What letter?"

"An anonymous one, with letters pasted onto a sheet of paper from your father's notepad. I wrote on it myself for him."

"That's crazy," he said, but his tone rang flat in her ears.

"Why? Couldn't you bear the idea she left you for a woman? That she chose Kim Potter over you?"

"I have no idea what you're talking about, but I'll sort it out. I swear."

"Go. Just go. Don't you ever come close to me again." She stifled a sob.

Ben left, his eyes filled with a rage that chilled Eve to the bone.

CHAPTER 25

*E*ve's brain worked on auto-pilot as she made her way towards the "Green Dragon". She needed someone to talk to.

"Eve? Are you okay?" The second man to ask her this question, but at least Chris was no-one to fear.

She sniffled as she saw the kindness in his face and burst into tears.

"I don't know what to do," she said.

He handed her a tissue and gave her a gentle hug. "You can tell me."

There was something about his voice, and the sympathy in his face, that broke down her barriers. "It's Ben. And his father."

"Is anything wrong with them?" Chris asked, frown lines creasing his forehead.

"I think they knew," she blurted out. "About Donna's love affair with a woman. And I think he killed her because of Kim."

Chris caught his breath. "What? I don't believe that."

"Neither did I. Promise me one thing, if anything happens to me, tell the police."

He reached for his wallet and took out an old invoice. On the back, he wrote something down and pressed it into Eve's hand. "Call me, if you want to talk. Day or night."

She shoved the paper into her pocket and searched for a tissue. "I appreciate that. I don't usually unburden myself on unsuspecting people."

The "Green Dragon" was empty apart from Grace. "Hayley's taken her nan for an eye examination," the bar maid said. "She'll be back this afternoon."

Eve huddled on her sofa, a blanket wrapped around her body to stop the shivering. A thought pierced through the fog in her brain. She had to talk to Kim. Her friend needed to hear the truth.

As soon as Eve's thoughts cleared, she'd call her. But first, she had to stop her thoughts going in circles and driving her insane. One moment she was convinced of Ben's guilt, the next she could swear he was innocent. And doing something so out of character as to unburden herself on Chris, was the final proof she'd become unhinged.

Ben drove home with a reckless disregard for his own safety. Deep inside, he'd always been aware of the inevitability of this moment. Five years, all that he'd done to prevent this, were for nothing. The tires screeched as he turned the corner onto the driveway. The electric gate was barely open as he squeezed through.

Ben marched unannounced into his father's room.

John's one moveable eyebrow rose. "Is the house on fire?"

"What have you done? How could you?"

John's mouth dropped open. "What are you talking about?"

"The letter. How dare you threaten Eve? Would you have

killed her too?" Ben stood over his father, hands clenched in his pockets, so he wouldn't choke the old man.

John's hands shook. "You're crazy." He tried to move the wheelchair away from Ben.

"I've protected you all these years," Ben said. "I've buried myself with you in this mausoleum, to make sure nothing bad would happen again."

"Protected me from what?"

"Don't lie to me. I should have let you rot in prison. You're lucky the police never really looked at the cripple, after your stroke."

"Ben." John's speech was strained. Normally, Ben would have panicked. Now he no longer cared if his father suffered another stroke.

"You were the one who'd have lost everything he loved if Donna had walked away with half my property. You were already in the house, and she'd never have thought twice about turning her back on you. Did you take the brick earlier and hide it in your clothes, or was it a spur-of-the-moment thing?"

Ben's anger rose with every word. "You could easily drug yourself, the moment she lay dead at your feet. Did she know it was you? Did she cry out for help?"

"You're crazy," John said again.

"I blamed myself for bringing Donna here. I thought sitting in this chair was punishment enough for you, but threatening Eve." Ben shook his head. "You shouldn't have done that."

"I never threatened your girl, and I never laid a finger on your wife. I thought it was you." Dribble formed in the left corner of John's mouth. "I've been protecting you."

"What? No."

"Who else could it have been? Who else would be careful enough to give me a dose that sent me to sleep but was small enough to be harmless? You were angry with her, about threatening to take this place away from us."

"Away from you, you mean."

"You did it for me. I never blamed you." John fumbled for a handkerchief.

Ben wiped his father's mouth in an automatic gesture. "How could you believe I'd kill for this pile of stones? It's a millstone round our necks."

"Who else could it be?"

"I don't know," Ben said.

The notepaper. Eve mentioned the notepaper.

"Your notepad. That's what Eve recognised."

"It was left over from a ten-pack Donna bought. She gave them away to a few people. Should we call the police?"

"And tell them what? That we both suspected each other, but have reason to believe there's a murderer at large who uses the same notepaper you do, courtesy of the original victim?" Ben sank onto his father's bed and buried his head in his hands. "It's all a bloody mess."

Eve woke up from a nightmare. Ben had chased her through the woods, a rock in one gloved hand, the other reaching for her throat. An owl hooted from the cabin roof, and Eve's feet sank into a black bog as she struggled to escape.

She wiped the clammy sweat off her brow and reached for the phone. The ringtone echoed in her ears, but Kim didn't pick up. "Please leave a message …

Eve hung up. She'd try again later, before her courage failed her completely. How could she have been so gullible?

Kim heard a faint ring as she locked the shop door a few

minutes early. She'd forgotten to pick up the marrow bones for Laika from the butcher's.

She groped for her key on the way to her back door. A shadow fell on the path, and a sickly-sweet smell hit her nose before she drifted off into oblivion.

CHAPTER 26

When Kim regained consciousness, she had no idea how much time had passed. The skin around her mouth burned, and she had trouble breathing. Sticky tape prevented her from uttering any sound.

She slowly opened her eyes. She was surrounded by darkness. The air smelt dusty and stale. She was tied to a chair with thick ropes around her chest and her ankles. Her hands were tied at the back. Her muscles screamed.

Kim tested the ropes. They were lashed tight enough to only allow her a fraction of an inch of movement.

Despair engulfed her. She fought it down. Whatever was going on, she needed to stay calm. What did the kidnapper want from her? She was neither rich nor important. Maybe it was all a mistake, and the person would let her go once he realised his error.

Her eyes adjusted to the dark. She saw the outlines of a bedstead without a mattress, two chairs and a table. A sliver of daylight shone through a chink in a window shutter; it must still be before sunset. If she'd been unconscious the whole night, she'd be parched and ravenous.

Kim held her breath and strained her hearing for another sound in the room. All she heard was the pounding of her own heart. She carefully turned her neck. She was alone. Her feet stood on a rough wooden floor. She wiggled her left foot. A few grains of sand crunched under her sole.

At least Laika was safe, at home. If she didn't appear for work, somebody was bound to look for her, and find her dog.

In the meantime, all she could do was wait.

Ben circled the fish pond. Incessant exercise might help put his thoughts into an orderly fashion. Right now, they merged into a thicket of ideas and impressions. How could his own father consider him capable of murder and live with the idea? It had been hard enough for Ben to sit across the old man day after day and keeping his own anger and sadness at bay. But for a helpless cripple in his wheelchair the constant worry and fear about what was going to happen next must have been almost unbearable.

No wonder John insisted on keeping Ben away from other people. The first murder was supposed to be the hardest. Once that threshold had been crossed, taking a life got easier and easier. How many murderers went on a killing spree the moment they sensed danger to themselves?

Eve; he had to keep Eve safe. Ben strode faster. She wouldn't see him, she'd made that clear, but he could go and ask Hayley for assistance. Eve listened to Hayley. All he had to do was go to the "Green Dragon" and enlist her help.

The clump of lead in his stomach dissolved, now he had a plan of action. He'd walk down to the stream and take the footpath to town. He didn't trust himself behind the steering-wheel until he'd solved the problem of Eve.

Ben hurried down the path to the cabin. He thought he'd spied movement between the trees and slowed down as a searing pain shot through his neck and his legs buckled under.

Kim's mobile phone still went straight to the mailbox.

Eve's unease increased with every try. She'd drive over and wait for Kim to come home.

The lights in the apartment were out. Eve pressed the doorbell, without any clear idea what she hoped to achieve. She leant against the door.

She was on the verge of giving up when she heard a faint noise in the building. Eve rang the doorbell again and pressed her ear against the keyhole. There it was again, a noise gaining in volume; a dog's bark.

The fine hairs on Eve's arms rose. Kim would never leave Laika alone at this time of night unless for a good reason. Something must have happened.

Bile rose in Eve's mouth. She'd told Ben she knew about Donna's love affair with a woman. It didn't take much for him to come up with a name, if he'd been unaware as to Kim's identity until then.

A man who could ignore his wife cheating on him with another man but was driven to a murderous rage by the simple fact she preferred another woman to himself, might bear enough of a grudge to strike again.

John had tried to tell her, but she'd been too blind to understand. Now she'd lead Ben directly to Kim.

He wouldn't have killed her in her apartment. She'd told him enough about Kim's security measures to stay well away. One point in Kim's favour.

Where could he have taken her?

She searched in her backpack for her phone. She had to warn Hayley, before Ben hurt her as well, for knowing too much.

Eve's fingers touched a slip of paper. The invoice Chris gave her. *Thank God.* Chris and Ben were close; if anyone had an idea where Ben might have taken Kim, it would be him. And he was strong, strong enough to wrestle Ben down.

She smoothed the paper. Chris Ripley, written in spiky, slanted letters. A handwriting imprinted in her memory. *"If God chose, I shall but love thee better after death."* He had. Elizabeth Barrett Browning's sonnet had been both a declaration of love and a threat.

CHAPTER 27

*E*ve sat motionless in her car. She should have seen it. Brown-haired Chris, who loved health bars. Chris, who had a key and was considered part of the family and John's confidant. Chris, who'd been the sole person able to coax Donna out of a bad mood.

He had easy access to John's notepad, and he must have watched Eve's cottage for any sign of her reaction. She remembered the prickling of her skin which she'd attributed to her frayed nerves and overactive imagination.

Where could he have taken Kim?

She called Ben. No answer. Eve bit her lip until the metallic taste of blood stopped her.

This was all her fault. She'd mentioned a woman in Donna's life to Chris. His shock had been real. It would have been easy for him to find out who Eve was talking about and where his prey lived. She imagined Donna, innocently mentioning Kim and the shop, a happy smile playing on her lips.

Where did Chris feel safe from discovery?

The door opened without a noise. The hinges must be freshly oiled, Kim thought incoherently.

She dropped her chin onto her chest and feigned unconsciousness. If her kidnapper noticed his error, she only posed a threat if she could identify him.

A kick made the door fly wide open. The unknown person grunted, as if struggling with a heavy load. Wheels creaked closer and closer. The door shut with an almost imperceptible noise. A feeble light came on, too weak to shine through the chink in the shutter.

Kim risked a sideways glance out from under her lowered lashes. A man in jeans and tennis shoes with silent soles, and another man, sitting in a foldable wheelchair.

She glanced up for a scary split second and saw a tanned face under a shock of blonde hair. She choked back a groan, all hope vaporised in thin air. Despite the dim light she recognised the second captive. Ben Dryden, Donna's husband. They were both here to die.

The man behind the wheelchair gave Ben a vicious kick against the kneecap. It took all of Kim's willpower not to react, but Ben stayed motionless. Maybe he was already dead.

She mustn't cry. If anybody had seen her being dragged away from her building, a rescue team could be on its way.

He probably had used the wheelchair to bring her here. People didn't look twice at a patient being wheeled to a car, except her neighbours would know Kim was perfectly healthy.

The man stood in front of Kim. She willed herself to stay slack. He touched her neck with two fingers, to take her heartbeat. The skin contact made her sick, but she kept control. She would fight for her life, whatever it took.

He prodded her cheek. She let her head loll gently to the side.

The man sat on one of the chairs, legs crossed and a revolver in his hand. He put the gun on the table, whistling softly. Kim's heart sank a notch further. He'd have to be convinced no-one could hear them. Where were they?

Eve wiped away tears of frustration. She'd left a handful of frantic messages for Hayley. Who could tell when she would find a moment to listen to them, on a Saturday night?

Eve had considered calling the police, but what could she report? That a grown woman, whose secret lover was murdered five years ago, left her dog alone?

Wasn't twenty-four hours the minimum wait before the force would even look at a disappearance?

It was up to Eve to save Kim, but she needed help. Why didn't Ben pick up his bloody phone?

Eve grabbed a paper bag and breathed into it, to calm down. Hyperventilating never saved anyone. During her tenth deep breath, inspiration struck. She left yet another message for Hayley and snuck out into the dark.

Ben's ankles were tied with duct tape over the socks. There would be no marks on the skin, Kim thought. She couldn't see his hands, but suspected they were secured as well.

Their abductor took the coil of rope and tied Ben's wrists in front of him. He wore surgical gloves on his hands. A sickening smile flitted over his face as he pressed the pistol in Ben's right hand.

Kim prayed inwardly that Ben would stir and pull the trigger. The bullet would hit the man in the leg, or if they were lucky, in the stomach and lead to instant shock.

Ben stayed motionless as the man took the pistol away and put two bullets into an empty chamber.

He'd thought of everything.

The man propped up Kim's left eyelid. She let her eye ball look up, so the pupil almost disappeared, in the desperate hope it would fool him into believing she was still unconscious.

He dropped her eyelid and turned around as Ben stirred, just in time to overlook Kim's involuntary start as she remembered his face. She'd seen him with Donna a few times, when they were nothing more than friends. A nice bloke, but nothing more than a harmless flirt, Donna had said. She'd been wrong.

Ben moaned and stirred in the wheelchair.

The man kicked him again. Ben's eyes fluttered open for an instant and closed again.

Kim struggled to keep her breath even and shallow. The longer it took for them to be officially awake, the better.

Their kidnapper had put two bullets in the chamber. If one of them missed, they had a slim chance to survive. She'd concentrate on that. It was better odds than Donna had.

The kidnapper lost patience. He slapped Ben. The smacking sound echoed in Kim's ears.

Blood trickled down Ben's lip and an angry red mark appeared on his left cheekbone.

"Sorry, old mate," the man said. He wiped away the blood. "We don't want any marks, do we?"

Ben's eyeballs skittered back until he finally could focus them on their adversary. "Chris," he murmured.

"Glad you're back with us. I thought the sedative was a bit strong. Now what shall we do about the lady?" A trick of the light turned Chris' open face into a menacing grimace.

Eve sneaked closer to the cabin. She had to cover twenty metres of open ground, littered with small twigs and other debris left after recent high winds.

Something crunched under her foot. It rang out as loud as a shot in her nervous ears. She stopped, motionless.

The windows of the cabin were shuttered, the first sign she was right.

Eve cowered on the ground and texted Hayley again,

with the location. *Please,* she prayed silently, *bring the cavalry.*

Inch by inch she crawled along the grass verge, as deep in the shadow as she could, well out of sight from windows or door should they be opened.

Chris took a long, sharp needle out a bag under the table. He held it up to the lamp and chuckled.

"We'll see if that brings her back to the land of the living," he said in a conversational tone to Ben. "What do you think, where should we stick it? Under the finger nail? Humans have lots of tender nerves there."

Kim moaned. And again, a little louder. She let her left hand stretch out and slacken.

Chris put the needle on the table.

He squatted in front of her.

She slitted her eyes, in an obvious effort to open them.

An obscenely tender look came into his face. He stroked her cheek, his finger following her jawline down to the jugular.

She could hardly breathe.

"Look at the competition, Ben," Chris said. "Isn't she gorgeous?"

"What do you want from us?" Ben spat out the words.

Chris raised his hand to strike him but stopped himself mid-air. "You see, it's all your fault."

"What is?"

Kim gave Ben an encouraging nod. The longer Chris talked, the longer they had to perform a miracle.

"You see, I thought it was you," Chris said.

"Chris, mate, I swear, if I ever did anything to hurt you, I'm sorry."

"I'm not your mate. I never was. I'm nothing but the hired help, and you're the lord of the manor."

"At least let the lady go."

"The lady? That's what you call the slut?" Chris' fingers curled into claws for one tiny moment. The gesture and the insane hatred in his eyes scared Kim more than the revolver and the needle.

"I've never met her, so I couldn't say," Ben said.

Chris jerked the wheelchair closer to Kim and ripped the sticky tape off her mouth. "In this case, let me introduce you. Donna's worthless shit of a husband, meet the woman you made her sleep with."

He turned back to Ben. "You see, she loved me. She told me so. Over and over again. She loved me, and one day we'd figure out how to be together forever."

"You both could have left," Ben said.

"No, we couldn't, could we? You'd tied down all the money, her money, and that's how you trapped her." Chris' voice shook with anger, but his hand was perfectly still. "And then one afternoon she got off the bed in this cabin, dressed herself and told me she'd changed her mind. It was over." He sobbed. "You took her away from me."

"No. I didn't," Ben said. "She was leaving me, remember?"

"You did alright. You repulsed her so much, she couldn't bear to be with a man any longer. Otherwise she'd have stayed with me instead of falling into bed with this one."

Chris hit Kim with the back of his hand. Her head whipped back.

"No marks." Ben stared at Kim with an anguish that, given the danger they were in, struck her as almost comical. He should focus on surviving, not on sparing her a little pain. "You said it yourself, Chris, no marks."

"On her they don't matter. Stop interrupting me."

They fell silent. Kim thought she'd picked up a sound from outside, but it would be the wind.

"I told Donna she made a mistake," Chris said. "But she laughed and said, we had a great time, but all good things end. She was right."

"But you stuck around." Ben flexed his wrists, anxious not to let Chris notice. The rope held fast.

"I waited for her to change her mind, and she finally did. She moved into the attic, as far from you as possible."

"What happened?"

"I asked her again to go away with me, and she called me stupid. I knew you had a business date the following week. All I had to do was let myself into the house, drop a crushed sleeping-pill in John's tea-pot and return half an hour before you were supposed to be home."

Ben winced. He could imagine the rest.

"We would have been happy together," Chris said. "You two ruined Donna's life. You ruined everything."

"But you didn't kill me then," Ben said.

"Why should I? You have no idea how much I enjoyed watching you there, being imprisoned by your own stupidity. I made sure John kept you on a tight leash, and you danced. Every time I made him pull a string, you danced. But then you had to find another woman, didn't you? You were going to be happy. And then she told me why Donna left me."

"What are you going to do?" Ben's voice was calm enough to give Kim a little comfort.

"I'll make you pay for what you did to us. When they find you both, you'll have shot your wife's lover through the heart." Chris made a circle with his finger on Kim's chest. "And then you shot yourself, with a gun you asked me to buy for protection. You have no idea how surprised I'll be."

He smiled. "Don't worry about your old man. I'll be there to look after John, if the shock doesn't finish him off."

Eve overheard the last sentences, her ear pressed against the side of the door. In her left hand she held the can with the self-defence spray.

Cold sweat trickled down her armpits. If she didn't act now, Ben and Kim would be dead. She slid the key into the keyhole and, in slow motion, tried the handle. The door was unlocked.

Eve slipped out of her shoes and socks and placed the baseball in a sock, holding it in her left hand. In her right, she held the self-defence spray. Praying fervently under her breath to no-one in particular, she kicked the door open.

Chris swivelled around. Ben stretched out his taped ankles to trip him up or at least slow him down.

Eve let out a blood-curdling scream and hit Chris with

the full spray-load directly in his eyes. He screwed them shut and clawed at his blood-red face as she swung the sock with the baseball at his temple.

Chris fell to his knees.

Ben kicked out and hit Chris on the head as Eve darted past them and grabbed the revolver.

"I'll kill you." Chris snarled at Eve. "You won't get away from me."

He struggled to get up.

Eve shrank back, the revolver aimed at his chest.

"Police. Drop the gun," someone yelled.

Eve's hand opened. The revolver clanged as it hit the floor. Someone pushed her aside, and two burly police officers stepped between her and Chris. In the background she thought she spotted Hayley.

One of the officers said, "Chris Ripley, you're under arrest."

Eve sank down and put her head between her knees. One of the officers picked up the weapon. The last thing she saw before a police woman led her outside, was Ben, still tied up but with a blissful expression on his face.

The police woman offered Eve a blanket, but she declined. "I'll be fine in a minute," she said and pointed towards the chestnut tree. "If you're lucky, you'll find evidence on the video camera."

She waited for what stretched into an eternity, until Kim and Ben emerged side by side, orange blankets around their shoulders. Kim's face already turned blue and purple, but she'd live.

An ambulance siren wailed.

"I'll take you home now," a police woman said.

"What about my statement?" Eve asked as the ambulance pulled up.

"That can wait until tomorrow. A few hours won't hurt."

Eve looked at her hand, surprised to see it tremble now. Belated reaction, she thought, but now she no longer needed a steady hand. "My baseball."

"Pardon?"

"It must be in the cabin. It's signed and belonged to my mother."

"I'll take care of her, if that's okay," Eve heard Hayley say. Miraculously, she held Eve's baseball in her hand.

"Eve," Kim called out as a police officer helped her into the ambulance. "My dog." She handed her keyring to a police man who delivered it to Eve, while another officer sealed off the cabin.

Eve stumbled towards the ambulance. Kim threw her the keys to her apartment. "I'm sorry I lied to you," Eve said. Kim gave her a small nod before the ambulance doors closed.

Hayley put an arm around Eve's shoulder. She also insisted on driving Eve to pick up Laika and packing together a few things for the dog.

"I understand you're exhausted and shaken," she said, "but I want to hear every single thing. I almost had a heart attack when I read your messages. Going after the bastard alone."

"I was a tad scared," Eve said, stroking Laika's soft fur. Her former panic had given way to a strange sense of serenity.

"But not enough to need a change of pants."

"Between you and me? It was close. Very close."

CHAPTER 28

*C*old, hard nose pressed against Eve's cheek. She stared into a pair of huge blue eyes, in a furry face.

"Down," she said. Laika wagged her tail. The dog obviously had the good taste to prefer Eve's 400-ply organic cotton sheets and duvet to the rough woollen throw Eve bolstered the basket with.

She dragged herself into the bathroom. No word yet from Ben or Kim. She decided to take a quick shower. She was due at the police station for her statement soon and intended to dazzle them with her coherence and her natural beauty, in case she ran into someone she knew.

A thick layer of mascara and a hint of blush made her appear human again.

Doorknocker and bell were agitated simultaneously. Laika barked. Eve jumped.

The post woman stood outside, eyes bulging with excitement. In her hand she held another of the ubiquitous promotion letters.

"Have you heard?" she asked.

"Sorry?" Eve feigned ignorance. If her involvement in last night's shenanigans was still a secret, she might get away with it. She had no interest in becoming as notorious as Ben, thank you very much.

"They've got him." The postwoman leant in to Eve's face. "The man who offed the Dryden woman."

Eve let her jaw drop. "You must feel so much safer now in your beds."

The postwoman crossed her ample chest. "You can say that again. It's been preying on our minds all these years, with the beast out there."

"Good." Eve lessened the gap. "My mail?"

The woman handed her the letter she could easily have shoved through the letterbox and went off, no doubt in search of another listener.

Eve took Laika along to the police station. The poor dog had been deserted enough, and the doctor insisted on keeping Kim at the hospital overnight.

The interrogation was endless. She thought it would all be straight forward. After all they had Ben's statement, the footage from Eve's camera, and her own description of events. She'd even brought baseball and defensive spray along, to corroborate her words.

Instead, the police officer insisted on hearing the whole story, from her first meeting with Ben, and later Chris, and Kim, up to the moment she hit Chris with a particularly well-aimed ball.

Reciting it all made Eve squirm. She sounded like a meddlesome, lovestruck teenager.

After an eternity of talking and repeating herself for the sake of clarity and a recording that was constantly paused when someone knocked on the door, Eve was free to go.

She and Laika hurried away from the police station.

A finger tapped her on the shoulder.

Eve stifled a scream. "Hayley, you scared the living daylights out of me."

"They needed my statement too, and when I heard your voice in the room next door I thought I'd wait."

"What did they want to hear from you?" Eve asked.

"I've kept it brief and professional. If anybody spills about your private life, it should be you."

"Thank you."

~

Laika stayed another night before Eve took him home. She and Kim had a few things to talk about, and if Kim visited her at Ivy Cottage, the gossip was bound to become part of the local lore.

The skin around Kim's mouth and nose was puckered where the chloroform had burnt it, but her bruise had changed colour already. She buried her face in her dog's fur.

Eve stood in silence, unsure what to say.

Kim surprised her with a hug. "Thank you," she said.

"I never intended to lie to you," Eve said. "I just didn't know what else to do."

"I might have done the same, for someone I care about." Kim smiled, a painful little smile that tugged at Eve's heartstrings.

"It's still not justice, is it? I've always wondered about that expression. You can't get justice for a murder victim."

"But you can get closure. Which we have, thanks to you. We're all free again." Kim paused. "He seems like a good guy. Ben, I mean."

Colour rushed into Eve's cheeks.

"It's okay. If I don't see him, because it might be awkward for him, tell him one thing. Donna picked fights with him because she used to care so much about him, in the beginning. It's much easier to say good-bye if it doesn't mean anything."

"I'll tell him. And, Kim?"

"Yes?"

"I hope we're still friends."

"In that case, next Friday at eight, at Andrea's wine bar? I'll pay."

"I'll be there."

Eve sang on her way back. If she listened closely, her voice sounded slightly less off-pitch than it used to. Or happiness caused a mild form of delusion.

Outside the "Green Dragon" stood a short queue, and all the parking spaces along the roadside were taken.

Eve dropped off her car and walked to the pub. Inside, she struggled to squeeze through the mixed crowd. Grace and Dom were hard pressed to keep up with customer demand. The Pink Panthers for once had no interest apart from their drinks in the young man. They all focussed on another person of interest. Next to Letty, whose eyes sparkled with delight, sat John in his wheelchair. A half-empty pint stood on the table. He winked at Eve and raised his left thumb towards the ceiling.

"I said all along, Ben Dryden would never hurt a fly," Eve heard Bob of all people say as she sneaked towards the passage.

"That Chris always had a shifty eye," a Panther said.

Upstairs, Hayley pulled her inside the flat. "I thought you'd never get here."

"What's going on?"

"Curiosity, bad conscience and thirst in equal measures I'd say." Hayley chortled. "You should have seen the faces, when John appeared. I swear, the Pink Panther who spread the word in town broke any speed record, on five-inch heels."

"I'm glad he came." Eve frowned. "How did he get here?"

Hayley patted her on the head. "Not so smart now, are we? Have a guess. I'll be downstairs, if you need me."

She gave a shrill whistle. Ben poked his head around the corner. Hayley tiptoed away.

They were both lost for words.

"Hi," Eve said after what felt like a lifetime. "How are you?"

His hand went towards his cheek. "Chris has got a killer swing."

For some reason, the remark broke her up. "He does."

"Mind you, you took him out with one strike."

"Because he stood close. At a distance, I can't hit a barn door. Plus, the ball belonged to my mother. It was her good luck charm."

"She saved us. You saved us," Ben said.

"How did John take it?"

"Better than I'd thought. All he cared about was he no longer had to doubt me, and I don't suspect him anymore. It's as if a crushing weight has been lifted. He's even talking about taking a holiday with Letty. In all decency, of course."

"That's fantastic."

Ben gave her a crooked smile which sent tingles down her spine.

"He's thinking of November. Which would free me up in case you need someone to carry your luggage when you visit your family."

"That's a lot of water down the Thames."

"Or we could go away for a break. Sort of a test drive."

"And your father?"

"We're not taking him. You've got a valid passport?"

This went a bit too fast for Eve. "What's going on?"

"Well, if you want to start a relationship being watched by the Women's Institute and the bowling team and the rugby fans, it's up to you. I'd rather have a bit more –"

He broke off his sentence to kiss her. His hands caressed the small of her back.

"Privacy," she whispered as he covered her neck in butterfly kisses. "Then how the hell do we get out of here?"

He pointed towards the fire ladder. "Or we could walk through the pub and get the rumours over with."

Eve slipped her finger underneath his shirt. "Or we could stay here."

He stopped her from undressing him. "Let me drop off my father first."

She gave in. They strolled downstairs, hand in hand. As if on a silent command, every customer turned towards them and gaped.

"There you are," John said, breaking the spell. "Why don't you two go on home and Dom will drive me later?"

They made one stop on the way. Eve nestled in Ben's arms as she watched the owl take up its perch on the cabin roof.

"It's a female," Ben said.

"How do you know?"

"If you take a close look, you can spot eggs in the tree-hole."

"Another romance, right under our nose." Eve shook her head. "We should give them their privacy."

"We should."

"I'm sorry I suspected you. I didn't mean it," she said.

"You did. And you had all the reason in the world."

"Okay." She pulled him away. "How long do we have until your father returns?" She took her phone.

"What are you doing?"

"Texting Hayley. '*Keep John locked up until further notice.*'"

"Does that mean you'd be willing start over again?"

"I might," she said. "If that's really what you want."

"No more secrets, or lies?"

She held out her hand.

He shook it. "Deal. So, what are we supposed to do now?"

"We could talk about all those things we skirted around on." She paused. "You look like you could still do with a decent rest."

"A lie-down would be good." His eyes twinkled.

"That's what I thought." She slipped her hand into his, to set off for home. Behind them, the owl screeched in what to Eve sounded like a triumphant fanfare.

She half-turned and blew a kiss into the approximate direction of the owl. "Your job's done. And thank you."

"Do you always talk to animals?" Ben asked.

She snuggled into his arm. "If you're lucky, you might find out."

If you enjoyed this mystery, please consider leaving a review where you bought it or on Goodreads and BookBub. Reviews are important to authors and I want to thank you in advance.

More books by Carmen Radtke

The Jack and Frances mysteries

A Matter of Love and Death

Adelaide, 1931. Telephone switchboard operator Frances' life is difficult as sole provider for her mother and adopted uncle. But it's thrown into turmoil when she overhears a suspicious conversation on the phone, planning a murder.

If a life is at risk, she should tell the police; but that would mean breaking her confidentiality clause and would cost her the job. And practical Frances, not prone to flights of fancy, soon begins to doubt the evidence of her own ears - it was a very bad line, after all...

She decides to put it behind her, but it's not easy. Luckily there is the charming, slightly dangerous night club owner Jack. Jack's no angel - six pm prohibition is in force, and what's a nightclub without champagne? But when Frances' earlier fears resurface, she knows that he's the person to confide in.

Frances and Jack's hunt for the truth puts them in grave danger, and soon enough Frances will learn that some things are a matter of love and death ...

Murder at the Races

Nothing is a dead-cert against a cold blooded killer ...

1931. Frances Palmer is overjoyed when her brother Rob returns to Adelaide as a racecourse veterinarian. But all is not well on the turf, and when a man is murdered, there is only one suspect – Rob.

Frances and her boyfriend, charming night club owner Jack Sullivan, along with ex-vaudevillian Uncle Sal and their friends have only one chance to unmask the real murderer, by infiltrating the racecourse. The odds are against them, but luckily putting on a dazzling show where everything depends on sleight of hand is what they do best.

But with time running out for Rob, the race is on ...

Meet Jack Sullivan in False Play at the Christmas Party, a novelette set in 1928.

A charity ball in aid of veterans sounded like rich pickings ...

Coming soon: Death under Palm Trees

Meet Alyssa Chalmers, Victorian emigrant, reluctant bride, intrepid sleuth.

The Case of the Missing Bride

Setting sail for matrimony – or something sinister?

1862. When a group of young Australian women set sail for matrimony in Canada, they believe it's the start of a happy new life.

But when one of the intended brides goes missing, only Alyssa Chalmers, the one educated, wealthy woman in the group, is convinced the disappearance is no accident. She sets out to find out what happened.

Has there been a murder?

Alyssa is willing to move heaven and earth to find out the truth. She is about to discover that there is more to her voyage into the unknown than she bargained for, and it may well cost her life …

Inspired by true events.

Glittering Death

Gold, wedding bells - and murder …

1862. A group of brides from Australia have arrived in British Columbia, and love is in the air - until the happiness in the prospectors' town "Run's End" is shattered when the hotel-owner is found dead. To make matters worse, something is wrong with the stored gold at the hotel, and an epidemic makes it impossible for anyone to leave town.

The brides pin all their hopes on their friend Alyssa Chalmers to find the murderer and restore peace in their new home. But the killer is cunning, and desperate ...

Walking in the Shadow

Quail Island, 1909. Jimmy Kokupe is the miracle man.

On a small, wind-blasted island off the east coast of New Zealand a small colony of lepers is isolated but not abandoned, left to live out their days in relative peace thanks to the charity of the townspeople and the compassion of the local doctor and matron of the hospital.

Jimmy Kokupe is a miracle: he's been cured. But he still carries the stigma, which makes life back on the mainland dangerous and lonely. To find a refuge, he's returned to the camp to care for his friend, fellow patient old Will, and disturbed young Charley.

Healed of his physical ailments and dreaming of the girl he once planned to follow to a new life in Australia, Jimmy meets 'the lady', the island caretaker's beautiful but troubled wife who brings their food. Can she help Jimmy forget his difficult past and overcome his own prejudices towards his mixed parentage, and find the courage to risk living in freedom?

Inspired by true events.

~

You can catch up with Carmen Radtke on her website (www.carmenradtke.com), on twitter or on Goodreads or follow her on Bookbub.

Lightning Source UK Ltd.
Milton Keynes UK
UKHW010639230222
399120UK00001B/205

9 781916 241053